Final Breath

JOHN FRANCOME

Final Breath

headline

First published in 2008
by HEADLINE PUBLISHING GROUP

1

Cataloguing in Publication Data is available from the British Library

ISBN 978 0 7553 3728 6 (hardback)
ISBN 978 0 7553 3729 3 (trade paperback)

Typeset in Veljovic by Avon DataSet Ltd,
Bidford on Avon, Warwickshire

Printed and bound in Great Britain by
Clays Ltd, St Ives plc

HEADLINE PUBLISHING GROUP
An Hachette Livre UK Company
338 Euston Road
London NW1 3BH

www.headline.co.uk
www. hachettelivre.co.uk

Final Breath

Prologue

He had waited a long time for this moment. All day hanging around, some of the time in his car but most of it on the beach or at the bar across the way from the complex of holiday chalets, nursing a soft drink. That had been the worst of it, trying to fit in with the tourists around him hell-bent on chilling out. It went against his nature not to hop on the happy train with everyone else. But if he allowed himself to down a cold beer and shoot the breeze he'd lose his focus. He wasn't here for good times. It was much more important than that.

So he'd sipped his juice, nodded to the pair of cheerful Texans who'd been trying to rope him in to their conversation, and headed back to the beach. He had a spot from where, looking over the page of his paper, he could keep an eye on the entrance to the chalets.

The problem was not that he did not see her. She was in and out on several occasions – she even came down to the beach, passing no more than twenty feet from where he sat. But she was never on her own and, for his purposes, he had to get her away from the others. He'd hoped – naively – that she might take a walk by herself, preferably along one of the paths that branched off the road at the top of the beach. He could catch up with her there. And do what had to be done.

But she wasn't the kind of woman who liked to slip away on her own. Someone else was always with her, which made it awkward. It was important that none of them saw him. He wore a hat and sunglasses and a loose beach shirt he'd bought down the street from where he was staying. It was not his usual apparel but he didn't kid himself he couldn't be easily recognised if the wrong person looked his way. Not that they would be expecting to see him.

The afternoon wore on. He quit the beach for the hillside where there was more shade and kept a lookout through his binoculars, cursing the cracked lens. But the binos had been a gift from his father – he couldn't bear to replace them. Finally, the heat eased its intensity and the sun sank lower in the blue, blue sky. There were still stragglers on the beach but most people had packed up, heading for the many bars and restaurants of the holiday township. He himself went back to the bar where he could eyeball the entrance. Thankfully the Texans had gone and he was able to drink his iced Vanilla Thunderclap – the house speciality minus the rum – in peace.

Finally she emerged, accompanied as before. This could go on for days, he thought. Days before he could get her to himself. But if that's what it took, he would see it through.

She was laughing – how could she laugh like that? She looked carefree and, as ever, magnificent. Her raven-black hair hung loose to her bare, bronzed shoulders, her beautiful body wrapped in a flower-patterned sarong of turquoise, beneath which – he knew because he'd observed her late-afternoon swim – she wore a lemon-yellow bikini. She walked off up the beach road, away from the shops and holiday apartments, in the direction of the headland overlooking the beach. Despite the heels on her sandals she strode out eagerly, her hips swinging fractionally, just enough to set his senses jangling.

2

He followed them. What choice did he have? Watched them turn off the beach road on to the cliff path that led to the bar. He knew she'd have to come back this way and so he sat on the other side of the sea wall and pretended to observe the view. But the curving coastline and placid, mill-pond sea greying in the fading light did not hold his attention. His gaze was fixed to the path on the other side of the wall, fringed with palms. She'd be returning this way, her companion still glued to her side no doubt. Today looked like being a write-off. But he was prepared for that.

People came and went at intervals. A familiar figure rounded the bend ahead – one of the cheerful Texans from earlier. He looked a little the worse for wear. Had the guy spent his entire day checking out the bars? He ducked behind the wall, out of sight. The last thing he wanted was to be hailed by some half-cut holidaymaker.

He waited till he was sure the man had gone. Then he waited some more, as the light faded to charcoal grey and the fairy lights that festooned the trees began to twinkle in the dark. He stayed where he was, a tourist wringing the last drops of enjoyment from the picture-perfect scene.

Laughter disturbed him, ringing out faintly from the beach road behind him. Maybe he was the only person on the island not sailing on a sea of rum-soaked jollity. He wondered whether to cut his losses for the day.

And then there she was. Coming towards him. The light was dim but he could see her clearly, a vision in turquoise walking towards him along the cliff path. Alone.

Finally, this was his opportunity.

Chapter One

They were short of time. Two men on an unscheduled journey to retrieve a racehorse. As the lorry barrelled down the country lane the fixings on the partitions rattled in their slots. The vehicle was doing over fifty, which maybe wasn't wise but there weren't any speed cameras off the main road. Anyhow, they'd be taking it easier on the way back once they'd picked up the horse.

'Give it a bit more welly, can't you?' said the man with blond hair who sat in the passenger seat. The hair, abundant and glistening, was the result of regular trips to a hair stylist in Swindon. Patsy Walsh didn't care who knew it. Little embarrassed him. 'Think I'm a natural blond?' was one of his regular lines to stray women. 'Want to find out?' Funnily enough, many did.

'Don't miss the entrance. It's just round this bend.'

Steve, the lad at the wheel, shot Patsy a look that contained a hint of irritation. He knew this route backwards. But whatever his feelings, Steve kept them to himself. Patsy might have a woman's name and a hairdo worthy of a shampoo advert, but he wasn't a man to pick a fight with.

Patsy noted Steve's reaction and ignored it. He liked a bit of spunk in the lads at Latchmere Park but most of all he liked loyalty, deference and complete obedience to his word. That's how the owner, Adrian Spring, liked it too, only he would never say so. And, since Adrian relied on Patsy to enforce his will, he didn't need to.

They turned through a stone gateway on to a smoothly tarmacked drive in far superior condition to the public road and cruised through a small copse of winter-bare trees, ignoring signs that urged a maximum of 10mph. Ahead lay the huddle of buildings that made up the yard run by Timothy Appleby, where Adrian Spring kept several of his Flat horses.

There would soon be one horse fewer and the thought of removing Sherry Darling from Appleby's clutches gave Patsy grim satisfaction. He'd not been in favour of Appleby getting his hands on her in the first place and he'd made his feelings known to Adrian at the time which, since he had a share in the animal, he was entitled to do. But Adrian was the majority owner, not to mention the guy who picked up the training bills, and Patsy had been overruled. He'd not lost sleep over it. He knew who buttered his bread.

But he'd been right all along. Sherry Darling had run five races for Appleby and not finished better than fourth in any of them. It had been clear to Patsy that the horse needed a longer trip but the trainer insisted on running her in sprints. Last night had been the final straw – dead last in a six-furlong burn-up on the all-weather at Kempton Park. This time Patsy had had no opposition from Adrian and here he was, first thing on a Sunday morning, to take the horse away. And not before time.

Sunday or not, the yard was busy. As Steve stopped the lorry with a crunching halt on the freshly raked gravel, the hissing as he pulled on the air brakes earned inquisitive looks from the lads mucking out in the nearby stalls.

A burly fellow in a battered Barbour jacket was striding in

their direction, shouting something. Gordon, the head lad. He had a small mouth, pink cheeks and looked decidedly cross.

Patsy sprang from the cab and faced him. He was a head taller than Gordon. In racing yards, Patsy was a head taller than most people.

'There's a speed limit here, you know. It's not bloody Brands Hatch.'

Patsy shrugged. 'We're in a bit of hurry. Come to pick up Sherry Darling.'

Gordon stared at the horse box which Steve was now manoeuvring up to the loading ramp.

'No one's told me about it.'

'I'm telling you now. I'd be obliged if you'd get one of your lads to fetch her out.'

Gordon's face turned redder. 'Hang on. You can't just pitch up and nick one of our horses. It's got to go through the governor.'

'You'd better go and fetch him then.'

Gordon didn't like being told what to do. His little mouth twitched uncertainly.

'Get a move on,' Patsy added. 'Some of us have got better things to do than hang around here all day.'

He watched Gordon consider his options. For a moment, it seemed, he might tell Patsy to get lost, to take his lorry and clear off until arrangements had been made through regular channels. He was a solid barrel of a man, as densely muscled as a prop forward. If he'd been accosted by Steve or any of the other Latchmere lads he'd have dismissed them with contempt. But Patsy was not a man to be brushed off and Gordon knew it. They were old adversaries.

Gordon turned on his heel, spat on the ground and stalked off. Patsy watched him go with a grin. He was heading past the nearest row of stalls to a door in the low building of yellow brick on the far side of the yard where Appleby kept his office.

'Come on, Steve,' he said. 'We'll get Sherry ourselves if these tossers won't help us.'

Patsy knew precisely where the horse was housed and was leading her across the yard by the time the dapper figure of Tim Appleby emerged, followed by the sour-faced Gordon.

'Patsy, what on earth are you playing at?'

Appleby's voice, a parade-ground tenor, reverberated around the enclosed area.

Patsy let Steve continue with the horse and turned to face the trainer.

'Morning, Tim.' He extended his hand.

Appleby ignored it. 'You've got a flaming nerve.' He was a man in his fifties, ex-army – it was known he'd served in the Falklands – and accustomed to command. 'Put that horse back at once.'

Steve's step faltered but Patsy called out, 'Carry on, Steve', and the lad obeyed.

Normally a cool customer, Appleby was glaring with fury. 'On whose authority are you taking that horse? This is tantamount to theft.'

'Don't be daft, Tim. As you well know, I'm joint owner of Sherry Darling and quite within my rights to remove her. Considering what a hash-up you've made of looking after her you've been bloody lucky to be earning fees off her for the past six months.'

'Now hang on a minute.' Appleby's tone shifted from the indignant to the unfairly maligned. 'No one is more disappointed than I am that she didn't run well last night. It's a setback, I agree, and maybe she does need a longer trip, but—'

'It's too late. You've had your chance and Adrian's patience has just run out.'

Appleby looked startled. 'Are you saying that Adrian has sent you here to start throwing your weight around?'

Appleby and Spring were golf buddies from way back, which explained Spring's patronage. In Patsy's opinion, it had gone on long enough.

'I can't believe,' continued the trainer, working himself back up into a lather, 'that Adrian would approve of this loutish behaviour. Did no one ever teach you any manners in that bog you come from?'

Patsy gave him a weary look. 'Insulting a man's nationality is no way to resolve a dispute, Tim.' He took a phone from his pocket and pressed Adrian's number on speed dial. 'Perhaps you should have a word with Adrian yourself.' He held out the phone.

Appleby snatched it from his hand without a word and held it to his ear. 'Adrian? Look, I've got your man Walsh in my yard. What the hell is going on?'

As he stepped a few yards off to conduct the conversation, Patsy amused himself by smiling pleasantly at Gordon. What a bunch of wankers they were in this set-up. Self-important windbags the whole lot. They boasted about their big winners but there were nearly two hundred expensive horses here. It would be impossible not to have winners with that amount of ammunition. However, give them an animal with a bit of temperament or one that needed imaginative handling and they were lost. They didn't have a clue.

He couldn't hear the other side of Appleby's conversation but he could see the effect it was having on the trainer. Acceptance of the inevitable was written on his face. Occasionally he started to utter excuses for the horse's poor form and his long-term strategy for the future but he was not allowed to elaborate. Once he'd made up his mind, Adrian was very good at chopping down dead wood. You couldn't present him with any proposal that wasn't well thought through.

Patsy had spent a deal of time thinking through the proposal he himself had made to Adrian the night before, after Sherry Darling's last failure. He'd not travelled to Kempton – why go to the trouble when he knew it would only add to the frustration? He'd watched in a betting shop and seen quite enough to know that this time Adrian had to listen to him. And to be fair, he'd raised no objections.

'OK, Patsy. Do what you want. Tim's blown it. I suppose you're going to say I should have listened to you in the first place.'

Patsy had refrained from rubbing it in but, as they both well knew, he could have done.

Now Appleby rallied as the call came to an end. 'Sure thing, mate. I'll dust off my clubs and we'll make a date. Give my love to Christine.'

His voice was cheerful enough but there was cold dislike in his face as he put the phone back in Patsy's hand.

'There's fees for the quarter owing,' he said. 'Considering we've had no notice, I think they should be paid in full.'

Patsy withdrew a slip of paper from his breast pocket, a cheque made out to Appleby and signed by Adrian Spring.

'If you fetch the account while I'm sorting the horse then I can settle up before we go. I suppose I can spare another couple of minutes.'

He almost laughed out loud as he regarded the expression of distaste on the trainer's face. But he didn't tell Patsy to sod off. He'd seen the cheque and he wanted the money.

Steve had the engine idling, the horse stowed safely in the back, when Gordon lumbered up and shoved the bill wordlessly through the open window of the cab. Patsy gave it a jaundiced look and filled in the amount on the cheque.

'Tell Mr Appleby,' he said as he handed it over, 'that he's

lucky Mr Spring is a generous man. Considering what a crap job you've done, I reckon you're bloody lucky to get a penny.'

'Jesus, Patsy,' Steve grumbled as he drove the box back down the drive, this time at a sedate pace, 'you really know how to make friends, don't you? Gordon's never going to buy me another pint after that.'

'Course he will. Tell him if he doesn't I'll come round and pull his head off.' And then he laughed half the way back to Latchmere.

Steve did not join in.

The sight of her new home lifted Tara's weary heart. Even though she'd not been driving, the three-hour car journey from Manchester had been tedious and she'd hardly slept for days – the anxiety of her departure had seen to that. But suddenly she was invigorated. Even on this dreary January morning, it was as if a shaft of sunlight had burst through the cloud.

Danny had stopped the car at the top of the lane and pointed to the white-walled building below, visible through the gap in the high hedge. 'How do you like it?'

Tara thought she'd never seen such a cute English country cottage this side of a chocolate box.

'That's where you live?' she said.

'That's where we live,' he corrected her. His smile faltered as he looked at her. 'You don't like it?'

'Oh no, Danny.' She reached for his hand and squeezed, returning the beam of contentment to his face – at least one of them was easy to please. 'It's fantastic. I just wasn't expecting anything so lovely.'

And it was indeed lovely. They parked by the gate and Tara took in the immaculate front garden with its freshly tended rose beds and neat gravelled path. She could possibly have done without the stone hedgehog by the porch but she was not here to criticise anyone's taste. She heard a whisper of running water – the path by the lawn to the left of the building must lead down to the river. In high summer with the roses in bloom this would be idyllic. She wondered where she would be when that time came.

Danny was hauling her bags from the boot. She tried to help him but he waved her away.

'You've hardly got anything,' he said.

That was true. Her luggage consisted of one suitcase, a large squashy holdall, a box of books – and the black leather handbag she'd clutched the entire journey, which contained £4,250 in cash zipped into the middle pocket, all she'd held in her current account plus the proceeds from the sale of her Peugeot. From now on, she wouldn't be using her debit or credit cards and she'd be entirely dependent on Danny for transport. It was going to be strange.

He opened the door and dumped the cases inside. Then turned to her with a look of intent, one arm snaking round her back, the other reaching behind her knees as he bent—

'No, Danny!' she squealed as he hoisted her into the air. 'Put me down, you idiot.'

'Why?' He held her weight easily but that was no surprise. Like all jump jockeys, Danny had tremendous upper body strength. 'Why can't I carry you over the threshold?'

'Because we're not married. It's bad luck if you're not married.'

'Rubbish.' His grinning face was inches from hers, his eyes gleaming.

'It's bad luck to me. Put me down.' She pressed her lips to his cheek. 'Please, lovely Danny.'

He set her down gently. She knew how to get her way.

She drew his arm round her waist as he ushered her through the doorway ahead of him. It was important not to forget his feelings in the turmoil of her own. He was a good, sweet man and without him right now she'd be doomed.

Inside, the cottage held no trace of the dampness she'd been expecting. The downstairs front rooms were snug and cosy and the big kitchen held an Aga and a dining table and two Welsh dressers, not to mention all kinds of up-to-the-minute appliances, most of which, Tara could see at a glance, had barely been used.

She reflected that there might be worse things to do with her new life than turn into a homebody.

Danny didn't linger downstairs and, though the motorway coffee seemed hours off, she didn't feel enough at ease to put the kettle on herself. So she allowed him to lead her upstairs where there was a nicely kitted out study with a computer and games console, a small exercise room with weights and a rowing machine, a large comfortable bathroom, and a bedroom with a view down to the river.

Danny put her suitcase down by the fitted wardrobe which ran the length of one wall. Its mirrored doors reflected the view through the opposite window of bare trees and a winter sky the colour of an old bruise. Here, inside, it was warm. The bed in the centre of the room was large and welcoming.

'Well,' he said. 'What do you think?'

She thought a lot that she couldn't say, but there was one thing she had to ask him.

'Is this where you were going to live with Kirsty?'

His happy face clouded over. Kirsty – the girl he'd been going to marry. Her own best friend. Murdered.

The ghost in their lives that had brought them together.

'Yes,' he said. 'Adrian had it done up for us as a wedding present. Kirsty told him what she wanted.'

That explained why it was so luxurious.

'Does that matter?' he asked.

'No.' How could it? Kirsty had been dead for a year and a half – nearly. Life went on.

He looked relieved. 'And you like it?'

'It's gorgeous, Danny.'

He slipped his arm cautiously round her shoulders. 'I hope you'll be happy here with me, Tara.'

'Of course I will.' She forced the smile back on to her face.

As he kissed her, he shuffled her backwards towards the bed. She didn't object as he toppled her on to the soft counterpane. In the circumstances, how could she?

Adrian Spring slipped his mobile phone back into the pocket of the lightweight zip-up jacket he wore for his Sunday-morning run through the woods of Latchmere Park. He treasured the moments he spent on his regular exercise – he tried to get out most mornings – but it was hard to be parted from his phone. Even ten minutes out of touch could mean that some fool in his employment would make a wrong decision.

Fool, however, was not a description he would ever apply to Patsy Walsh. At least not now. Ten years ago, when Adrian was still working full time in the advertising business and just dipping his toes into the world of horse breeding, Patsy had waylaid him on a visit to Christine Clark's yard. All he knew about Patsy was that he was related in some fashion to the trainer. He was a raw-boned lad, far too big to be a rider, who probably owed his place on the stable staff to the family connection. Adrian owned a couple of jump horses under his future wife's care.

Patsy had bent his ear about a horse, a small grey mare owned and trained by a local farmer. 'Believe me, Mr Spring, she's quick, like her mother – comes from good stock. Old Gilligan's got to raise some money fast, that's the only reason he'll let her go. I'm thinking you could race her for a couple of seasons and then breed from her. If I've heard right, that's the kind of thing you're interested in, isn't it?'

Adrian had been duly cynical of this pitch but Christine had vouched for Patsy. 'He's a bit of a rogue but he's the smartest lad in the yard. He's Dermot's stepbrother and their dad breeds a few horses over in Ireland, so he knows what he's on about.'

Dermot was Christine's late husband, a roistering Kerry man who'd been too fond of the bottle.

At the time Adrian was in the process of selling his business for £85 million and so the £12,000 the farmer asked for the mare appeared little more than spare change and worth a punt. But it had turned out to be more than a casual speculation. Miss Brown had won three Group races for Adrian on the Flat, after which he'd retired her to stud where she'd produced a string of talented colts. She was still a valued member of the Latchmere Stud, with her offspring commanding impressive prices at the sales. Adrian had never sat down to work it out, but over the years his initial outlay of a few thousand must have earned him close on a million.

The story of Miss Brown was, for once, win-win all the way down the line. Apart from the obvious, it had illustrated to Adrian that Patsy Walsh was more than just a pretty face and since then the two of them had forged a working relationship that was of more value to him than all the riches accruing from Miss Brown. And he'd made sure that Patsy had reaped the benefit from this and every other venture they had been jointly involved in, though Patsy, being a smart fellow, had never been slow to look out for number one. Adrian had noticed, the day after Patsy had brokered the deal for Miss Brown from farmer Gilligan, that he had swapped his dodgy old Mini for a three-year-old Nissan that started at the first twist of a key. Adrian had no doubt that this was due to a 'drink' the Irishman had extracted for the sale and he didn't begrudge it. In his experience, self-interest was a powerful motive in an employee; he just had to ensure that their aims were mutual.

The knock-on benefits of Miss Brown had also extended to Adrian's love life, adding to the bond that was developing between himself and Christine. At the time he'd been a workaholic with no time for significant commitments outside the office. His appetite for women had been strictly fast food, with a taste for leggy brunettes. The succession of slinky companions whom he squired around town barely counted compared to the all-consuming complexity of his business life. It had been that way ever since he'd told his father to stick his hopes of seeing his only son become the first Spring to go to university and talked his way into a Soho ad agency instead. He'd not spent long toiling amongst the office pond life. By the age of twenty-one – the age when he might have been graduating from some no-account redbrick uni with a wanky arts degree, as he put it to his father – he'd been running ad campaigns for multinationals, overseeing television shoots with agency-busting budgets and pulling in a top salary. But Adrian wasn't a salary man at heart. By his mid-twenties, he'd teamed up with a couple of smart creatives and sweet-talked backers into launching his own agency. The day his father put money into the business was the best of his life to that point. And the business itself – winning over clients, making memorable campaigns, acquiring other companies, kicking the shit out of the competition – was his all-consuming obsession. No woman could compete with the buzz of that kind of endeavour. The girls came and went, leaving no lasting impression, all of them transient no matter how hard they tried to become permanent fixtures.

It was a long time before the thrill of his company's success began to pall and when it did the signs came from an unlikely quarter. Adrian had forced himself to take an interest in horseracing when he was wooing a telecoms billionaire who'd dragged him along to the Cheltenham Festival. By the time four hilarious and exhilarating days were over, Adrian found he'd agreed to buy a horse himself from his friend's trainer, an attractive dark-haired mother of two who owned a small yard in Lambourn. He'd heard she was tough, a widow who had survived marriage to an alcoholic with a temper. He saw for himself that beneath the long-limbed elegance there was steel and the strength to manage an unruly horse, or haul a belligerent drunk up the stairs to bed. As it turned out, Christine Clark was only the part-owner of Latchmere stables. Half of the interest in the yard had passed into the hands of the bank, thanks to her thirsty husband who had spent the money acquiring the diseased liver that had sent him to his grave before his fortieth birthday.

At first it had just been his horse, Spring-heeled Jack – he'd not resisted the pun – that had captivated Adrian's attention. Jack had been a game stayer, never happier than when battling over obstacles on bottomless ground. When Adrian realised that watching his horse come a game third on a foul and muddy day amongst the brollies and bacon-butty smells of Fontwell Park gave him more of a thrill than any boardroom victory, he knew his advertising days were numbered.

If he played his cards right Adrian realised he could walk away with enough money to keep him in clover for the rest of his life. But – to do what? At the time he wasn't yet forty – the same age that Christine's husband had met his undignified and painful end. The irony wasn't lost on him.

He knew that once he retreated from advertising he

17

would lose half his acquaintances at a stroke. He had good friends, colleagues he'd fought with and against over the years; he wouldn't lose them entirely but there would be an unavoidable slackening of bonds. What drove their lives and took up their time would no longer have a claim on his. Once he was no longer a player he wouldn't be of much interest to those still in the game.

He had no family to speak of in England, beyond a few distant cousins. Both his parents were gone and Rachel, his only sibling, had put down roots in Israel. He saw her and his nephews twice a year at most. And, of course, he had no children of his own.

The bottom line was that he had time, energy and money to make another way of life, if only he knew what it should be.

For such an inveterate planner it was strange the way he let the horse business take over. He found himself spending time at race meetings and in Christine Clark's yard. He bought a couple more horses and began researching the breeding side of the business. At first it was the money that caught his attention – the vast sums that could be won and lost dealing in bloodlines – but to get into any business he knew you had to understand the hands-on basics. And the hands-on basics here were a pregnant mare and a quivering newborn bundle of horseflesh tottering around a stall in the middle of the night.

He witnessed his first birth at the Latchmere yard by Christine's side, having made her promise to call him once she thought her mare was due, whatever the hour. He'd driven down from London at three in the morning and made it just in time. She'd been pleased to see him – at least, he hoped she had been. She wasn't a woman who was easily impressed. Neither his Bentley nor his Porsche had drawn a comment from her and his Christmas gift of diamond circlet earrings from Tiffany had been met with a simple, 'That's very generous,' and he had yet to see her wear them.

In the early morning, though, with the foal safely delivered after a three-hour labour, Christine's cool façade finally began to melt. She leaned back against Adrian's body and for a moment he thought she was going to fall. He held her up, his arms round her waist, his face in her dishevelled mop of dark hair.

'You must be dead on your feet,' he said. She'd been up all night.

'It's just the relief,' she said. 'I'll be fine in a moment.'

They stood in silence, Adrian savouring the weight of her. She smelled of hay and blood and horses with, somewhere in the distance, a note of citron, her customary perfume. In front of them the new mother set to with her tongue to clean her foal, who was all legs and matted hair. Adrian knew he would never forget this moment.

Christine turned languidly in his arms to face him. Her eyes, deep-set and unreadable in the dim light, were just a couple of inches lower than his. He could feel the knots in her spine beneath the wool of her sweater. Her face was lined with fatigue.

'Thank you,' she said.

'What for?' All he'd done was make her cups of tea in the office across the courtyard.

'It helped,' she said. 'You being here.'

He didn't reply. The whole scenario was alien to the life he had lived – the bucolic birth, the smell of horse shit, the unglamorous woman in his arms. But it all added up to something. It was real. He wasn't going to make a bloody commercial out of this.

The moment was broken by the noisy arrival of Stephanie, Christine's eleven- year-old daughter, eager for news. 'Oh wow,' she squealed at the sight of the foal.

But what stuck in Adrian's mind was the way Christine sprang from his arms at Stephanie's arrival, as if she had something to hide. He realised then that maybe his attempts to burrow beneath the woman's cool exterior were having some effect after all. Which, in the event, had proved to be the case.

Six months later they were married, Adrian had paid off the bank loan on the yard and bought the next door farm where he was in the business of establishing his own stud. Along with a wife, he had acquired a National Hunt trainer, two stepchildren and an entirely new way of life. At the time he had thought it the best takeover of his career.

From his jacket came the summons of his phone. He pulled it from his pocket. Christine.

'I'm just checking you'll be here for lunch.'

'Lunch?'

'Danny's bringing Tara. Don't tell me you've forgotten.'

Of course he hadn't forgotten – he never forgot anything, as Christine well knew. But she was anxious about the occasion, with Danny showing off this girl who'd just moved in with him. The girl who was taking Kirsty's place.

He'd not met Tara yet. When, recently, Danny had brought her to the yard, taken her racing and teamed up with Christine and Stephanie for a get-to-know-you session in the pub, Adrian had been elsewhere. It hadn't been entirely accidental. He wasn't sure he wanted to encounter Kirsty's replacement.

But there was no way out of it today unless he was prepared to cause a major rift in the family. Not that he was afraid of that. His marriage to Christine was a business arrangement as much as anything else – one she had been more than happy to embrace.

He'd proposed to her in Paris – it had been the furthest he could persuade her to travel for a night from the yard and the kids. He'd made it as romantic as he could: an old-fashioned Left Bank hotel, a restaurant free of tourists with unbelievable food and a walk by the Seine at midnight on a balmy May evening. He'd proposed to her on the narrow Pont de l'Archevêché in the shadow of Notre-Dame.

When he'd said, 'Will you marry me?' she'd replied, 'How would that work exactly?' So he'd told her what his money could do for her and the children and for Latchmere Park. He told her he loved her too, and that he wanted to point his life in a new direction – if she'd lead him there.

'OK,' she'd said. 'I conditionally accept.'

He'd laughed. He had his arm round her waist as they looked down at the black waters of the river. 'That's not the most romantic response, Christine.'

'It wasn't the most romantic proposal.'

He thought he'd tried but he didn't argue the point. 'What conditions?'

'The training yard stays in my name. I built it from nothing and it stands or falls on my ability. If you want to bale me out with the bank, I'd be delighted but that doesn't give you a say in the yard. Not that I won't be happy to listen to my husband's opinion.'

'Is that it?'

'One more thing.' She turned her face to his. Her pale, handsome features were grave, set in stone. 'You have to promise you'll love my children as much as any of your own.'

The words took him by surprise. Then he took in their implications.

'Do you want us to have kids?' he said.

'Do you?'

He'd not thought about the matter, not in any specific sense, though he'd always assumed that one day he would be a dad. Maybe that day was closer than he'd thought.

'Yes,' he'd replied. 'Let's give it a try. But whatever happens I promise to be the best stepfather I can.'

Her eyes had lit up. Her lips were no longer stony. He kissed them to seal the deal. And he had been a good stepfather. It was just a pity that they'd never managed to have children after all. It lay between them like promise unfulfilled.

But he didn't like to think about what might have been. There was a lot to be said for seeing marriage as a contract. Although it was not possible to keep emotion off the page entirely. He might not want to meet Tara but he could hardly throw her off his land in a fit of emotional revulsion. Just because she wasn't Kirsty.

'Don't worry,' he said into the phone. 'I'll be there in my best bib and tucker.'

'Thanks, Adrian. Sorry to nag.' There was relief in Christine's tone.

'That's all right, darling.' He used the endearment deliberately. 'I'm looking forward to it immensely.'

He sounded sincere but, an adman all his working life, he'd always been a bloody good liar.

Tara stirred and pushed the bedclothes from her face. It took her a second or two to recognise her surroundings – the thick cream carpet, the pale apricot drapes framing a view of fields and sky. She was in bed at Danny's cottage with Danny's arms wrapped round her and his breath warm against her ear. She wondered if he'd lain here with Kirsty just like this, the covers pulled snugly over their half-naked bodies after they'd made love on the counterpane. If making love was an accurate description of what they'd just done.

On Danny's part it undoubtedly was. He'd always liked her, from the moment Kirsty had introduced her to him as 'my best friend in the entire world'. They'd met up on their own once or twice, mostly to discuss the upcoming wedding in which Tara had reluctantly agreed to be the maid of honour. On one occasion, after an evening in a wine bar, Danny had even spent the night on her sofa in Manchester. And never, in that honeyed period before Kirsty had been killed, had he cast a lustful glance in her direction. He'd been in love with one woman and others didn't interest him – which was how it should be.

And after Kirsty's death, that's how it had remained. There had been long middle-of-the-night conversations and the occasional meeting when they'd pooled their distress. Good friends with the same bleeding wound, that's how she saw it. They'd needed each other to lean on, him more than her, which she understood. After six months she'd tried introducing him to other girls, just to cheer him up. But he'd told her to stop it, he'd find his own women when he was ready and that having her to talk to was more important than any meaningless fling. She'd been impressed by that.

Then her own world fell apart and she'd needed a way out. The only escape route she could see was the one that she had just taken – and she'd done it by deceiving her closest friend.

But when a bruiser the size of a house has shown you the vial of acid he will use to melt your face, it drives all thoughts of loyalty out of your head. Sheer terror had kept her from telling Danny the truth.

She knew she wasn't just in danger herself. Danny had invited her into the centre of his life. Latchmere Park was hearth and home and his working world, inhabited by his family and closest colleagues. They would be at risk too.

It had been easy to change the nature of their relations. She'd never counted herself as much of an actress but it wasn't hard to think of Danny as a suitor, to turn the regular confessional dinner into an occasion with a hint of promise in the air. They'd both run out of dissecting the past anyway. She allowed one thing to lead to another and soon overnight accommodation for Danny was no longer her lumpy old sofa.

It was barely six weeks since she'd rerouted him into her bedroom. She'd made herself pretty tipsy to get over her nerves, to help with the subterfuge or maybe just anaesthetise herself. If she hadn't still been shell-shocked by the catastrophe of her affair with Tom she doubted she could have gone through with it. As it was, she'd felt neither pain nor pleasure, just – as Danny looked tenderly at her the next morning – an overwhelming sense of guilt.

She was getting used to the guilt now, even with the additional burden of lying here in the bed her best friend had once shared with the same man. But she could cope with that – Kirsty would have understood and the dead have no choice but to be forgiving. She wasn't so sure about the living, however. Danny had fallen for her like a lost soul clutching at salvation and she couldn't bear the thought of hurting him. Maybe, in time, she would be able to love him as he deserved. Maybe this – the new life in the country, the perfect cottage, the handsome man at her beck and call – would be the solution to all her problems.

'I'm getting to like it,' Danny murmured into her ear.

She chuckled. 'I thought you always liked it.' It was the kind of things lovers said.

'Not that. Your hair. It shows off your gorgeous neck.'

Her hair. She hadn't thought the new haircut – the drastic shearing, as it had turned out – would be so hard for him to take. To be fair, she hadn't considered his reaction at all when she'd got Sharon to set to work.

'You sure about this?' Sharon had said as she stood over her, scissors in hand. 'It's a bloody long time since I did more than give anyone a quick trim. And you've got such lovely hair.'

'I'm sure,' she'd said. 'I'm fed up with having it long. New life, new look, that's what I want.'

'But . . .' Her landlady had still hesitated. 'Won't your folks want to see you with your old look? My mam would have gone bananas if I'd massacred my hair.'

Tara had told Sharon she was going back to Ireland to live. 'At least I won't have to deal with the psychos who live in this dump,' she'd said.

That, at least, had been true. She couldn't let on to Sharon where she was really going.

To have done the job properly, and that had been her original intention, she'd have got Sharon to dye her hair as well as cut it. But the ragged crop looked so radical – reframing her face, the thick honey-blond hair standing up in spikes across the crown of her head – that she thought it might be good enough. Face it, if Tom came after her himself, no amount of hair colouring would disguise her. That bastard knew every inch of her body.

So Danny's reaction had not been uppermost in her mind. The poor man. Little did he know what a bad deal he was holding in his arms.

He was breathing softly into her ear, teasing her lobe gently between his teeth – the way hungry lovers did.

'I ought to unpack,' she said.

'No,' he said. 'Later.'

'But shouldn't we be getting ready? We've got lunch at the farm.'

'That's not for ages.' His hand found her breast.

She turned in the circle of his arms and studied his expression. Would he look as happy as this if he knew the truth?

She could tell him now. Come completely clean about

Tom and the trial and Benny Bridges who would peel the skin from her flesh with a penknife if she did not retract her statement.

And Danny might put her bags back in the car and drive her far from the warm and welcoming sanctuary of Latchmere Park. Get rid of the ticking bomb before it blew up in his face.

She considered telling him the truth. But she didn't have the guts to take the risk.

Chapter Two

The wind gusted into Rick's body, whipping flecks of rain into his eyes. He ducked the peak of his riding hat into the breeze and his mount shuffled unhappily. Maybe this wasn't the best weather to be giving a first jumping lesson to a couple of four-year-olds. The clouds were moving in from the west, blotting from view the ridges of the Cambrian Mountains. A deluge was on its way.

'Come on, Rick.' Hugh's voice rang out above the wind as he set off at a steady canter up the side of the field. Hugh's horse Gingerbread looked a sight more eager than the one Rick was now digging in the belly with his boots, just to get him going, but that was no surprise. Treacle Toffee was a lazy sod. All the talent in the world but bone idle. Rick didn't mind riding lazy horses so long as they made the effort when pushed, which in five runs on the Flat was something Treacle Toffee had never done. Still, jumping might be just what he needed to give him an interest.

The two horses had done plenty of schooling as young-sters on the stud before Hugh had sent the pair away to be trained. Not that he had ever planned on racing them but the two were jinxed when it came to sales time – as if they were never meant to be owned by anyone else. As yearlings they had missed out on a new home, through injury in the case of Gingerbread and failure to reach a decent reserve in the case of Treacle Toffee. Then at the end of their second season of racing, having recovered barely half of their training fees in prize money, they had been set for the horses-in-training sale, only for them both to get ringworm. So here they were on a filthy wet Sunday morning in January, taking the first steps on a new career as jumpers.

Rick had spent the last year living with Hugh and his family, helping out with the horses at Hugh's modest stud. It was a far cry from the big racing enterprises Rick had been involved with when he was trying seriously to make it as a jockey. That had been before his sister's death. In reality, Hugh and his wife Gwen had been grief counsellors as much as employers. They were terrific people. Horses were at the heart of their lives, and no matter what went wrong, they never faltered in their enthusiasm. If ever a couple deserved a decent horse it was them, but to date they had had little to show for years of effort.

Hugh and Rick cantered around the field a couple of times to get the horses warmed up and then took them in to show them the first flight of hurdles. The obstacles were laid out in the field in lines of three some eighty yards apart. There were three different sizes, all with large white plastic wings on either side to help prevent the horses from running out.

'Come on, you leary bollocks.' Rick had to give Treacle Toffee a gentle slap down the shoulder to make him walk up close to the hurdle. Rick could feel the animal's heart pounding in his chest as he took him close enough to sniff the top rail, but once he realised the hurdle wasn't going to jump up and bite him he seemed to relax. Treacle Toffee was well bred but his career to date was one of unfulfilled promise, reluctant to show the speed he possessed on the familiar gallops of home. Now his Flat career was over; did he have what it took to become a jumper?

That was what they were here to find out.

Meanwhile Gingerbread was taking it all in his stride, as if he had schooled a hundred times before. The baby hurdles were only about eighteen inches from the turf to the top of the padded rail. The idea was to get the horses jumping and enjoying themselves. Gaining confidence. Once they were happy over the babies, then they could move to the next size up before taking on the regulation-height hurdles which measured an inch over three feet.

'Are you ready?' Hugh said as he wheeled Gingerbread round. 'We'll sit upsides nice and sensible, you keep on my left because he is less likely to run out there.' Rick did as he was told. He might have been the race rider with most experience, but Hugh knew these horses inside out. If truth be told, he couldn't wait to be jumping again, even on this modest scale.

The pair turned and trotted back fifty yards before turning in to face the line of baby hurdles. Treacle Toffee was now keen to get going and Rick had to talk to him to keep him settled. For one moment Rick felt him move to run out to his left. Luckily he was riding with a good length of leather and a firm squeeze with his left leg got him straightened up.

The two horses took off simultaneously. Treacle Toffee sprang into the air as if he was expecting the hurdle to jump up and grab him. By the time he landed, Hugh and Gingerbread were twenty yards in front. Hugh steadied up and waited for Rick to get upsides again.

'OK?'

'He's fine – just a bit windy.' By the time Rick had replied, the next hurdle was upon them. He gave Treacle Toffee a good kick in the belly to make him jump forward and this time when he landed he was almost upsides Gingerbread who, Hugh was proudly informing him, felt a complete natural. Rick could feel Treacle Toffee's confidence growing as he powered across the wet turf towards the last flight. This time the horse couldn't wait to jump. His stride quickened and he took off and landed running like a veteran.

Hugh was beaming from ear to ear as they slowed to a walk at the end of the field.

'Somebody very talented must have schooled these at some stage.'

The tongue-in-cheek comment brought a smile to Rick's face. Hugh was the most modest man you could find. He was well aware Rick knew he had schooled them both while breaking them in.

'Come on, let's try the middle ones.'

These were appreciably higher but, at two foot six, hardly formidable. What would Treacle Toffee make of them?

Not much, it seemed. His confidence was such that he now wanted to be in front of Gingerbread rather than alongside him. Rick kept a tight hold on him to make sure they helped each other. The horse negotiated all three as if he'd been jumping such insignificant barriers all his life. He hardly seemed to be aware they were there.

'Good lad,' Rick shouted, patting the horse's neck with enthusiasm as they pulled up again. 'Let's see what they make of the big ones.'

Hugh looked dubious. 'Is that wise?'

But Rick wasn't going to debate the matter. Hugh might be his boss but he knew when a horse felt right. And Treacle Toffee, for almost the first time in their acquaintance, appeared to have an appetite for work.

'Come on. They're fired up now.'

Schooling was like a drug to Rick. He could hardly wait to get going again.

They trotted back down to the start and this time set off at a quicker pace to gain momentum. The horses took more notice of these larger obstacles. Rick felt a moment of hesitation as Treacle Toffee wondered whether these were too big for him to jump. But a moment was all it was as the horse surged forward and took the hurdle in his stride. Rick patted his neck. At the next flight he sensed that his mount was going to have to make some adjustment to his stride to get over it quickly. He sat still, waiting for Treacle Toffee to shorten his step, but instead the horse came up a whole stride early. Rick thought they were bound to hit the top bar and come crashing to the ground. He held his breath in anticipation and sat as still as he could so that Treacle Toffee had the best chance of balancing himself. He needn't have worried. The horse stretched out his front feet as far as he could and seemed to extend his entire body in mid-flight. Ears pricked, he landed almost as far on the other side of the hurdle, as pleased as Punch with himself.

'Bloody hell, how good is that?'

Rick and Hugh looked at each other in disbelief. Maybe they'd found something Treacle could do well – at last.

A vicious squall of wind and rain blasted into them, interrupting their reflections. The rain was now running off the end of Hugh's nose on to his jacket. He took out his handkerchief.

'Come on, let's go home and do some planning.'

No, he'd never met this Tara before, Adrian decided. The slender girl with the urchin haircut would surely have stuck in his memory. He would not have forgotten the mismatched eyes – one more green than brown – and the little gap between her front teeth. These imperfections simply reinforced the impact of a spectacularly pretty woman shivering slightly by Danny's side in the hallway of Latchmere House. Was she nervous or just cold? Whatever the reason, Adrian's impulse was to throw a protective arm round her. So much for his loyalty to Kirsty's memory.

In the event he just took the small hand she proffered and offered her a drink. 'Something to warm you up,' he said. 'How about a Scotch? Or a brandy? I've a rather special cognac that would be just the thing.'

She declined the spirits in a voice with an Irish lilt but agreed to a glass of red wine – to be agreeable, he suspected. Before retreating to the kitchen to fetch it, he stood aside to allow Danny to usher her into the sitting room.

Latchmere House was built on a large scale. When Adrian had first set foot inside it, it had been shabby and badly maintained, for the obvious reason that Christine had no money to spend on it. Their marriage had changed all that. A new roof, a conservatory extension and a radical programme of redecoration had transformed a ramshackle Victorian farmhouse into an airy and impressive mansion that had been featured more than once in glossy lifestyle magazines. Some of the longer-standing stable staff, Adrian knew, considered the big house 'too posh' these days and always used the back door for fear of making a mess. But that, Adrian considered, was as it should be.

He watched as Tara crossed the room towards Stephanie, who was holding out her arms in welcome. As the two young women embraced, an image flashed into his head – of a slender girl walking away from him into the welcoming hug of her friend. The friend had been Kirsty and the willowy girl, with thick burnt-honey hair tumbling to her shoulders, had been Tara, he was suddenly convinced of it. She must have cut her hair since that summer evening eighteen months ago. He'd not seen her face – he'd been trying to keep a low profile, watching from the Starbucks across the street from Kirsty's block in Manchester – but that walk brought back memories, a weightless glide into the arms of the other woman. Even though, back then, it was his future daughter-in-law who had obsessed him, he had been able to appreciate her friend's allure.

Some thirty minutes earlier, Kirsty had insisted he leave her flat, saying she was expecting someone. She'd been coy, refusing to give a name or even her visitor's sex. She could be like that, the little witch. She liked to wind him up, to exercise her power over him. For a man like him, rich and influential – in line for significant public honours if he played his cards right – it had been a strange sensation to find himself putty in another's hands.

He'd sat in the cafe letting his expensive froth go cold in front of him, untouched, wallowing in the strange sensation that he knew must be jealousy. Who was Kirsty's visitor? It must surely be a man. Not Danny, that was certain – he was 170 miles away with two rides at Fakenham.

Kirsty was sloe-eyed and curvy, husky-voiced and effortlessly flirty. The kind of girl who attracted men like wasps to a jam pot. Young as she was, there'd been a few who'd offered her a piece of their heart, Adrian was sure of it. At first, when Danny had paraded her with pride, Adrian had been sceptical and he'd had her checked out. He had not turned up anything to disqualify her as a daughter-in-law. Her parents were worthy enough – her father taught at an independent school in Shropshire and her mother was manager of a charity shop. Her younger brother, Rick, was easy to assess. He'd been working at another Lambourn yard as a conditional jockey and, after Danny had recommended him, he'd joined the Latchmere staff. Kirsty herself had dropped out of a law degree at Manchester University and was working at a PR firm in the city. All of which was unremarkable enough. And when Christine had set her seal of approval on the match, who was he, merely the stepfather, to throw cold water on proceedings?

He'd made an unnecessary detour through Manchester to

drop in at her office unannounced. She'd been unfazed and cleared her diary to accept his invitation to lunch. It was the first of many once he'd realised what an utterly beguiling young woman she was. Middle-aged man falls for female half his age – he was well aware of the familiar script. But in this case, he told himself, it was entirely excusable. After all, she was about to become his daughter-in-law.

It was this paternal enchantment which had led him, ultimately, to his pathetic vigil in a cafe. He tried justifying his actions by telling himself he had Danny's interests at heart. But he knew the roster of his imperfections and self-deception was not among them. He was spying on Kirsty to assuage his own jealousy.

So it was with feelings of profound relief that he had realised the girl with the dancer's step was Kirsty's visitor. And now here was that same girl in his own home, having just unpacked her bags in Danny's cottage and about to take Kirsty's place in all their lives. There was a symmetry in this turn of events but he wasn't sure that it was to his liking.

For one thing, just how closely had Kirsty confided in her 'best friend'?

There were some matters that had died with Kirsty, which Adrian did not relish being brought back to life.

As he poured wine for his guest in the kitchen, he wondered exactly how much she knew.

'So what are you going to do with those two horses?' Rick said as he entered the kitchen of Hugh's farmhouse. He was briskly towelling his thatch of sandy-brown hair. Hugh sat at the table amidst the ruins of the family lunch, flicking through a newspaper. The rest of the family – Gwen and their two daughters – had gone off showjumping for the afternoon.

Hugh got up at Rick's appearance and made for the oven. 'Here you go,' he said, placing a brimming plate on the table. 'Gwen says sorry if it's a bit dried out but it's your own bloody fault.'

Rick had stayed on in the yard, sorting out the two horses who'd needed extensive cleaning and drying before being fed after their exhilarating but mucky morning. Hugh had done his bit but Rick had insisted he went back on time for Sunday lunch. He knew Gwen and the girls had to leave by one thirty.

Rick sat down and picked up a fork. Dried out or not, any hot food was welcome at this point.

'I want to run them over hurdles,' Hugh said, busying himself at the kettle. 'Why else were we out there this morning arsing around in the wet?'

Rick found himself grinning. 'I enjoyed it.'

'Me too.' Hugh plonked a mug of industrial-strength tea by his elbow. 'They did all right, didn't they?'

'They did. Treacle's got real promise.'

'He's always had that. It's just that he never delivers on it.'

'He might this time.' This was a familiar conversation but Rick intended to turn it in a new direction. 'When I asked what you were going to do, I meant do you plan to train them yourself?'

Hugh sipped his tea and considered. 'I'm not sure. We've got a great schooling ground but we don't really have a decent gallop. You know that. And I don't want to be fooling around putting them in the lorry every time I need to work them. What do you think?'

'I suppose we could try and bring them on here.' Rick took another mouthful – the beef was overdone all right. Too bad. 'But I would have thought they would be better off getting the best training facilities you could afford. You've got a fair amount tied up in them.'

Hugh's investment was as much emotional as financial. The pair had been named by his daughters and had become part of the family.

'So what would you do if they were yours?'

'If they were mine,' Rick said, 'I'd ask Christine Clark to take them. She's a genius with difficult horses.'

'Is she? I thought she was just coasting on her husband's money.'

'That's not fair. She was training long before Adrian came along. She kept the business going when her first husband got ill.'

'Oh.' Hugh looked surprised. 'I thought you'd fallen out with that lot.'

This wasn't entirely true, though he was almost as surprised as Hugh to find himself advocating Christine. His sister had been killed while holidaying with Danny and her future in-laws. However, what had happened to Kirsty was not Christine's fault, any more than it could be laid at the door of the other members of her family. A tourist murder on a Caribbean island paradise – they were as much the victims of the event as he was. Only he'd been four thousand miles away and they'd been right there. They'd taken his sister away, alive and laughing, delighted at the prospect of everything that lay ahead of her. And they'd brought her back in a coffin. It was tough to get over.

His feelings were complicated but they were also irrelevant where Treacle Toffee and Gingerbread were concerned.

'Believe me,' he said, 'Christine's brilliant. She's got a sixth sense when it comes to animals. The vet at her yard says she can tell when a horse is out of sorts before its own lad can. She takes endless care. Very imaginative. She's better with horses than humans, if you ask me.'

'You're pretty good with horses yourself.'

'Thanks, but I don't know enough to train them like she

would. Schooling them like this morning is one thing, getting them up for a big race is quite another.'

Hugh nodded. 'Tell you what. I'll send them to Christine Clark on the understanding that if she gets them racing, you'll be riding.'

That was a shock.

'I'm not sure I want to get back into that, Hugh.'

'Why not? You can't hide away here with me for ever. It's a waste. If you ask me, you're twice the jockey most of the regular guys are.'

'That's kind of you.'

'No, it's bloody not. It's true. And what's also true is that you've got to get over your big sister. It's a terrible thing, I know, but Kirsty's gone and she's not coming back. And me and Gwen aren't going to mollycoddle you for ever. You've got to get out there and start living your own life.'

Rick felt the blood rush into his face. He wanted to tell Hugh to mind his own business. He wished he'd never opened this can of worms. He felt like getting up and running out of the room. Except, of course, Hugh was right.

'You and Gwen have been talking about me, haven't you?'

'What do you expect? Once we've finishing discussing our own kids we move on to you.'

'You want me to move out.'

'Not yet, not till you're ready. You can stay here for ever as far as we're concerned but we don't think that's in your interest.'

'Oh.' Rick felt in shock. 'So where does that leave us now?'

'It leaves you ringing Christine Clark and sounding her out about my horses. If she's interested, I'll take over and tell her you'll be riding for me.'

Rick had the feeling he'd been manoeuvred into something against his better judgement. But he trusted Hugh. Maybe he knew best. And there was the prospect, remote though it seemed at the moment, of race-riding again. One thing his friend had said struck a chord – it was time to get back into the saddle.

Maybe it was the wine but Tara found the lunch party she had been dreading was passing without pain. She was sitting next to Danny's sister, Stephanie, whose only topic of conversation, on this occasion, was the difficult pregnancy of a favourite mare at Latchmere Stud. Steph was a horse obsessive, rarely seen out of sloppy sweaters and riding trousers. Today she sat awkwardly in a blouse and crumpled skirt, a sop to Sunday lunch formality, so Tara assumed.

On another occasion Tara might have found this breathless drama of premature birth less than riveting. Today she was simply content to sit back and prompt her neighbour to keep going. This way, nobody was asking her questions that she might prefer to avoid answering. And on her other side sat Christine, who was far too polite to put her on the spot – on this occasion, at any rate.

At the head of the table the three men present, Adrian, Danny and a latecomer, a broad-shouldered fellow with long blond hair, were also discussing horses. Specifically an animal called Sherry that Patsy, the long-haired fellow, had removed at short notice from another yard that morning. Exactly what to do next with the horse monopolised their interest to the exclusion of all else, and they soon sucked Christine into the discussion.

Tara was grateful her presence caused so little stir. Possibly they were as keen as she was for her to simply blend in. After all, not so long ago Kirsty would have been sitting in her place. And all of them, apart from Patsy, had been on the holiday from which Kirsty had not returned. How did the rest of them feel about the murder? she wondered. They must have talked about it together. Maybe round this table at Sunday lunchtimes. Now that was a spooky thought.

Tara found herself staring at Patsy. Since he was sitting directly in her eyeline, it would have been hard to avoid doing so. Unlike the others, he appeared to have made no concessions to a Sunday dress code – unless frayed jeans and an open-necked shirt was his idea of dressing up.

Kirsty had told her about Patsy – he'd not been in her good books. 'He thinks he's been put on this earth as a gift to women,' was what she'd said. 'Well, he's not my idea of a gift.'

Tara had asked whether he'd made a pass at her, which might explain her animosity. Kirsty had denied it. 'He's not an idiot. He knows I'm off limits. I'd go straight to Danny and Adrian and he'd be screwed. He owes everything to Adrian.'

All the same, Kirsty was a natural flirt. Tara wondered if she could have given an unsophisticated operator like Patsy the wrong signal and caused some kind of a blow-up between them.

On the other hand, despite the earring and the elaborate coiffure, Patsy was evidently a sharp fellow. No man held in high esteem by Adrian Spring, as Tara knew Patsy was, could be any kind of fool. Danny had told her Patsy was a kind of uncle, one of the family. The way he was talking to Christine – arguing his case with confidence and firm good humour – did not imply any lack of social sophistication. Maybe Kirsty had got him wrong. She was the kind of girl who liked to be the centre of attention and this golden, god-like man might have been too much like competition.

Luckily Patsy did not appear to notice her interest but the same could not be said of Adrian. Tara was conscious of his flinty grey eyes flicking in her direction at regular moments throughout the meal.

Though he must be fifty or so, there was still a youthful air about him. His handshake was vigorous and his voice warm. His hair was now more salt than pepper, but a lock fell boyishly over his forehead which he swept back with long aesthete's fingers. There was no hint of middle-aged tummy and she remembered that Kirsty had commented on his fitness regime. All in all he was an imposing package, as befitted a millionaire ex-advertising man.

These days Adrian was a regular in the press, enjoying an increasingly prominent public profile as a spokesman for the racing industry and a benefactor of charities, notably in support of research into liver disease. Tara knew Christine's first husband had died of liver failure. Adrian was a powerful man with a public image as well as a private persona to protect. He would be curious about this new woman who had moved in with his son-in-law.

As pudding plates were cleared away and the meal came to an end, Tara steeled herself. She wouldn't be able to hide for much longer.

There was talk of coffee. 'I'm not going to stick around,' said Stephanie. 'I must see how Mitzy's getting on.' Mitzy, Tara had gathered, was the mare who had just foaled. 'You can come too, if you like.'

It was an escape route but Tara hesitated before accepting. 'Can I come along later?' she said as she followed Stephanie into the hall. She really ought to stay and talk to the others, Adrian in particular – he was the boss, after all. She didn't want to appear rude.

Adrian was just behind her and she turned to look directly into those inquisitive eyes. 'It's so lovely here,' she said. 'The cottage is a dream. I can't tell you how grateful I am for the chance to stay.' She was aware she was gushing but she was sincere. Grateful did not cover how she felt.

'You don't have to thank me, my dear.' Up close he was no

less attractive. He was more lined and less boyish, but that only made him seem more authentic. Tara could understand how Kirsty had appreciated his attentions. 'If Danny is happy to have you by his side,' he continued, 'then I am overjoyed. He's had a very hard time.'

'I know that.' She held his gaze. 'I've got his best interests at heart, believe me.'

It was important to make this statement of faith. And Danny was dear to her. She had no intention of letting him down.

He smiled suddenly and for the first time she felt a hint of his menace. Those fine white teeth looked expensive. They gave him a hint of crocodile.

'Danny says you're a solicitor.'

'I'm still a trainee. Was a trainee.'

'Are you intending to get a job down here?'

'Not as a solicitor. I'd like to do something else.'

'Really? Why's that?'

There was a long answer to the question but she had no intention of giving it. 'I'm not sure I'm cut out for the law. I'd just like a change.'

'I see.'

He was about to press her further, she could tell, when a telephone sounded from the table in the hallway. Adrian looked around but there was no one else on hand to answer it. 'Excuse me,' he said and lifted the receiver. He looked puzzled for a moment and then his face was transformed by another smile, totally different from the one he had directed at her – there was no crocodile about this. 'Rick,' he cried. 'How fantastic to hear from you.'

Despite it being his idea, it hadn't been easy for Rick to pick up the phone to Latchmere. Though he hadn't dialled it in over a year, he knew the number by heart. When Kirsty had first been engaged to Danny, while the cottage was being gutted and made over for the pair of them to live in, she had stayed at the house.

He hadn't expected to get Adrian on the line although, if he'd thought it through, he might have remembered that Sunday afternoon was the one time he was likely to be home.

'Hello, Adrian,' he said, wondering if he ought to start the conversation with an apology. They had not parted on good terms. It had been just a week after Kirsty's funeral and he recalled blaming Adrian for her death. 'Someone has to be responsible,' he'd shouted. 'It was your idea, your holiday and you took her. As far as I'm concerned, she's dead because of you.' It had helped him to say those things, though he'd had time since then to reflect that he'd probably been unfair. He'd quit the yard that day and gone back to his old job down the road – not that he'd stayed there for long. It was a crap yard compared to Latchmere.

Adrian, it was clear, held no grudges for that outburst. He just sounded delighted to hear from him.

Adrian had written to Rick after their rift, had said he could understand how he felt and that he would always be welcome at Latchmere. Christine had sent him cards on his birthday and at Christmas. Stephanie had called him several times and tried to make arrangements to meet for a drink but he'd made a string of excuses. She'd sounded sincere, as if she needed to confess her bystander guilt, but he'd not thought he could bear to listen to it.

The only one of them he'd had any dealings with was Danny. He'd seen him at racecourses but in the hurly-burly of the weighing room nothing personal had been exchanged. Danny had been in a poor state, wearing his grief like a shield, warding off all conversation. And he'd been riding like a maniac with reckless regard for his own safety. Rick had tried to calm him down, feeling bad about it in a funny kind of way, as if he bore some of the responsibility for his sister disappearing from Danny's life. Then he'd reminded himself that it was Danny who had accompanied Kirsty on a tropical island holiday from which she'd not returned.

That was one of the reasons he'd stopped riding, so he didn't have to see Danny. Now he felt that might have been feeble of him – taking a coward's way out. Kirsty certainly wouldn't have approved.

He felt differently now, though. Hugh was right. He had to take charge of his life again.

'I've got a proposition for you,' he said to Adrian. 'For Christine really. Do you want to put her on the line?'

'In a moment, young man. First you've got to tell me when we're going to see you.'

In the dim light of the stall Tara peered at the foal nuzzling into his mother's side. He was her in miniature – the same white stripe down his muzzle and a tawny brown coat of the exact hue. It was remarkable how baby animals often emerged so fully formed, she thought. Here he was, less than a day old and standing on his feet. He already looked quite capable of looking after himself. How unlike a human being – and how admirable. She could see why the girl by her side was so obsessed.

When it had become clear back at the house that the phone call had gripped all of Adrian's attention, Tara had turned to Stephanie, now dressed in working clothes, who was about to leave the house. 'I'd like to come with you after all,' she'd said. 'Do you mind?' Of course there had been no objections, though having got wind of the phone call, Stephanie had insisted on saying hello to Rick on the phone. Only when the receiver was finally passed to

Christine did they leave the house. The way Tara looked at it, she'd been reprieved.

It was a mile and a half drive to the stud on the other side of the estate which was bisected by the public road. Even in mid-winter the sweeping green curves of the meadows, defined by neat copses of woodland, lifted Tara's spirits. To see so much sky was a pleasure in itself. She was used to an urban landscape where a person's gaze was rarely raised to the heavens.

Stephanie had driven her muddy Polo at a hair-raising pace. It was plain she'd begrudged every moment spent over lunch away from her animals. Now she was explaining how the stud farm worked and, as her breathless monologue rolled on, Tara found the details slipping by her. She focused instead on the little foal cuddling up to the mare and heard herself saying, 'Do you think an extra pair of hands would be useful?'

'You mean you?' said Stephanie.

'Yes.' She supposed she did. She couldn't hang around the cottage all day while Danny was riding. She'd been thinking along the lines of a temporary office job in Swindon or Newbury but she'd have to solve the transport problem before she could start looking. Working within walking distance of her bolt-hole had a lot of appeal. Especially when she looked at the nativity scene in front of her. 'I wouldn't want any money,' she added. 'I'd just like to lend a hand.'

'Oh,' said Stephanie. 'I don't know. It's a highly professional set-up here. They don't normally let volunteers just pitch up. Do you know anything about horses?'

Tara was about to answer, truthfully, 'Only a little,' when a voice from behind them spoke for her.

'Of course she does. She's from Ireland – it's in the blood, isn't it?'

Tara turned to find herself looking up at Patsy. He'd appeared out of nowhere, it seemed. He held out a hand to her.

'Patsy Walsh. We're compatriots, I hear.'

His grip was warm and firm. It occurred to her that he would be a reassuring presence to have on her side were she to be tracked down. 'Where are you from?'

'I'm a Kerry man. You sound like you're from the north. Belfast – am I right?'

She nodded. 'Is it obvious?'

'Well, I can tell you're a city girl. But you'll have no trouble fitting in here. Common sense is what counts with horses.'

Stephanie didn't look convinced. It occurred to Tara that the girl had probably scrapped hard to be taken seriously and was jealous of her status. Well, she had no intention of being a threat.

'I was only thinking of making tea for the real workers. And helping muck out or clean kit.' She remembered the terms. As a child she'd had a pony-mad friend and had spent time in the local stables.

Stephanie looked mollified. 'Well, I suppose that might be useful on occasions. What do you think, Patsy?'

The tall man pretended to consider the matter seriously, though Tara noted the mischievous glint in his eye.

'I think,' he said finally, 'you can never have enough smart Irish women in any organisation. I'm sure we can find something for Tara to do when she's ready.'

For the first time that day Tara found herself smiling as if she meant it.

As Rick had intended, his father answered the phone. At this time of night his mother would be in bed.

'Hey, Dad.'

'Richard.' His father was the only person who ever called Rick by his birth name. Growing up, Rick had wondered why but now he had come to like it. Though recently retired, his father would never shed the air of a school-master and the slight formality seemed appropriate.

Rick got straight to the point which, he knew, would be appreciated.

'I've decided to leave Hugh and go back to riding. I mean, proper race-riding.'

His father didn't seem surprised. 'You always wanted to be a jockey. That's the reason you left school, after all.'

Left school at sixteen, his father meant, in the face of all academic advice. It had been a sore point and might still be, unless Rick recaptured his original drive to succeed as a rider.

But that battle was in the past, overtaken by other, more painful, events.

'The thing is, Dad, I'm going back to work at Latchmere. For Christine and Adrian.'

'Ah.'

Rick hadn't expected an outburst of emotion. His father didn't wear his heart on his sleeve like the female members of his family. As a schoolteacher he'd kept control by remaining detached from drama. The boys who'd tried to wind up Mr Jordan had been perpetually frustrated.

'Why?' he asked.

There were several reasons but Rick did not want to explain all of them. His father didn't need to be told that he'd been hiding from the life he'd once fought for and now he had to get out and pick up the pieces. Or that he liked the people at Latchmere, that they'd once been like a second family to him and it felt right to reconnect with them once more. Even, that they too were victims of Kirsty's death.

Instead, he said, 'Hugh's got two promising jump horses

and I've recommended he sends them to Christine. She's the best person to bring them on.'

'And you're going too?'

'Hugh wants me to ride them. It's a top yard, Dad. She's got great horses there and she says I'll get my chance. I won't get an opportunity like this anywhere else.'

'I see. So you've made your mind up.'

'Yes – unless you couldn't bear the thought of it. I won't go if you and I are going to fall out.'

'We won't fall out, son.' He could picture his father's gentle smile, the resigned look in eyes magnified by rimless spectacles. 'If you believe it's the right thing to do.'

'Kirsty was very happy there, Dad.' He blurted it out, as if he needed his sister's approval to justify his decision.

'Richard. You do what you think is right and I'll back you. You're my only child.'

The only one left – but his father didn't say that.

Christine removed her reading glasses as the words on the page began to swim before her eyes. She made an effort to read at bedtime every night, usually a novel, something unconnected to racing. But worthy literary offerings gathered dust at an alarming rate on her bedside table. She rarely finished any of them.

She heard footsteps in the hall in the seconds before the door opened. Sleep retreated in an instant as Adrian stepped into the room.

'I saw the light,' he said, 'but I can go away.'

'No.' She didn't want that. Visits from Adrian at this time of night were not to be squandered however tired she felt. She pulled the covers back from the other side of the bed in a gesture of welcome. When, she wondered, had it become awkward to receive her husband into her bed?

They'd been occupying separate bedrooms for the past

few years. They had never discussed it or made a conscious decision to sleep apart but had somehow fallen into it. His habit of working till past midnight in his study and her need to be out of bed often before dawn had made it seem a natural arrangement. At least, that's how she chose to think of it. And, after all, it made his late-night visits more of an occasion.

'So, are you happy about Rick coming back?' he asked as he settled himself beside her, lifting his arm so she could nestle against his side. The silk of his dressing gown was cool against her cheek.

'Yes.' What else could she say? The decision had already been made by the time Adrian had passed her the phone – in principle, at any rate. And how could she deny her husband the pleasure of taking the lad back into the fold? Anything he could do to make recompense, no matter how tiny, for what had happened to Rick's sister while she was under his care in the Caribbean would be precious to him.

And then there was Stephanie. She'd been carrying a torch for Rick for years – she'd not forgive her mother easily for discouraging his return. But, more important, if Rick wanted to come back, who was she to say no? The emotional difficulties were surely far greater for him.

'I promised him some decent rides,' she said. If he was going to return to the yard she might as well make the most of his ability. He'd shown a lot of promise before, when Kirsty was still alive.

But the bottom line for Christine was Danny. He'd looked as pleased as Punch when she'd consulted him. If he'd been reluctant she'd have knocked the idea on the head, whatever anybody else's feelings. For Christine, Danny always came first. And though she'd promised Rick some good rides, the very best were reserved for her son.

For once Adrian seemed to have picked up on her thoughts. 'Danny was pleased about Rick,' he said. 'Of course, he'd have been pleased about anything today.'

She knew what he meant. With his new girlfriend by his side at lunch, Danny had exuded contentment. Her firstborn was so transparent. His eyes had scarcely left the small urchin-cropped figure of Tara throughout the entire occasion.

'The girl was very quiet,' Adrian said. 'I tried to get a few words out of her but then Rick rang and when I turned round she'd gone.'

'Maybe she's shy. It's intimidating to step into a room full of strangers.' Actually, Christine didn't think Tara was shy so much as cool. She herself would have kept a low profile in those circumstances, being paraded before her boyfriend's family for the first time.

'She strikes me as a shrewd cookie. A trainee solicitor. Knows when to keep her mouth shut. And when to butter a man up.'

'I thought you didn't talk to her?'

'Just enough for her to say how marvellous the cottage is.'

'So?'

'Where did she spring from? If she was such a big pal of Kirsty's, why haven't we ever seen her before? I don't even remember her at Kirsty's funeral.'

Christine knew the answer to that. 'She wasn't there. Her mother died at the same time so she was back in Belfast.'

'That's where she comes from, is it? No one tells me anything.'

She laughed. 'What rubbish. You should talk to your stepdaughter more often. Stephanie's taken the trouble to get to know her. She's been up to Manchester a couple of times. She's given me the background.'

'So it's a whirlwind romance, is it? Tara and Danny.'

49

'It's friendship that's suddenly turned into something else. That's what Stephanie says.'

Adrian chewed on the information. When he next spoke the irritation had gone from his voice. 'And how do you feel about her? Do you mind her moving in out of the blue?'

'I only care about Danny. I just hope this girl can make him happy. He deserves it.'

Adrian nodded. Both of them knew how true this was.

'She's nothing like Kirsty,' he said finally.

He sounded wistful, which aroused an old resentment in her. Personally, Christine thought the difference was no bad thing. Kirsty had been no saint, everyone knew that even if they never admitted it.

Suddenly Adrian kissed her. She'd been expecting it, looking forward to it in fact, though the timing could have been better. She didn't want Kirsty on his mind if he was going to make love to her.

In any case, she was unsure whether to permit it. She pulled away from him. 'I'll see if I can find out a bit more about her. Just in case it might be serious with Danny.'

Adrian chuckled. 'There's no "might" about it. She's the first girl he's looked at since Kirsty. And she's given up her career so she can move in with him. That's got to be serious, hasn't it?'

She supposed so. And maybe it wasn't a bad thing – provided nothing went wrong. Danny was so vulnerable. After Kirsty she didn't think he could take any more emotional turmoil. Well, she would do her best to make sure it didn't come to that.

Adrian kissed her again, insistently. It was plain he no longer wanted to talk.

This time she didn't pull away.

*

As Tara lay in bed in her new home waiting for Danny, she felt some of the tension begin to ebb from her body. For the first time in weeks she could see a way forward. A way that did not involve lying broken and disfigured in a hospital bed.

The calls had started six weeks ago. Up to then she could still have persuaded herself that Tom loved her and, shaken though she was by what she had discovered, that she still loved him. After all, it was hard not to bend to the will of a man like Benny Bridges and she could understand that maybe he'd coerced Tom into taking a course of action that was unwise. But she was convinced she could make him see sense – she'd been sure of it. And so, when he'd tried to persuade her not to go through with her threat to talk to the police, she'd given him two days to withdraw his alibi for Benny Bridges. Two days to retract his statement that the pair of them had been conducting a meeting close by the Gallagher Ferguson offices at the time Bridges had been cutting an innocent man's throat in Clementine's Park.

But Tom, her commander in and out of the office, a man whose integrity she'd taken for granted, the tenderest lover she'd ever had, had turned the ultimatum on herself. Told her that her student idealism was unsuited to the real world. That she should grow up and leave her stupid moral gestures behind her – if she wanted to remain in one piece. He'd left her in tears, shattered as much by her own naivety as by his brutal cynicism.

After that the phone calls had started, warnings issued in a sly Mancunian voice which emphasised in detail the horror that awaited her. The calls had always been menacing but when the thug had actually shown up at her door, the threats he had made had pressed all her buttons and sent her rushing into Danny's arms.

'Listen, darling, do you want to look in the mirror and see

a face that's been fried in chip fat? Or would you prefer to spend the rest of your life in a wheelchair? That's if you get lucky. My friend might just decide to shove you in a canal with a few bricks in your pocket. Believe me, that's what'll happen if you don't change your mind.'

She'd known then that she had no choice but to abandon her old life and here she was, grabbing hold of a new one.

She heard the sound of Danny's footsteps on the stairs. There was a spring in his step and she knew that was because of her. She couldn't tell him the real reason she was here in his bed. At some point she'd tell him the truth but in the meantime she'd try to be as good to him as he was to her. And maybe, after all, she could come to love him as he deserved.

Right now anything was possible, provided she kept herself safe to testify in the Crown Court on 9 June against Thomas Ferguson, her former employer. Tom was the man who'd once sworn he desired her more than any other woman he'd ever met. And whose most fervent desire, she now believed, was to end her life.

Chapter Three

When Gareth Jordan was told of his daughter's murder, he did not weep or curse or fall into despair. He comforted his wife as best he could and summoned his son home. Then he'd packed his bags and booked the earliest flight to the British Virgin Islands. It was many weeks before he returned to England and he never went back to his job.

But though Gareth remained outwardly calm, inside he was bleeding. Kirsty's cruel death eviscerated him emotionally as thoroughly as any outward hysterics would indicate. So for Rick to return to work for the family who had taken Kirsty on that ill-fated holiday was not a piece of news to which he could be indifferent, though he might not show it.

Three days after Kirsty's death, shortly after he had arrived on Amana, he first heard the name Larry Owens, the man accused of the murder. At the time he was in a mental spin, aware that life-changing events were taking place around him against the unreal backdrop of a tropical island fairyland. Half-naked holidaymakers frolicked in the sunshine while his daughter lay on a mortuary slab with a battered skull.

He was staying in the same estate of beach chalets occupied by the Latchmere party – Adrian Spring had arranged it. The accommodation was just a few hundred yards from where Kirsty's body had been found.

He'd sat by the pool with Adrian while a middle-aged local policeman, his uniform shirt gleaming white against his dark skin, told them he had a man in custody. Larry Owens, an American tourist who had been in the Cliff Tops bar before the attack on Kirsty. It transpired that Adrian, who had accompanied Kirsty to the bar, had picked him out of an identity parade the day before. He'd been wearing a blue and yellow shirt – the colour of the island flag – which appeared to be significant.

Gareth had been confused. 'You were with Kirsty?' he said to Adrian.

'Yes.' Adrian spoke patiently, as if he'd explained this before and he probably had. 'The others were all busy,' he continued. 'Stephanie and Christine were coming back on the ferry from Tortola and Danny had gone sailing. We were all meeting up for dinner but I suggested to Kirsty we went for a drink first.

'While we were in the bar we noticed a man sitting by himself, wearing one of the island shirts. He seemed a bit drunk. He kept asking us to join him. To be honest, he asked Kirsty. I went to the toilet and when I came back I found he'd insisted on buying her a drink.'

'Then what happened?' Gareth recognised bits of the story now. He'd been told it but not really taken it in.

'When he saw he wasn't getting anywhere with Kirsty, he pushed off. We stayed and forgot about him.'

'What did you talk about?' Gareth was keen to know. He was jealous of Adrian spending the last few minutes of Kirsty's life by her side. He wished it had been him. But if it had been, Kirsty would not have been allowed to leave the bar on her own. He was coming to that.

Adrian was vague in his reply. 'We talked about the guy who'd tried to pick her up. We were going to have dinner at my favourite restaurant, the Wild Tamarind. We probably spoke about that a bit.'

The policeman butted in at that point. 'It's a real fine place,' he said.

Gareth remembered wanting to scream out loud.

'And, of course, the wedding,' Adrian continued. 'Kirsty said this holiday was like having the honeymoon first.'

Gareth had put some bite into his next question. 'Why did she leave on her own? Why did you let her?'

To be fair to Adrian, he looked dreadful. His usual air of sleek self-satisfaction had vanished. If a man with a suntan could look grey with fatigue and worry, that was an apt description.

'Believe me, Gareth, I wish to God I hadn't. I'd have sworn this island was as safe as my own house. Over the years Stephanie has been out half the night on her own and come to no harm.'

'All the same.' Gareth was determined to get an answer to his question.

'The short answer is that I got a phone call from home. A call about a charity I work for sometimes. It was going on a bit and Kirsty wanted to get back and change for dinner.'

'Who called you?'

For a moment Adrian looked nonplussed, as if Gareth didn't have a right to ask him.

'Charlie Pevsner – Sir Charles Pevsner, actually. He's the chairman of the Liver Cancer Fund.'

Gareth accepted Adrian's word. Later he would try and verify the picture Adrian had supplied. He tracked down an American couple who confirmed that they had been in the bar at the same time as Kirsty and Adrian and had seen her leave before he did; the husband had thought Adrian might have been on the phone at the time. Later still, Gareth asked a detective from London, Superintendent Ian Edwards, to approach Pevsner and he was able to confirm that the phone call had taken place just as Adrian had described.

At the time, however, Gareth wasn't thinking of talking to witnesses himself and cross-checking their stories. He was a shocked and bereaved father who trusted implicitly in the wisdom of the Royal Virgin Islands Police Force to solve the crime and provide Kirsty with justice. That was rapidly becoming the thing that mattered most to him.

He turned to the RVIPF officer. 'You say you've arrested a suspect?'

The man smiled. It seemed incongruous. 'We sure have. We've got the man who killed your daughter, Mr Jordan. I know that's no great comfort at this terrible time but you should sleep easy knowing the man that done it is going to pay.'

'Who is he?'

'Larry Owens. An American.'

Larry – he remembered it sounded such an innocuous name.

And it *was* a comfort they'd caught the bastard.

A week after the meeting with the policeman by the pool, Gareth visited Larry Owens in jail. He went not to vent his rage or gloat or to seek a confrontation but to see if he could help the poor fellow. By then he seriously doubted he could have been responsible for Kirsty's murder.

His first doubts had surfaced when he met Ron and Maureen Benson, the Americans who had found Kirsty on the path leading down from the Cliff Tops bar where they had been celebrating their wedding anniversary. They claimed to have seen a man walking briskly away from the spot where they discovered the body.

He asked them if they would mind returning to the bar with him. It was plain that they did but also that they were acutely conscious of the situation he was in.

They showed him the table they'd occupied at the front of

the bar area looking out over the sea. And they'd pointed out where Adrian and Kirsty had been sitting, next to the bar itself.

'It wasn't packed but it was pretty busy,' said Ron. 'We noticed your daughter, though.'

Gareth wasn't surprised. Kirsty was a girl people noticed.

'She was the prettiest girl in the place,' said Maureen tearfully. She blew energetically into a paper tissue. By this time, Gareth had a tight rein on his emotions and he fervently wished Maureen Benson could be similarly self-controlled.

Ron put a hand on her arm. 'We weren't here long. A half hour maybe.'

'Did you see a man sitting by himself? Wearing a blue and yellow shirt?'

'We know the shirt you mean. No, we didn't see a guy like that. Or, if we did, we don't remember.'

Gareth turned to Maureen. There were tears in her eyes and she had the tissue over her mouth. She shook her head vigorously. 'I didn't see him. There were people at the bar but no one on their own.'

'They were pretty much all couples,' Ron said. 'We remarked on that, it being our anniversary. We said we'd picked the right place, considering all the romance in the air.'

Maureen began to cry openly.

'Guess we got that wrong,' Ron added.

He asked them about the man they'd seen on the path, walking away from the spot where they found Kirsty.

'He was bending down near the wall ahead of us but when we came along he stood up and moved off real quick. He was only in sight for a few seconds. To be honest, we didn't take much notice of him.'

'Can't you describe him at all?'

He took notes of what they said but it wasn't much. A

white holidaymaker still in beach clothes. Wearing a blue and yellow shirt.

When he returned to the Arcadia Beach Rooms, where he had removed himself to regain his independence, Gareth was waylaid on the way to his room by Isaac, the landlord.

'There's a fellow been waiting for you in the bar,' he said. 'He's been stretching out one beer for two hours and I ain't going to retire on that.'

At the time Gareth wasn't well enough acquainted with Isaac to know how to respond. Instead he made for the bar and found an unshaven young man carelessly dressed in what were nevertheless expensive casual clothes. He rushed to grip Gareth's hand.

'Dave Carson. I'm a physician from Dallas, Texas. On vacation with a buddy.'

Gareth thought he seemed a bit young to be a doctor but now he looked closer he could see the man was in his late twenties. He was still gripping Gareth's hand.

'I'm terribly, terribly sorry about your daughter, Mr Jordan.'

Gareth hadn't yet learned the proper response to that. He never would. He nodded awkwardly. Surely this young man hadn't waited all afternoon to tell him this?

'I've got to talk to you about Larry.'

Then Gareth understood. Carson was talking about the man arrested for the murder. Larry Owens.

'I know he didn't do it,' the young man said. 'I've just come from the jail and what's happening to him is terrible.'

Gareth's instinct was to say that it was out of his hands and none of his business. Let the law take its course – your friend will have his day in court. But what harm would it do to listen to what the young doctor had to say?

'How about another beer?' he suggested.

The upshot was a trip to the north of the island with

Carson at the wheel of a hired car. He'd made this trip several times, he said as they drove over the mountainous spine of the island to a harsh flat terrain where there was no green, only burnt brown dirt and rock. A suitable place for a prison.

Carson said he'd wait in the car and Gareth left him with the aircon blowing at maximum, while he pushed his way into a low prefabricated building that had the neglected atmosphere of the temporary-turned-permanent.

The officer behind the desk told him to go away as they didn't allow visitors on Thursdays. Gareth told him he was Owens' legal adviser. Another man, a sergeant, appeared and said the American's lawyer had been in the day before. Gareth said that was an associate and demanded access. Then the first man, who'd been scrutinising Gareth closely, finally recognised him as the father of the girl Owens had killed. Their manner had then softened, and they advised him to go away in a less peremptory manner. They were sorry, he couldn't be admitted in case he assaulted the prisoner.

Gareth had been prepared for something like this, Carson had warned him the officials were obstructive sods.

He took a business card from his pocket and laid it on the desk where the RVIPF insignia could be plainly seen. Next to it he placed two other cards, one belonging to the Deputy Governor and the other a Legislative Council member. Officials had not been slow to offer their condolences and assistance while he had been staying with Adrian. He began to dial the first number.

'Yeah, OK, man,' said the sergeant as Gareth was connected to the office of the Police Commissioner. 'You can have ten minutes.'

In the event he had longer than that. They kept him hanging around for half an hour and searched him

59

cursorily before finally showing him into a shabby but clean interview room where he waited. Eventually the door was opened and a stocky young man in a T-shirt and sweatpants was pushed into the room by a uniformed guard of considerable size. The door closed, leaving the pair of them alone. Gareth felt a stab of anxiety. Was it wise to leave him alone with a suspected murderer?

But one glance at his companion dispelled all fear. This unhappy character was no threat.

'Jesus, you came. I never thought you would.' Owens seized his hand and clung on to it. 'I am so, so grateful, believe me.'

'How do you know who I am?'

'They told me just now. They made me shave and put on clean clothes so I knew you must have shaken the bastards up.' He looked around. 'This place ain't so bad but it's a hellhole back there. Scorpions and cockroaches and shit crawling all over the place. And the people are way worse. Don't get me started.'

Owens spoke in an exaggerated Southern drawl that Gareth recognised from the movies. He had a round snub-nosed face that in happier days might have been called cheeky. Now, however, there were dark sacks under his eyes and no sign of a grin. Gareth noticed that his hand shook as it rested on the chipped formica-topped table that separated their seats.

'Dave Carson said you'd been asking to see me.'

'Yeah, but I never thought you'd come. I want to tell you the truth about my involvement . . .' He paused and reconsidered. 'Hell, there is no involvement. I just want to explain how come I got mixed up in this.'

He stopped again.

'Go on.'

'Jeez, you're a cool customer, Mr Jordan. I can't decide if

60

you're about to jump across the table and rip out my throat.'

Gareth was hit by a wave of sympathy for the pathetic young man in front of him. He pushed it to one side.

'Please just tell me what happened.'

'OK. I was in the Cliff Tops bar when your daughter came in with a guy. I was at the bar and they sat at a table just over the way. There were plenty of other people around but it wasn't that busy. They were close enough so I could see them. I didn't notice the guy much, to be honest. He was a lot older. But she – well, I know you're her father but I hope you don't mind me saying she was a very beautiful woman.'

Gareth nodded. He'd never known how to gauge other people's reactions on meeting the adult Kirsty. He'd wiped her nose and fed her mashed-up fish fingers and ironed her school blouses. But she had indeed grown into a beautiful woman.

Owens carried on. 'Anyhow, she looked like a heap of fun and here she was sipping mineral water with this serious older guy who seemed as boring as hell. I thought, she should be with someone her own age. Heck, I thought she should be with me. So I invited them over for a drink. I was probably a bit bombed. Anyhow, when the guy got up to go in back I bought her a drink anyway, a real one. She was very nice about it, said thanks an' all, but she said she had plans for the evening and it was plain they didn't include me. Then I got a call on my cell from Dave, saying he had a taxi waiting down on the beach road and to get on down quick. So I did. Said goodbye nice and polite to your daughter and left. And, I swear to you, that's the last I saw of her.'

Gareth had his notebook out, scribbling down Owens' version of events. The other man made no objection.

'Why do you think the police are so convinced that you are responsible?'

Owens hit the table with the flat of his hand. 'Because of the goddamned shirt I was wearing. Apparently it looked the same one the bad guy had on. But a lot of guys are wearing that shirt. It's like a local souvenir. I was in a bar earlier that day with a guy who had the same one on. It don't prove nothin'.'

'What about the blood?'

The police had told Gareth there were bloodstains on the shirt Owens had been wearing.

'Oh yeah. When they finally get the shirt back from the lab they'll find that's my blood. Look.' Owens lifted his arm and showed Gareth a two-inch scab below his elbow. 'I scraped it on a rock when I was snorkelling. That's why I wasn't swimming that day. I wanted to let it heal up.'

'That's why you were in the bar on your own?' Gareth said.

'Correct. Dave had gone to the beach and I decided to hike up to the cliff bar. Worst decision of my life.'

And maybe of mine too, thought Gareth. That's if this twitchy, verbose young American is guilty.

'What happened when you left the bar?'

'I went straight back to the road and found Dave in the taxi. We went for dinner on the other side of the island – place called Mexican Mike's. You might think it's plain stupid for guys from Texas going for a Mexican meal on a Caribbean island but that's what we did.'

'Can you give me some times?' Gareth had his pen poised. This was crucial.

'You bet, though I wasn't looking at my watch the whole time. I guess I left the bar around ten after six, got to the restaurant just before seven. It's about a forty-minute drive.'

Gareth wrote down the figures and compared them with the times the Bensons had given him. Ron had estimated they had arrived at the bar around six fifteen and left half an hour later. Which would verify the time of departure Owens had just given him. But who was to say that the Texan had not hidden on the path and waited for Kirsty? She had left just before the Bensons.

'I know what you're thinking,' said Owens. 'Can I prove I was out of the area before your daughter was killed? And I can.'

Gareth waited for Owens to back up his statement of innocence.

'When I joined Dave in the taxi I realised I'd just about run out of cash. So the taxi driver – he's called Solomon Davy, a good guy – drove us down the road to an ATM. The records will show the time of my transaction. And Solomon and the waiters at the restaurant will verify the times. I just wasn't anywhere near your daughter when she was killed, Mr Jordan, and I can prove it.'

'So why are they still keeping you locked up?'

Owens shrugged. 'Because they're incompetent. Because they don't care provided some outsider gets the blame. Because they don't like Americans. Because they're stupid. Because they've told everyone I've done it and they're only interested in being proved right. I could go on. I just know they're determined to stick it on me.'

Gareth must have looked doubtful.

'You don't think that can happen? They've just moved another American into my cell, a real sleazeball. He's very friendly, wants to talk all the time. I know what he's up to.'

'What's that?'

'He's trying to get a confession out of me, in return for some favour, I've no doubt. And if he doesn't get it, he'll just make it up. Man, am I stuffed, rotting here in this shithole while my folks go crazy. My mom's out here while my pop tries to stir things up back home but I reckon they're out of their depth. Dave's got me a local lawyer but he's just another cog in the system. If this was back in the States there wouldn't even be a case to answer.'

'If things are so bleak, what do you think I can do?'

'First off, Mr Jordan, you can believe me. If I know you don't think I'm guilty of killing your daughter I'll find some way to keep on fighting. It would be a big help, I swear.'

Gareth looked him in the eye. 'If what you tell me is true then I do believe you. I had my doubts before I even set foot in here.'

Owens closed his eyes, exhaled deeply. 'Thank the Lord,' he said.

'I intend to talk to this taxi driver.'

'Hell, man, you talk to who you want. Dave will take you to him. Thank you, Mr Jordan. Just having you on my side makes me feel a whole lot better.'

Gareth couldn't see why. He felt sorry for the man but Owens was not his primary responsibility. And then he realised that, in a sense, he was.

Owens realised it too. He was grinning for the first time as he said, 'You know, don't you, that as long as they've got me here, the police ain't gonna be looking for the guy who really did kill your daughter.'

And that made all the difference.

The first time Gareth met Superintendent Edwards and his colleague, DS Harper, he was aware that he'd put his foot in it. Edwards was not much younger than himself, he thought, or maybe it was in the nature of a policeman's job that it wore a man down prematurely. He wore steel-rimmed spectacles and blinked in the harsh sunlight. Harper was half his age, with all the confidence of youth. He seemed impatient to wrap this murder business up.

Notwithstanding his position as the victim's father and thus, he assumed, to be treated with kid gloves, Gareth was concerned that what he had discovered should not be ignored. Though perhaps it wasn't politic to try and drive a wedge between the British detectives and their colleagues in the RVIPF.

He talked to them on the verandah of the bar at the Arcadia. Though they'd been three days on the island this was the first time they had spoken to him. He had no doubt they had already interviewed Adrian. The irritation fuelled his opening remarks.

'I hope now you're here you'll put a boot up the investigation,' he said.

Harper's eyes narrowed. 'How do you mean exactly, sir?'

'I mean that the police here are not out interviewing witnesses and looking for the killer of my daughter.'

'I don't think you quite understand, sir. They have drafted in dozens of extra personnel to search the area where your daughter was attacked.'

'And have they found anything?' If they had, he suspected he would be the last to know but from the expression on Harper's face he could tell they had discovered nothing.

Edwards spoke for the first time. 'Are you aware that the police have a man in custody?'

'Of course I'm aware. But it seems to me unlikely that he had anything to do with it.'

'Really, sir?' Harper's beaky face stopped just short of breaking into a grin. 'Our colleagues in the RVIPF are confident of building a solid case against this particular suspect.'

Gareth ignored him and looked directly at the senior officer. 'I've met Larry Owens and I find his version of events more than plausible. It's extremely likely the local police are barking up the wrong tree with him and in the meantime the real culprit has had time to destroy evidence and get away. I hope you two haven't travelled out here just to connive with this incompetence.'

Harper looked outraged. 'We've not been informed you've had access to Owens,' he said, as if that were the point at issue.

Edwards said, 'What makes you think the suspect is not responsible?'

'Because he was on the other side of the island at the time Kirsty was killed.' Gareth told him about the timing of Owens' visit to the Cliff Tops bar, the phone call from his friend, the ATM transaction and the taxi journey to the distant restaurant. 'A lot of this is easy to corroborate. I've talked to the Benson couple – they didn't see him in the bar. I've also spoken to the taxi driver. His name is Solomon Davy but I assume you know that.'

It was plain from the blank look on their faces that they didn't even know of his existence. Harper was scribbling in his notebook.

'I wouldn't presume to tell you how to do your job,' Gareth continued, 'but I also assume you can check the time of the phone call Mr Owens received in the bar and the cash machine records.'

They didn't stay long after that but two days later Larry Owens walked into the Arcadia. He looked a transformed man, light shone in his eyes and his grip was firm.

'I'm on my way to the airport. But I had to see you before I went. You saved my life, man – literally. Much longer in that shithole and I'd be dead.'

'I'm not sure how much it's got to do with me.'

'It's got everything. You spoke to the Scotland Yard guys, didn't you? They shook the whole case up. They even got my shirt back from the lab and, guess what, the blood was mine, like I said. If you ever come to Dallas, you're not paying one dollar for anything, believe me. I owe you.'

Gareth was pleased he'd helped an innocent man walk free. It gave him the first lift he'd felt since he'd arrived on the island – until he talked to his wife that evening.

'You're saying the police had a man in jail and you helped get him out?'

'He was the wrong man. He didn't kill Kirsty.'

'How on earth can you say that? You're not a detective. I think you'd better come home, Gareth, before you do any more damage.'

Eighteen months on, there'd been no further arrest and no trial. The murder of their daughter had not been solved. And Gareth knew his wife held him accountable for that.

Chapter Four

There was a time when Danny considered Wincanton his lucky track. He'd had his first ride there as a conditional jockey and, later that season, his first winner. On another occasion, one dry autumn day, he'd been dumped at the head of a field of eighteen runners. Rolling himself into a ball, he'd pictured his bones being smashed into the hard ground by every pounding hoof. To his amazement, the charging pack had danced over him without landing one kick and he'd stood up untouched, dizzy only from the storm and speed of their passing. Kirsty had been watching that day and in the evening, still tingling from his reprieve, he'd kissed her for the first time. Just how long ago was that? Two and a half years – maybe less. It felt like another lifetime.

He put Kirsty out of his mind – funny how it was possible to do that now – and began to pull on his boots and breeches. On the other side of the room, he could see Rick doing the same thing and it added to his sense of well-being. Rick had been back at the yard for almost a week, following his surprise call after lunch on Sunday, and with him had come two horses for Christine to put an edge on.

Rick's arrival had been low-key – even Patsy hadn't made much of a fuss – but his return had cheered everyone. It just seemed right that Kirsty's brother was back where he belonged. Steph had cried, of course, and Adrian had made sure he was on hand to welcome him. Nobody had been happier than Christine. People said his mother was a cold fish but Danny knew how keenly sensitive she was to the things that mattered in life. Much of what exercised people was transient and she, as he often told people, didn't do trivia. But he had noticed how tightly she had hugged Rick to her lean frame before turning her sharp eyes on the horses that had accompanied him.

It seemed to Danny that the miracle of Rick's reappearance had somehow to be attributed to Tara. Not that she knew him at all well, so she said. She'd been Kirsty's friend in Manchester and the only time she had gone racing had been when he'd taken her. She was here today though and, to her credit, had spent the last week performing odd jobs at the stud for Patsy and Steph, fitting herself into the set-up at Latchmere, a world that must be completely alien to her.

He couldn't quite believe that Tara had chosen to throw her lot in with him so completely. There had been no talk of long-term commitment but she'd burned a few bridges to join him and that had to mean something. Unless she was just using Latchmere as a stepping stone, a temporary refuge before she headed off somewhere else. He was wary of asking her outright about her plans – he was too scared of how she might reply.

He'd skirted around it though. 'Have you got another job?' he'd asked back in Manchester when she'd told him she wouldn't be going back to the office of Gallagher Ferguson.

She shook her head; those glorious honey-blond locks had danced across her shoulders in the candlelight. They were sitting side by side on her sofa. 'I've had enough of the law.'

70

'But you've got a degree – you're only six months from qualification.' He'd left school after GCSEs and that was none too soon. He couldn't imagine the study that had gone into getting Tara to where she was. How could she think of chucking it all in? He'd said as much.

She'd laughed softly. 'Are you my dad now or something?'

That had stopped him. Her dad, like his, was dead – it was one of the ties that bound them. He had no intention of being a father substitute. They'd only been lovers for a few days at that point and his ambitions were decidedly more carnal than that.

'I've had enough of it,' she'd said. 'There's got to be a better way of life than working in this cesspit. I'm getting out.'

'You can come and stay with me, if you like.' He'd tried to sound casual, as if he didn't care whether she said yes or no but, to his own ears, his need was naked. On reflection it had been little less than a proposal of marriage.

And she'd said yes – after a fashion.

'Don't feel you have to offer, Danny. I can always go back to Ireland.'

'Stay with me first,' he'd said. 'Come and live in the country. Fresh air and green grass. We'll get you out on horseback.'

'Sounds blissful.'

'You'll come then?'

She'd laid her head on his shoulder and pulled his arm round her waist. 'You'll look after me, won't you, Danny?' was her reply.

The next morning the conversation had seemed like a dream but she'd been quick to make arrangements to leave with him. It had been a deal done swiftly and without second thoughts, as far as he could tell.

'You're not on the run from the bailiffs, are you?' he'd

asked with a grin as they'd thrown her bags in the car in the black light of their early-morning flight from Manchester.

'Don't be daft,' she'd said, but she'd looked anxiously behind her as she'd hunkered down in her seat, her face white and unsmiling beneath her new shock crop.

He'd wondered, once or twice, what he was getting into with her. Whether he might come home after a race meeting and find she'd gone off, leaving a note that just said thanks, with no forwarding address or contact number. She'd dumped her mobile phone. Who does a thing like that? He'd bought her a new pay-as-you-go, which she'd insisted on paying him for, but he didn't think she'd used it except to take his calls.

He knew the job she'd been doing had been stressful – how could dealing with the lowlife handled by a criminal practice in Manchester be anything else? But she'd told him that was why she did it, to be in the heart of the action, to see life on the other side of the tracks and try to make it better. At least that's how she'd started out her traineeship. But that had been a couple of months before Kirsty's death, when he'd not known her that well. And after, as they'd bonded in the grieving, her issues had barely been discussed. He just knew she was fiercely committed to a difficult job that he could neither do nor understand. He'd not exactly been curious, selfish bugger that he was.

Well, he could make up for that now by providing her with sanctuary at the very least and maybe a whole lot more. Really, he shouldn't be anxious about her. She had her mysteries but so did everyone. He'd learned that the hard way. People who seemed utterly straightforward often proved to have something to hide. Give Tara time and when she realised how much he adored her, she'd be bound to trust him with her secrets.

She'd agreed to come racing this afternoon, after all. At

first she'd refused, saying she didn't want to be in the way and, anyhow, race meetings were not her scene. He'd not pressed her – the last thing he wanted to appear was possessive – and to his surprise she'd suddenly changed her mind.

'I want to cheer you on to victory,' she'd explained. 'You're my saviour, Danny. It's the least I can do.'

He doubted that he was likely to ride a winner but her change of heart had certainly put him in a positive mood. And there was Rick's reappearance too. There was a new woman in his life and his old mate was back at the yard.

Danny couldn't remember when he last felt so good.

The moment he entered the parade ring, Rick felt the pressures of the last week slip from his shoulders. Returning to Latchmere where he'd worked for nearly two years, where every building and blade of grass reminded him of his dead sister, had been an ordeal. But he'd survived, keeping his emotions tightly bottled, acting like a proper grown-up, determined to make Hugh and Beth proud of him. It hadn't been easy and ahead of him now was a different kind of ordeal. Two miles and five furlongs over fences on a tricky horse demanded complete concentration. There was no room in his head for the anxieties of his situation.

But that was the reason he was here, to rediscover the part of him that made him a jockey. Because deep down he knew that race-riding was what he was meant to do. When he was on a horse, nothing fazed him. He had total confidence in his own ability and, no matter what happened, he knew he could cope. He relished the challenge in front of him and, for the first time in days, he felt his head begin to clear. Kirsty's death had thrown him seriously off course but now it was time for him to get his life back on track.

Beneath him was Rock Solid, a five-year-old gelding,

owned by Patsy Walsh. Rick suspected it was Christine's idea to give him the ride but it had been Patsy who made the offer.

'I've got no expectations,' the Irishman had said. 'He's the only jumper I've got and I only bought him to make the deal on a fast little filly I fancied.' He'd paused to allow Rick to acknowledge the double entendre.

Rick had raised a smile. Kirsty had fallen out with Patsy for some reason and her dislike had always coloured his opinion of the big Irishman. However, he was now starting afresh at Latchmere and was well aware of Patsy's importance. Besides, the guy was offering him a ride and for that he was truly grateful.

'I've looked up his form and spoken to Danny,' Rick said. 'He just doesn't seem to settle, does he?'

Patsy gave him a lopsided grin. 'That's something of an understatement. He's had three outings this season and run himself into the ground each time. If you can get any sort of tune out of him, you'll be doing well.'

Rick appreciated that Patsy had levelled with him. It was rare to be riding for an owner who had a realistic opinion of his horse's chances. Most of them were blinded by hope and the crazy expectation that the money they spent chasing their dreams on the racecourse had to yield some dividend, as it did in most other spheres. Horseracing, of course, was a different kind of business. And no one, Rick was aware, knew that better than an operator like Patsy Walsh.

But Patsy's expectations were neither here nor there as far as Rick was concerned. This was his first ride under rules in almost nine months. It mattered more to himself than anyone else.

He'd ridden Rock Solid a couple of times at home and found him a nice horse, if hardly a champion in the making. The moment he put his feet on the gallops, how-ever, he wanted to run away. Christine had assured Rick there was nothing physically wrong with him that might be causing pain, which was usually why horses pulled so hard. The reason had to lie in his thick head. One saving grace was that he jumped well; in fact the only time he settled was about six strides before a fence. The barriers seemed to make him concentrate on what he was doing.

Danny had ridden Rock Solid on the previous five occasions that he had run and hated him. Rick could understand why. There's nothing a jump jockey dislikes more than a puller – an animal you have no control over. Invariably you spend the first half of the race trying to hold on to the horse and the second half pushing him. And in between you are in the lap of the gods – anything can happen. The only certainty is that you are both guaranteed to finish thoroughly exhausted.

There was another runner in the race from the Latchmere yard, Willoughby, who was being ridden by Danny. He was only a young horse but had won all three of his starts over fences and looked to have a decent chance today.

Christine was legging Danny up. Once she'd seen him settled she came over to Rick, who was checking his girths.

'Just try and get him anchored, will you?' she said. 'I'm sure this running off is just a bad habit.'

'I'll do my best.'

The moment Rick's backside touched the saddle, Rock Solid began jig-jogging and plunging forward, completely ignoring the stable girl who was trying her best to hold on to him.

'Let him go,' said Rick, 'or he'll walk all over you and climb on top of that horse in front.'

The girl didn't need asking twice. She undid the buckle on the lead rein and ducked under the rail out of the way.

Rick let Rock Solid break into a trot and got him moving forward. So long as he was on the go he didn't seem so bad. Rick made straight for the exit and got away before the others, out on to the path leading to the course. As soon as they were on the grass he hacked away, trying hard to keep a nice long rein so that the pressure on the horse's mouth was as light as possible. Rock Solid dropped his head and, surprisingly for him, kept to a nice even pace all the way down to the start.

'How is he?' Danny inquired as he arrived ahead of the rest of the runners. Willoughby looked cool and disdainful which, given that he was possibly the classiest horse in the field, he well might.

'He was behaving like a twat to begin with but he seems better now.'

Rick had hold of a chunk of Rock Solid's skin just below his withers and was pinching it as hard as he possibly could between his thumb and forefinger. It was a trick Hugh had taught him. He didn't know how it worked but, provided Rick kept the pressure up, Rock Solid stayed calm. The second he released his hold, the horse was off jig-jogging again. The only problem was that it made Rick's fingers ache. At Hugh's yard he'd used an old crocodile clip – he could do with it now.

Patsy watched Rick's every move from the stand. He'd been a reasonable rider himself. Good enough to know that the lad he was watching had a proper feel for what he was doing. You couldn't teach people instinct. You either had it or you didn't.

He had never taken much notice of young Ricky when he had first been at Christine's. Now, seeing how Rock Solid was behaving, he had an idea that he might be seeing a lot more of him.

Alongside, Tara was observing Rock Solid closely – Patsy had been telling her about the horse's unruly ways. 'He doesn't look that wild to me,' she said, sounding almost disappointed.

Patsy chuckled. It was extraordinary. That horse would normally be dripping with sweat by now, and knocking into the other runners assembling before the start.

'Maybe young Ricky has slipped him a handful of Valium,' he said.

'Are you serious?' Her big greeny brown eyes were boring into his.

'It's a joke, sweetheart. Keep your hair on – not that you've got much of it.' And for the first time that afternoon he laughed properly.

'Sod you.' She scowled at him. 'And I'd rather you didn't call me your sweetheart because I'm not.'

'More's the pity. You're a gorgeous creature, hair and all.'

'Oh, sod off.'

Was that a hint of smile on her sexy little mouth? He resisted the temptation to tease her further. The race was about to start and Rock Solid had gone down to the start like any other sensible beast. Whatever happened from now on was a bonus.

It might have been a while since Rick had worked at an ambitious yard with expensive horses, but he'd not wasted his time under Hugh's tutelage. He'd ridden all day and every day on a variety of horses and now he had far more guile when it came to dealing with tricky animals. Hugh had taught him that when you got into a fight with a horse there could only ever be one winner, and that was the animal. A pat down the neck or a little bit of cunning or know-how always got you further in the end and with longer-lasting results.

Now, as they lined up along the tape, Rick felt able to concentrate on the real business of the afternoon. This was almost like having his very first ride all over again, but with the benefit of hindsight. He knew now that for your first few rides you always ended up being further back in the field than you imagined. And with Rock Solid the only thing he really had to concern himself with was getting the animal to relax. The horse was a rank outsider, a 50–1 chance in a field of fourteen, so there wasn't much of a downside for him.

Wincanton is a medium-sized rectangle of a course with sharpish bends and a long downhill run from the far side of the course to the winning post. It is also one of the few tracks where you jump four open ditches in two-and-a-half mile races. On most other courses there are only three. Danny lined up at the front of the field, waiting to get a good break once the starter let them go. Rick was some twenty yards behind him. He had already warned the starter that he wanted to miss the break.

'Come on, jockeys. Away you go.'

The instant the tape flew up and the race began, Rock Solid jumped straight on to the bridle and wanted to be away but Rick was ready for him and pulled him hard to the left as if he was going to run him in a big circle. As soon as they got level with the hurdle track on the inside, Rick pulled him hard back the other way. By the time they were back to the inside of the course, Rock Solid had stopped pulling, confused by what was happening. Then in an instant they were inside the wings of the first fence and Rock Solid had to spring up off all fours to get over. He landed in a bit of a heap and by the time he'd got himself back on an even keel, Rick figured they must have been the best part of fifteen lengths behind the last horse. But he had done what he'd set out to do and that was to bewilder his horse. Far from running away, Rick now had to squeeze with his legs to keep him going. The second fence, the ditch, saw Rock Solid do what he excelled at and that was jump. But this time he didn't try and tear off afterwards.

'Good lad,' Rick shouted into the perky brown ears just in front of him. God knows whether his words had any effect on his companion but they made him feel upbeat. As if they were a team.

He let Rock Solid carry on at his own pace along the back straight, round the first right-hander and down the slope to the turn into the home straight. Most of the runners were still well ahead of them – he noted Danny's red and yellow chevrons out wide on the left. Rick had Rock Solid tight to the inside rail. Each time they came to a fence, the horse cleared it with seemingly no effort whatsoever and Rick felt them get significantly closer. As they passed the stands for the first time and turned back out into the country to complete the first circuit, Rick gave him a nudge and a squeeze. 'Pick it up, boy,' he commanded. This was a test – would his partner respond?

There seemed a terrible time lag while Rock Solid made up his mind. They were now racing away from the stables and if there was one thing you could rely on a horse knowing, it was the way back home. They were almost better than pigeons. If anything, Rock Solid seemed to slow up. The first in the back straight was fast approaching and for a split second Rick wondered if he was going to refuse. He gave him a slap down the neck and suddenly they were off again.

Oh yes! This was more like it. Rick kept him towards the rail and they overtook a horse who was blowing hard. Approaching the ditch for the second time, there was a wall of horses in front and barely any room to see the fence, never mind jump it. Instinctively, Rick looked for gaps in the line. Was there an opportunity to thrust Rock Solid into the heart of the contest?

But he couldn't see a way through. Unless – was that a chink in the wall? A hint of a gap between the inside horse and the rail? There was only one way to find out.

God, it was good to be racing again.

'Go on! Get stuck in, Ricky boy!'

Patsy was enjoying himself. He wasn't one to keep quiet during a race but he'd expected to be cursing Rock Solid for being the flakey donkey he'd turned out to be – up to this point, that is.

Little Ricky – that's how he'd always thought of Kirsty's young brother. A wet-behind-the-ears wannabe jockey who'd never make it in a man's world. And race-riding was that, all right. Some jockeys were hard as flint and wise beyond their years, no matter what it said on their birth certificates. Piggott had won the Derby at eighteen, after all. But other riders would never have the balls, no matter their age. And he'd put little Ricky Jordan in that latter category until now.

It looked as if Kirsty's brother had come of age during his time away. Patsy didn't mind being proved wrong about him, especially when Rick was riding his horse.

'He's doing all right, isn't he?'

Tara had perked up now the race had started. He'd lent her his binoculars – she didn't seem to mind the cracked lens. She looked as if she was enjoying herself for once.

'You're not kidding, sweetheart. I've never seen him run like this.'

It struck Patsy that the reason he'd never seen the horse perform before was because this was the first time he'd had a jockey on his back smart enough to settle his nerves. Danny had never managed it, but then Danny was nothing special as a jockey.

Look at him now, he thought, taking the safest way round the course on the outside. Even though you're on a decent horse you don't win a tight race taking the long way round.

He kept the sentiment to himself. Though he didn't set much store by being polite, it might not be wise to mention it to Danny's new lady love at his elbow. He didn't want to piss her off.

Now Rock Solid was making progress down the far side. It looked as if he was going up the inside of the short-priced favourite who was ridden by the champion jockey Sean Boyle. How about that for cheek.

'Go on, Ricky!' he bellowed. 'You can take him!'

The rider ahead of Rick heard him coming. 'No, you bloody don't,' he shouted, moving to close the gap between his mount and the white running rail. But Rick was not to be bullied. He had thrust Rock Solid into the hole and he was damned if he was going to be squeezed out.

For a second or two it seemed as if the other horse would block him off. The second open ditch in the straight was coming up and Rick wondered if he was asking too much of his horse. Hold your nerve! he screamed inside, as much to himself as to Rock Solid.

The two horses seemed glued together, flank to flank, with the other jockey's lean mud-spattered face turned in their direction, spitting curses into the wind.

Tough, thought Rick. He's left a gap and I'm going through it.

He slapped Rock Solid on the shoulder and, with a surprising change of gear, the horse wrenched himself clear and flew over the open ditch, leaving their furious adversary in their wake.

Next it was round the bend and into the dip, heading for

the home straight and the long run-in past the stand.

Rick could hardly credit it, but they were in the lead.

'Hard luck, Patsy – he came so close.'

Patsy was hoarse from shouting but the sympathy in the greeny brown eyes of his companion dulled the edge of his disappointment.

In fact, as he now recovered from the excitement of the finish they had just witnessed, he could hardly claim to be disappointed at all. Second, after all, was a flaming miracle.

'It was the shock of being in front,' he said. 'That horse has never been first to a winning post in his life.'

The truth was that Rock Solid had run out of gas. As he'd set off up the home straight, the strength had slowly drained from his legs and he'd been caught just before the last. Rick had rallied him as they'd cleared the fence but there'd been no room for a comeback and he'd lost by half a length. All the same, it had been an eye-opening performance.

And, what's more, the outcome had been a success for the yard since it had been Willoughby, with Danny on board, who had reeled Rock Solid in.

Patsy was forgetting his manners. 'Congratulations, sweetheart. Your Danny's bringing home the prize money. He'll be wanting you at every meet from now on.'

'Oh God, I hope not.'

He laughed. 'Don't tell me you didn't enjoy seeing your man come home first.'

She blushed. 'Yes, of course. It was great. Well done, Danny.'

'Right enough. Let's go and tell him, eh?'

But as Patsy manoeuvred Tara through the crush of punters down to the winner's enclosure, he couldn't help wondering how easily Willoughby would have won had Rick been riding.

*

'I want a word, you little turd.'

Warm words of congratulation were still ringing in Rick's ears – Patsy had been particularly effusive – so to be greeted in this fashion as he stepped into the changing room took Rick off guard. He'd forgotten about his tussle with Sean Boyle out on the track, though he'd heard he'd been a faller at the second last – which might have contributed to his foul temper.

'I want an apology out of you,' Boyle hissed. He wasn't known for his charm and, like all the junior riders, Rick had always steered clear of him. As champion jockey for the past four seasons, Sean Boyle was lord of the changing room and the field force of gloomy intensity that surrounded him was grudgingly respected by all the other jockeys. Right now his long bony face was flushed pink, a picture of outrage. 'What did you think you were playing at going up my inner?'

Rick shrugged. 'There was a gap, I went through it. It's what happens in a race.'

The pink darkened to maroon. 'Don't you get smart with me. What you did was outrageous. There was no room on the rail.'

Rick grinned – deliberately, he couldn't resist. A year ago he'd not have dared to say boo to a man who was already a racing legend. But he'd just beaten him fair and square on an unranked horse and he didn't see why he should be abused for it.

'Of course there was room. If there wasn't room then how come I got through? Just because you're the champion jock doesn't mean you've a divine right to go where you want. The inside is the inside, not three yards away from it. Are the rest of us supposed to sit on our hands and wave you through?'

He wondered if he'd said too much. There was a steely coldness in the other man's eyes as he said, 'Maybe it's true what they say about you. You've gone off your rocker since your sister kicked the bucket.'

Rick's defiance stuck in his throat. He'd not seen that coming. Is that what they said about him? He considered where he was going to thump the champion jockey.

'Hey, Sean, cut it out.' Danny stepped between the two men. 'You're just pissed because you got dumped on the run-in.'

Boyle glared at him but considered his words. 'The pair of you ganging up on me, are you?'

'Hardly.' Danny grinned. 'I'm just suggesting you cool it. You can't win every race, mate.'

The older man took a pace backwards. The colour had left his cheeks and he considered them wearily. 'I don't know why I'm wasting my breath. You can't ride for shit, either of you.' And he walked off back to his peg on the other side of the room.

Danny put his hand on Rick's arm and said softly, 'What you might call a sore loser.'

Rick said nothing. This was his first time in the changing room of a racecourse for nine months.

Welcome back.

'Would you like me to drive?' Tara asked.

Danny looked at her with something like incredulity on his face as he unlocked the car door. 'No fear,' he said, then added quickly, 'I mean, I always do my own driving.'

Tara took her seat beside him. She didn't know why she'd asked, except she'd not been behind a wheel for over a week and she was used to getting herself around. Also, she'd thought it might be helpful – maybe Danny needed to switch off after riding all afternoon. However, looking at him, she could see he was still wired from the events of the day. He'd be a lousy passenger.

'You all right?' he asked as he steered them out of the car park.

She gave it a moment's thought. She hadn't wanted to come – the idea of leaving her country haven had spooked her. But, on reflection, she'd realised she'd be more vulnerable hanging around at the cottage or in the yard while Danny and the others were elsewhere. Suppose Tom or one of his guys had tracked her from Manchester and was waiting for an opportunity to get her on her own? Saturday afternoon while the main men were at the races might just provide it.

And the afternoon at the races had been OK. Better than OK, even if she'd had to put up with Patsy's constant jibes. But standing in the shadow of that blond giant she'd felt safe. His chauvinist oaf act was wearing but there was much that was reassuring in his Celtic blarney and she couldn't help liking him. In small doses, she told herself.

Her only moment of alarm had come when Patsy had dragged her into the winner's enclosure to congratulate Danny on his win. In the corner of her eye she'd noticed a man in a suit holding a microphone. 'Is this being televised?' The thought shot through her like an electric current and she'd hung back, dipping her head, hiding in the crowd in case she should be caught on camera.

Tom was a racing fan. He'd spent many Saturday afternoons at her flat with the racing programme on. As she'd fallen deeper under his spell he'd even had the nerve to bed her to coincide with the racing schedule – and laughed about it when she caught him out. 'Why do you think there's half an hour between races, babe? Time for a quick shag and a phone call to the bookmaker.'

She cringed at the memory. Danny was under the illusion

she was an intelligent woman. But not where some things were concerned.

Finally she responded to his question. 'I'm feeling great. I'm going home with the hero of the hour, aren't I?'

He shot her a suspicious glance as they waited their turn to join the stream of traffic on the road.

'Honestly. I'm so proud you won.'

She laid a companionable hand on his thigh and he flashed her a happy grin, as she knew he would. God, it was a relief to be with a straightforward man for a change.

That was one of the things that had bound her to Kirsty – their taste for difficult men. They'd teamed up halfway through her first term at uni in Manchester. She'd noticed Kirsty in lectures and immediately pegged her as someone who wasn't her type. The law freshers were a pretty staid lot, quite a few of the boys wore collar and tie, the others sported acne grunge; the girls were former school swots and dressed accordingly – as she did herself in those days. But Kirsty wore bangles that jangled and bright crop tops that showed a lot of toned flesh above her little skirts. She usually arrived late and fled the class as soon as she could, never staying to socialise. Well, we've got that in common, Tara had thought.

She was hating her first term, had made no friends that counted and was seriously considering her decision to come to a big English city. She felt like an Irish hick. She should have stayed in Belfast.

Kirsty was in Tara's seminar group, to which, despite prompting from the leader, she contributed little. It was obvious she'd done no preparation. The questions directed at her became more probing and, sitting next to her, Tara shared her embarrassment. She rearranged her papers so that her summary page – colour-coded and bullet-pointed in her usual A-student style – was plainly visible between them and gave Kirsty a nudge with her elbow. It was the kind of thing she'd done often enough at school. After that, Kirsty began to hold her end up in the discussion and, as the class finished, she'd put a hand on Tara's arm and hissed, 'We're having lunch.'

There wasn't any arguing with her. She steered Tara away from the studenty pubs and noodle bars into an arty-looking chrome and plate-glass restaurant.

'I'm paying,' Kirsty said, taking in the look of panic on Tara's face as she conned the menu. 'I want to make sure you sit next to me every seminar.'

They were next to each other more often than that. They fitted together like pieces of a puzzle, their knowledge and instincts interlocking to make them a unit. Kirsty was city savvy, already tuned in to the best music and shops. She brightened up Tara's wardrobe and introduced her to people who wanted more out of student life than discussing crap TV and getting off their faces every night. She banished Tara's homesickness and made her forget all about packing it in. For her part, Tara organised her new friend's work and unruly way of life, playing Miss Sensible to the other's cheerful chaos.

There was never any doubt that when they moved out of college accommodation at the end of the first year, they would share a flat. By then it was Kirsty who had dropped out. For all Tara's prompting she'd mucked up her first-year exams and announced she had no intention of resitting. 'Don't worry,' she'd said. 'I'm getting a job and we're going ahead with the flat – I wouldn't leave you in the lurch.' And in less than a week she'd landed work as an office dogsbody in a PR company. And within the month she was sleeping with the guy who'd interviewed her – Chris, a twinkly-eyed chain-smoker almost twice her age. Kirsty didn't intend to stay long at the foot of the office greasy pole.

Tara couldn't take the high ground over the affair because

she was soon going out with Chris's friend, Zak, a slim and caustic TV producer with a passion for French movies and, so she believed for a blissful six weeks, her. Then Zak's wife turned up at the flat, called her a student slut and threatened to write to every lecturer in the Law School. But what really burst the bubble were the photos the poor woman showed her of Zak playing happy families with his three-year-old daughter and a babe in arms. She felt soiled – she was no home-wrecker – and she'd sworn to pick her boyfriends with care in the future. And three years on, she'd hooked up with Tom. He, too, was married, with two children, although that turned out to be the least of her problems. So much for learning from your mistakes.

Kirsty's eye for a suitable man didn't improve either, except that each liaison seemed to bring its own advantages – a fancy holiday, useful contacts, new clients. And when things went pear-shaped, she rarely shed tears. An evening of commiseration with Kirsty inevitably turned into a laugh-aloud bitching session about the ex.

Kirsty met Danny at a race meeting she'd attended as a corporate guest; her name was pulled out of the hat to present the prize to a winning jockey – Danny – and, she claimed, their eyes locked as she handed over the champagne. The fact that she had a brother trying to make it in the racing business eased the connection.

Danny had been quite a change of pace for Kirsty. He was her age, for a start, and a professional sportsman though hardly a household name. He wasn't married or carrying the burden of a lost love or crawling through some dark night of the soul with the aid of a vodka bottle. What's more, when Tara finally met him – for once Kirsty had been coy about making the introduction – the new boyfriend had turned out to be funny, guileless and kind. 'He's the first good man I've ever been to bed with,' Kirsty announced. Two months later, her brother was taken on at Latchmere and by the end of the year Kirsty and Danny were engaged.

And now, Tara reflected, here she was in her turn. Travelling home from a racecourse with the same victorious jockey whom Kirsty had snared. A saviour whose kindness and generosity to her appeared bottomless, who was prepared to open his heart and home to her as he had done to her friend.

Poor Kirsty. It wasn't right. She should be here in my place.

And I should still have a career and a home of my own and a car and my friends.

At least I've still got my life.

She realised her hand was still resting on Danny's thigh. She left it there. Just as Kirsty would have done.

Chapter Five

'Aren't you going to take me right up to the gate?' Sophie Ferguson's voice took on the teenage whine with which Tom was so familiar – and to which he was so sensitive. 'Please, Daddy. Don't make me walk in the rain.'

The shower had stopped a good ten minutes earlier but Tom knew better than to point that out. The school was only fifty yards off the main road and to deliver her by car involved a detour. He was running late but he obediently indicated left and turned off into the one-way system.

'You only want me to drive you because you like arriving by Ferrari,' he muttered.

'You bet.' She gave him one of her winning smiles. 'If you've got it, flaunt it – that's what you say, isn't it?'

As a matter of fact, that was one of her mother's bon mots and her daughter had adopted it greedily, along with many of Carol's other irritating habits. Perhaps he should be grateful she hadn't picked up his wife's other terms of reference for the beautiful blue ('Le Mans blue' according to the dealer) machine in which they now sat. 'Penis extension' was one of the more polite ones.

'Daddy?' They were stuck in the drop-off queue as parents deposited their offspring by the school entrance. To avoid trespassing on the yellow zig-zags outside the gate – the local bastard council had begun photographing offenders –

the convention was to stop in the middle of the narrow road. The process took a while.

'Yes, darling?'

'Why can't we book our summer holiday now? I really need to know when we're going.'

'What on earth for?' This was a topic that had arisen over supper the night before and he'd given it short shrift.

'I told you. Because I've got arrangements to make. All my friends are getting booked up and I really want to ask Chloe to come with us.'

Chloe was Sophie's best friend, a distractingly pretty nymph who would grace any poolside. In any ordinary year Tom would have been happy to book three weeks in the sun and invite her along. But this was not an ordinary year.

'The thing is,' Sophie was eager to make her point, 'I can't just be stuck at home for eight weeks while all my friends are away doing stuff. Considering what I'll have just been through, I think I deserve a good holiday. The best ever, actually.'

Tom nodded, absorbing her words. Sophie had just played her big card, alluding to the GCSEs she was due to take in the summer term. She was down for eleven and the school predicted an A in all of them which, typically, wasn't good enough for his wife – 'She's got to get at least eight A stars,' Carol had announced. 'Oxbridge won't look at anything less.'

'I'll talk to your mother about it,' he said, aware he was ducking the real issue. 'There are one or two problems to sort out.'

'Thanks, Daddy.' She laid her slender hand on top of his as it rested on the gear stick. He remembered only too vividly when those elegant woman's fingers were chubby little sausages wriggling in his palm. However much of a bastard he'd been in his life, he'd always loved his children with a painful intensity.

'I mean,' she went on, 'I know there's been a bit of a problem at your work but it's your firm, isn't it? Yours and Uncle Jack's. So they can't exactly sack you. And Uncle Jack's going to do everything to help, isn't he? I know Chloe's parents would pay for her and maybe we could go somewhere a bit cheaper or not for so long or something. So we should be able to afford a holiday, shouldn't we?'

He let her rattle on, her milky blue eyes bathing him with her youthful certainty, his stomach tumbling with terror. How could he tell her the question was not whether he could pay for a holiday but whether he would be at liberty to take her? And whether the entire foundation of her sheltered existence was about to shift. If his trial, of which she was still miraculously ignorant, went against him, she'd be facing a life stripped of more than a few weeks on a beach. No lifts in Italian sports cars. No fancy private school. No daddy of whom she could be proud. How long would those pretty blue eyes remain innocent once she'd begun visiting her daddy in prison? he wondered.

A beep from the car behind brought him back to the present. He took his foot off the brake and rolled forward. They were almost at the head of the queue now and Sophie began to gather her belongings.

'Don't forget your flute,' he said, almost by reflex. It was funny how he could operate on one level as if life was a humdrum affair and there was no pistol pointed at his head.

'We're starting orchestra rehearsals today for the governors' concert – it's mad, isn't it? It's not till next term. You've got to promise you'll come this time.'

'I promise.'

She leaned over to kiss his cheek as he brought the car to

a halt. 'Bye, best Dad. Thanks for driving me the long way round.'

He watched her retreating figure, taller now than her mother, as she merged into the stream of other girls and disappeared from sight. He regretted his ill humour of five minutes ago. He'd drive her the long way every day from now on, he decided. While he was still free to do so.

Christine tapped her fingers on the desk in irritation, then left another message on Jean's answering service. Where could the girl have got to? It wasn't like her to abandon her duties – at least, not without a proper explanation; a twenty-second message on the answerphone saying she couldn't come in hardly counted.

Jean had been a willing and efficient office secretary for the past nine months. Always eager and fiercely loyal, she'd made a proper contribution to the Latchmere Park team. Provided she was allowed access to the horses and time to ride out, Jean wouldn't think twice about staying late or taking work home to help out. The girl was horse-mad and Christine could hardly disapprove of that.

But now Jean had disappeared into the blue. There had been no word from her for four days and the office systems were beginning to suffer. A pile of post required a response – today's hadn't even been opened – and Christine was looking at a lengthy list of callers. As she ran her eye down the names, she could see that several would be hard work, which was one reason why she employed a full-time secretary. Jean was good at shielding her from time-wasters and, when her shield wasn't in place, Christine felt distinctly exposed.

A shadow passed the office window and a familiar figure appeared in the doorway. Christine tensed as Patsy entered. She never relished being on her own with the big man. There were things she knew about her brother-in-law that made her uncomfortable – and things he knew about her, too, of course. Their relationship had been forged through testing times and, so it seemed to Christine, whenever Patsy's blond head ducked inside the office doorway, it spelled trouble. She wondered what had brought him today.

'No Jean?' he said.

Of course, Jean would be the reason. Patsy had turned his attention on the poor girl at the Latchmere Christmas party and, so Christine had been informed, the pair had embarked on a heady seasonal romance. She tried to stay above the yard gossip but she couldn't afford to remain ignorant of the goings-on around her. Here was a case in point – not that she could have done anything to spare her secretary the pleasures and pains of allowing Patsy into her bed.

'I haven't seen her all week,' she said. 'And I haven't heard from her either.'

'Ah.' He had the grace to look embarrassed. 'That's probably my fault. We had a little misunderstanding.'

She waited for him to continue.

'Affairs of the heart, you know.' He shrugged.

'You broke it off with her?'

'It was never really on. Not in any lasting sense.'

But he'd moved into her flat on New Year's Day, that's what Christine had been told. Ever since his marriage had broken up, Patsy had changed addresses like most men changed socks. And a new girl was a regular feature of the costume change.

Now Christine understood what had happened to Jean. She wasn't the kind of girl who hopped from man to man. Naive and whole-hearted, she had fallen like a ton of bricks for a practised womaniser a good ten years older than she was. And now he'd shrugged her off, the girl had simply taken fright. Christine could imagine Jean would not be showing her face at Latchmere in a hurry for fear of running into Patsy.

'Where is she?' Christine asked.

'I'm the last person she's going to tell,' was the reply. 'But her mum lives in Swindon if you really want to get her back.'

Christine wasn't sure about that. Maybe she could sweet-talk the reluctant secretary into returning but did she want to? Frankly, it was feeble behaviour to bolt like this. Not to mention insulting to her employer.

Patsy was gauging her reaction. She felt like giving the thoughtless bastard a piece of her mind. He had no right mucking a girl like Jean around. She had no doubt he'd allowed her to entertain all sorts of fanciful ideas of a future together while having his fill of her curvy little body. And now he was bored with her. That kind of behaviour, thoughtless and cynical, made Christine sick.

But she bit her tongue. She couldn't afford to fall out with Patsy who, apart from family considerations, was her husband's right-hand man and partner in so many of their ventures. In the scale of things, Patsy's goodwill weighed far more heavily than the loss of a secretary.

'Look, I'm sorry about this. If she's got any sense she'll be back in a day or so and I'll keep out of her way, I promise.'

Christine said nothing. She just wished Patsy would go. The unopened post and the phone list commanded her attention.

'Anyhow,' he said, 'if you need a bit of help round here I've got a suggestion. Danny's new girl has been hanging around the stud trying to make herself useful. But I'm running out of things to give her to do and, to be honest, she's wasting her time making Steph and me cups of coffee all day. Why don't I bring her over?'

The thought had already occurred to Christine. Particularly this morning when she realised how disarray was overtaking her normally efficient procedures. But she'd rejected it.

'You'd be getting a bargain,' he said. 'Tara's a smart cookie.'

Christine had no doubt of it, though she hardly knew her. And she'd have the chance to know her a whole lot better if she came to work here in the office. But she was reluctant.

Two years ago Kirsty had stood in for a week when the secretary of the day was on holiday. Christine had imagined it would be the perfect opportunity to bond with her future daughter-in-law, but things hadn't worked out that way. It wasn't so much Kirsty's casual attitude on the phone to owners and racing officials or her slapdash attitude to paperwork. Even the indiscreet conversation Christine had interrupted with a journalist from the *Racing Beacon* had been excusable. But the heavy hints that Kirsty was always dropping about being allowed to race-ride – like her brother, she had talent in the saddle – and the long, giggly personal calls had irritated no end. And the way Adrian suddenly took to dropping in for a chat had not improved Christine's mood. When, on the fourth day, Kirsty returned late from a lunch with her own husband, Christine had had enough. She thanked Kirsty for her help and told her her services were no longer required. 'Thank God for that,' the girl had said. 'I'm bored out of my mind in here. I don't know how people stand it.' Christine had been sorely tempted to slap her beautiful, ignorant face.

All in all, Christine reckoned it was best to keep her son's girlfriends out of her workplace.

The phone on the desk burst into life. Christine glared at it, as if she could somehow shut it off.

Patsy picked it up. 'Latchmere Park, can I help you?' He was grinning at Christine as he spoke, enjoying her discomfort. 'I'm sorry, Mr Henderson, but Christine's up on the gallops – probably putting that fine horse of yours through his paces. I'll make sure she phones you back as soon as she can.' He replaced the receiver. 'Well, Christine, I'm not babysitting you all afternoon. Shall I fetch Tara or not?'

On second thoughts, this girl seemed nothing like Kirsty. 'Yes, please,' she said.

Rick studied Christine as he cantered Treacle Toffee back around to take the line of hurdles for the second time. He was eager to know what she thought of this newcomer to her yard – and her opinion of Gingerbread too, who Danny was riding. But Christine's pale oval face was inscrutable, as usual. She'd said nothing to him about the horses since their arrival and, according to Hugh, whom Rick had been calling on a daily basis, she'd been noncommittal in their only conversation so far.

But Rick knew that her silence was not an indication of indifference. The day the horses arrived at Latchmere he'd been preoccupied in sorting out his digs and had not turned up at the yard till gone noon the next day. He'd been dismayed to be told that Treacle and Ginger had not settled in well to their new quarters. 'The pair of them were sounding off the whole night long,' one of the lads told him the moment he arrived. 'Kept half the yard awake. And they're off their food too.'

Rick's alarm sent him straight to Christine who calmed him down. 'We've solved the problem. We had one of them in a barn stall and I don't think they liked being separated.

They're next to one another now – I don't think we'll have any more trouble.' And she'd been right.

So it was no wonder he was keen for her to share his opinion of Treacle and Ginger's potential as jump horses. So far she'd watched them go through their paces on the all-weather gallops among a string of other Latchmere animals. Their performance hadn't been much to get excited about, consistent with their form on the Flat, which was well known to be ordinary. It was their prospects as jumpers that mattered. And this was the first occasion the trainer had watched them school over hurdles.

He took Treacle Toffee up the sequence of hurdles again, with Danny on Gingerbread. They both jumped well, as if they were enjoying themselves. 'You're jumping like an old hand, aren't you?' Rick said to Treacle as they landed cleanly over the last. He shot a glance over his shoulder in Christine's direction, hoping to get some kind of acknowledgement of their progress. To his astonishment he found himself staring at the back of the trainer's olive-green jacket as she walked away, heading for her Land Rover parked on the edge of the field. The pocket of elation that had surrounded him evaporated instantly. Obviously she'd seen enough and wasn't particularly impressed.

Danny's eyes were sparkling as he pulled up and patted his horse enthusiastically. It was plain hc was a happy bunny. But then Danny appeared to be permanently on cloud nine these days and Rick didn't kid himself it was necessarily to do with horses.

His old friend was in love and, in theory, Rick was happy for him. In practice, his feelings were more complicated. So far he'd managed to give Tara a wide berth. It wasn't her fault she wasn't Kirsty but he'd not bargained for Danny being in so deep with a new girlfriend – they looked like they were engaged, for God's sake – nor for the fact that this fiancée once used to be Kirsty's closest friend. He'd known her briefly in that role himself. The whole business made him uneasy and he was trying hard not to give it much thought.

'What do you think?' he called over.

Danny gave him a thumbs-up. 'You've done a good job on these.'

'It's down to Hugh really. He's a smart operator.'

'Why didn't he want to run them out of his yard then?'

'Because he's not a jumps specialist like your mum. Who's cleared off, I notice. I thought she might want to give us the benefit of her expertise. She's plainly not impressed.'

Danny laughed. 'I can tell you've not been around lately. Mum doesn't need to see much to form an opinion these days. I bet she's well impressed.'

Rick stared at him in disbelief.

'What's not to like?' Danny continued. 'This feller's pretty good and yours is better. That's what Mum will say. Relax, mate. You'll see.' And he beamed his love-struck fool grin once more.

Rick said nothing.

The park, pretty at other times, was bleak in winter. Without leaves on the trees the town buildings on the perimeter seemed to loom over the green space and the low-slung sky was grey with a new threat of rain.

Tom found Carl sitting on a bench in front of a deserted children's playground. 'What kept you?' he moaned in flat nasal Manc. 'I'm freezing me bollocks off here.'

Considering Carl was built like a bear, even taller than Tom and twice as big round the chest, he didn't look vulnerable to the elements. Though maybe he could have done with some headgear to protect his gleaming scalp.

'Sorry I'm late,' Tom said. 'Bloody awful traffic.'

The other grunted. It went without saying. He got up and the pair began to follow the path that ran round the southern edge of the park. Tom knew they were an incongruous couple, a shaven-headed tough in leathers and a well-turned-out businessman in a tailored cashmere coat. So far, however, there was no one around to remark on it. All the same, it would be better to keep things short.

'I can't find her,' Carl said.

'Her' was Tara. Tom's most glorious triumph and his biggest folly. The woman who held his future happiness in her hand as, in a funny way, she'd done since the moment they'd met. Not that he wanted to romanticise the treacherous bitch.

'She's disappeared,' Carl added.

'How do you mean?' Tom asked. In some respects, the less he knew about Carl's dealings with Tara the better. Even the knowledge of the threats that Carl had issued to date was dangerous to a man in his position. After his last encounter with Tara, Carl had told him he'd left her 'wetting her knickers'. He'd not found it as amusing as Carl obviously did.

'I've been round to her place and, guess what, she's done a runner.'

'You're sure?'

'That's what her landlady told me. Gone back to Ireland. And there was no sign of her. I couldn't see her car.'

Tom thought. 'She was quite thick with the woman she rented from. She could just be covering for Tara.'

Carl shook his head. 'The flat's been re-let. I hung around. Two bloody hours before some skanky git turned up in a van. He went up to the second floor where your girlfriend lived. I saw him in the room before he pulled the curtains.'

'Maybe she's seen the error of her ways since your little chat and gone for good.'

Carl looked at him quizzically. 'Don't ask me, pal. You think she's the type to just piss off?'

Tom ignored him.

'What did the landlady say about Ireland?'

'Just that she'd packed in her job and gone back to her family in Belfast. I asked for an address – said I was a mate from uni and wanted to keep in touch. No need to look at me like that, I could be a student if I wanted.'

'Did you get the address?'

'She said she didn't have one. The girl left in a hurry.'

'Phone number?'

'Just the one you already gave me.'

And that was no good. She must have changed her mobile.

Tom wasn't happy. What family in Belfast? Her parents were dead and her sister was married to a banker in Hong Kong.

'Turns out,' Carl continued, 'she flogged her motor last week. It's on the forecourt of a dealer in Bury New Road. And she's cleaned out her bank account too.'

Tom looked at him. How on earth did he know these things? But he himself had supplied as many of Tara's details as he could glean from the personnel file. And a man like Benny Bridges – Carl's boss and Tom's most lucrative client – had his finger in many pies.

So Tara had gone. But without knowing her intentions, it did not solve his problem.

They'd taken a turn around the open field and followed the path down through the trees to the river, full from the past few days' rain. They stopped on the bank.

Carl cleared his throat and shot a ball of spit into the brown flow racing in eerie silence past their feet.

'Benny says I've got to go after her. Sort her out for good.'

The moment the words were uttered, Tom realised that was their only choice. Until Tara's silence was ensured they

couldn't leave it to chance – and Benny would have understood that straightaway.

'Only,' Carl went on, 'you've got to give me some idea
where to look.'

Jesus. 'That's not going to be easy.'

'Well, it's up to you to find out.' There was a hint of a
smile on Carl's face now. 'Like Benny says, you're the one
who was dicking her.'

Once he'd returned Treacle Toffee to his stall and seen to his
needs, Rick marched across the yard to the office, intent on
finding Christine. All the while he'd been rubbing the horse
down he'd been chewing over the situation. It was all very
well Danny saying Treacle and Ginger were in good nick but
it didn't much matter to him if they weren't. What mattered
was Christine's opinion and he didn't think he could wait
any longer before he heard it. Was she deliberately keeping
him in suspense?

He could see Christine through the office window,
standing by the desk, holding some papers. She was talking
to Tara who was seated on the other side of the room in the
place usually occupied by Jean, the secretary. God, it hadn't
taken the girl long to make herself at home. She was quite
the little cuckoo in the nest.

He didn't knock, just shoved the door open and thrust his
head through the gap.

'Can I have a second, Christine?'

He hadn't meant to sound so abrupt but his words sliced
through the conversation that was taking place and silence
fell.

'Of course.' Christine put the papers down on the desk and
took her coat from the chair. 'Let's go and look at these
horses of yours.' She flashed him a quick smile.

Rick was immediately disarmed and conscious of the

boorish impression he must be making. He turned to Tara. 'Sorry to, er, interrupt.'

She just nodded, her face grave as she stared at him. He felt uncomfortable under her gaze and stepped swiftly backwards into the yard. It wouldn't have hurt her to say hello, would it? But maybe she didn't remember him. It had been some years since they'd met.

He quickly put Tara out of his head as Christine joined him and they made their way across the yard to Treacle Toffee's box.

'I was wondering,' Rick began, 'what you thought of him. And Ginger. I know the form's not much on the Flat but Hugh reckons they could make jumpers. Hugh's a good man, you know.'

'And what's your opinion?'

Treacle Toffee stuck his head over the door and observed them. Next door, Gingerbread did exactly the same thing. As if they knew they were under discussion.

Rick put his hand out to fondle Ginger's ear. He spoke rapidly. 'I reckon they're doing pretty well. Treacle really likes jumping and that's half the battle with him. And this one's always been game, never gives in – maybe he'll have a better chance over hurdles. But,' he forced himself to slow down and take a breath, 'you're the expert. You're the reason I persuaded Hugh to send them here. You've seen them this morning, what do you think?'

She laughed softly. 'I think you're far too anxious, Rick. I like them.'

Thank God for that. He let out a sigh of relief. He'd been so afraid he'd misjudged matters and she'd say they were rubbish and not up to the standard of the others in her expensive and well-regarded yard.

'I think they have promise,' she continued, 'but it's about time we put their ability to the test. I was thinking that a run out at Haydock this weekend would be the next step.'

'Excellent.' That was just what he wanted to hear. 'Does Hugh know?'

'Of course. It was either that or Uttoxeter the week after but he preferred Haydock.'

He would do. Haydock wasn't far from Hugh's yard. Rick imagined that he'd bring Gwen and the girls along.

Christine was smiling at him. 'Does that make you feel a bit better?'

'Yes. The way you left this morning, I was worried you didn't think much of them.'

'Why would you think that? You must learn to trust your own judgement. I came back because I'd promised to call Hugh once I'd had a look at them schooling.'

All the same, he was convinced she'd been teasing him, keeping him on tenterhooks. Not that he cared now.

'There's another thing,' she added. 'Hugh wants them entered for the Triumph Hurdle.'

He stared at her. Just getting them on the racecourse was good enough for him. The Triumph Hurdle at the Cheltenham Festival, the best hurdle race of the season for four-year-olds, had not crossed his mind. He'd not have dared to think of it.

'It's a bit of a stretch, isn't it?'

'Agreed, but the entries are due in now. Hugh says it might be the only time in his life he has jump horses so why not? I can't argue with that.'

Neither could Rick. He was thrilled at the thought.

'Congratulations, you two,' he said to the horses, still attentive to their conversation. 'You might be in for the big time.'

She put her hand on his arm. 'I hope you don't take this the wrong way, Rick, but are you feeling all right about being back here?'

'What? Because I talk to the horses?'

'No. We all do that.' Her slate-grey eyes pinned him. 'I'm delighted you've decided to return here but I'm concerned. This place must have many bitter-sweet memories for you. I don't want us to part on bad terms again.'

He was surprised that she'd raised the matter. It was tempting to say that Kirsty's death and the angry manner of his parting was all in the past, but he didn't see why he should lie – certainly not to Christine.

'Honestly, Christine, I don't know what to tell you. I just felt it was right to come back. The fact that Kirsty was happy here is part of it. But that doesn't mean I'm ever going to get over her death.'

She squeezed his arm. 'I don't think any of us will, Rick.'

Tara walked well away from the stable buildings and up the track the horses used. Mobile phone reception was better up here but that wasn't the principal reason for getting away. She needed complete privacy for the call she was about to make.

Finally she reached a point high above the yard and, even on this damp January day, she took pleasure in the vista of green turf and open sky stretching to the horizon. Danny had told her the country life would be good for her soul and he'd not been wrong. Maybe she'd turn into a country girl after all.

Ahead, Christine's string of horses were returning from the gallops and Tara veered away from them to the far corner of the field, not wanting to be seen.

She called the Manchester number she'd programmed into her new phone, only the second in her list of contacts after Danny.

Some kind of receptionist answered. Tara said, 'DS Hammond, please.'

'I'll try for you, love, but I'm sure they're all out.'

And so it proved. The phone rang half a dozen times then clicked into answerphone mode. Damn. She ended the call.

'Hey up, what are you doing here?'

She looked up to see a figure on a nut-brown horse trotting towards her. Danny must have been one of the riders out on the gallop whom she had tried to avoid. It was just her luck that he had noticed her. There might be plenty of open spaces in the countryside but sometimes it was bloody difficult to get some privacy.

'Who are you calling?'

'Just a friend.' She knew that wasn't adequate the moment the words were out. He'd caught her on the hop. 'I mean, Sharon. I was just checking that there hadn't been any post for me.'

'And is there any?'

'She's not in. I'll try again later.'

He grinned indulgently at her. 'Use the office phone. Mum won't mind.'

She shrugged. 'I just wanted some fresh air.'

'It's brilliant up here, isn't it? I'm going to get you out on a horse next time.'

'OK.' She couldn't hide her lack of enthusiasm.

'You'll love it. I promise.' The steam rose from his mount in a cloud and she could see the animal was getting edgy. 'I've got to go. See you later.'

She watched the pair trot back to join the other horses, conscious she'd made some kind of blunder. God, she hated lying, especially to a man as transparently honest as Danny. The thing was, if she was to make a success of her current situation, she had to get a damned sight better at it.

Jack Gallagher manoeuvred his bulk through Tom's office door and closed it behind him. He sat heavily in the chair opposite the desk and sighed, his round pink face a picture of gloom. It was the morning performance Tom had become accustomed to during the past six weeks. He felt like an errant son in front of a reproachful father.

Tom hoisted a smile on to his lips. 'Morning, Jack. How's tricks?'

For the best part of fifteen years, Tom had basked in the glow of Jack's grateful patronage. It was Tom's energy and cunning that had transformed the old Gallagher practice from a moribund outfit entirely reliant on bottom-feeding Legal Aid miscreants to a money-making concern with heavyweight clients who expected to be billed accordingly. In a civilised society even Satan is entitled to a decent brief, Jack had told him on his first day in the office and Tom had laboured hard to ensure that Gallagher Ferguson would be the first number Old Nick dialled when the Greater Manchester Police came calling. Within two years of his arrival Tom had made partner and Jack Gallagher had become fat and rich on the younger man's efforts – at least, in these sour days following his arrest, that was how Tom saw it. And right now was payback time. He needed his senior partner's support more than ever before.

'Any news?' Jack said.

What was the man expecting him to say? That the police had changed their minds? That the CPS had declined to act and all charges against him had been dropped?

Of course not. Gallagher Ferguson had been successfully defending drug dealers, murderers and gangland racketeers for more than ten years. The firm – and Tom Ferguson in particular – were not popular with the law enforcement authorities. If they could put him on the stand for a parking offence they'd be pressing for jail time. The charges against him of perverting the course of justice would not be dropped if there was a one per cent chance of conviction.

And the odds were rather better than that. Not that Jack was fully aware of the statistical probabilities.

'I was wondering,' Jack continued, 'whether there was any news of the girl? Tara's not turned up, has she?'

'No.'

'Well,' his plump face lifted, 'I suppose that's good news. If she's not around to testify against you, they haven't got a case.'

How true. If only he could believe that Tara had gone for good.

'Maybe,' Jack continued, 'she's finally come to her senses and realised that making wild allegations about partners in her firm is no way to pursue a career in the law.'

Tom nodded. 'You may be right.'

Poor old Jack didn't have a clue. When things had blown up – after the embarrassment of being charged and bailed – Tom had owned up to the affair with Tara. By then the girl had resigned and fled the office. In a sorrowful confession, Tom had explained to his senior partner that Tara had taken the end of their affair badly and had refused to accept his decision to put his family first. And in revenge – it was the only way he could account for her behaviour – Tara had gone running to the police and made a series of accusations against him which, given Tom's unpopularity, had been seized on with excessive zeal. So far Jack had swallowed the line and long may that continue to be the case.

It hadn't been plain sailing, however.

'I must say I'm surprised about Tara. A girl from my own town.' Jack had started out in practice in Belfast – the connection had been a point in Tara's favour when she'd applied to the firm and was often referred to. Jack took her defection personally. 'You know, I'd never have taken her for a bunny boiler. Such an intelligent girl.'

'Are you saying she's too intelligent to fall for me?'

This exchange had taken place during one of their morning chats, after Jack's initial alarm had died down.

'I'm saying that she always struck me as dedicated to the idea of becoming a successful member of the profession. Sleeping with your supervising partner is not the brightest way of going about it.'

Tom had been tempted to disagree. In his experience that had been a profitable route for more than one lawyer he could name. But he'd been flippant enough already and this was not a joking matter for Jack. It had taken some persuading to ensure that Jack didn't invite himself round to see Carol and offer himself as a father confessor to her, too. 'Would it not be of comfort to Carol to know that I'm fully supportive of you? I wouldn't like her to think that the firm was not behind you one hundred per cent. Besides, I count myself as a family friend, Tom. And you need your friends at times like these.'

But Tom had persuaded him to limit contact to a phone call of commiseration. Jack was a good soul but Tom didn't want the pair of them comparing notes. Carol did not know about Tara although she was aware of other transgressions in his past. It was important for Tom that his business partner and his wife did not assemble the big picture. As far as Jack was concerned, Tara was a one-off, an irresistible temptation which Tom now regretted, having nobly cast the girl aside for the good of his family. As for Carol, she believed that Tom, being on a final warning, had given up his philandering ways. Truth to tell, there'd been a suspicious lack of curiosity in Carol's concern for his whereabouts for some months. This, together with her habitual frostiness, led Tom to believe that he'd lost her somewhere along the twisting path of their marriage. For all that, husband and wife provided a united front for the sake of Sophie and her younger brother, Cosmo. Staying together for the kids – there was truth in every cliché. But if Jack told Carol about his affair with Tara, all bets might be off.

Of course, should Tara take the stand against him at the trial, the result might very well be the same. His freedom and his marriage down the pan in one hit.

Carol would move for sure. Her parents lived in some splendour in Cape Town – he could imagine her running home to them with the children. Sophie was sixteen and all but an adult – she could soon make her own decisions. But Cosmo was only thirteen. When would he see his son again?

You didn't just lose your liberty when you went to prison. For a man like him, you lost your whole sodding life.

'Tom, are you feeling all right?'

Jack had been talking and Tom must have tuned him out. Now Jack was leaning across the desk, his poached-egg eyes swimming with concern.

'I'm fine, honestly. Just a bit preoccupied.'

'Well, that's understandable.' Jack studied him for a second then rose to his feet. 'I'll let you get on.'

Tom watched him walk to the door. Jack had made it clear that, unless a conviction was upheld against him, he was welcome in the office, though they'd both agreed it would be better for Tom not to show himself in court. And every morning Jack popped in to boost morale and offer his help, which was invariably declined.

Now, however, something occurred to Tom.

'Do you still have contacts in Belfast, Jack?'

The big face spread into a smile. 'It's a long time since I trained but I don't expect everyone's died off.' His expression darkened. 'You're thinking about Tara, aren't you?'

'She might have gone back there. Perhaps she's looking for some legal work. You could ask about her. Maybe pick something up on the grapevine.'

111

Jack shrugged. 'Seems unlikely. And what if I find her?'

'You could ask what her intentions are. As you say, she might have thought the better of her allegations.'

Jack weighed the thought. 'Wouldn't it be better to go through her family?'

'Her father's long gone and her mother died last year. Remember? She had time off for the funeral.'

Jack nodded. Then, to Tom's surprise, he began to chuckle. 'You could always try Monaghan's. The bakers in Castle Street.'

Tom stared at him.

'Des Monaghan's her uncle.' Jack couldn't help looking smug. He enjoyed occasions when he could display superior knowledge. 'The first conversation I ever had with Tara was about Monaghan's. The shop's just up the road from my old firm.'

That had a ring of truth to it. He could imagine Jack waxing nostalgic about his trainee days. And Tara would have been smart enough to exploit it at her interview.

'Are you sure, Jack? The man who runs it is her uncle?'

'That's what she said. On her mother's side, I assume.'

'You've got a good memory.'

'There's some things you never forget. Like a treacle farl or a Belfast bap.'

Tom nodded though he didn't know what Jack was on about. Nor did he care. His partner – possibly – had just handed him a lifeline.

Though not for Tara, of course.

It wasn't until later, when the horses were settled after their morning work and most of the yard workers were on their afternoon break, that Tara trudged back up the hill to phone Manchester again.

The same woman answered as before. She recognised Tara's voice. 'He's back now, love. I'll put you through.'

'Hammond.' He answered in his usual grumpy style, bored, with a hint of 'I know you're going to waste my time' in his voice. She couldn't imagine it went down well with his superiors.

'It's Tara,' she said.

The tone changed, as she knew it would.

'Tara. Where on earth are you? I've been looking all over the city.'

'Give up, Duncan. I'm not anywhere you're going to find me.'

A sigh came down the line. 'I'm concerned for your welfare, lass.'

'I'm aware of that. Perhaps if your colleagues shared your concern I wouldn't have had to take emergency action.'

When the first threats had begun – the vague but menacing phone calls – she'd appealed to the police for help. She hadn't been reassured by their response. And she'd had other knowledge, from her work at Gallagher Ferguson, of how well the authorities protected their prosecution witnesses. It wasn't fool-proof. She trusted DS Hammond, however. Perhaps it was the Celtic bond, the Scotsman and the Irish woman surrounded by the men of the red rose, but she felt safe with him. Though not safe enough to reveal her whereabouts.

'Look, Duncan, I'm OK. Nobody knows where I am and it's best like this. Just tell the CPS and whoever else needs to know that I am fully committed to appearing in court in June to testify against Tom Ferguson. So don't worry. I'll be there.'

'Tara, listen to me a moment. It's not safe—'

'Goodbye, Duncan. I'll be in touch.'

And she cut him off.

The first person she saw when she returned to the yard was Danny.

'Been back up the hill? Did you get her this time?'

What was he talking about?

He must have caught the confusion on her face.

'Sharon – isn't that who you've been calling?'

She remembered her fib about her former landlady. 'Oh, yes. She was in this time. There's no post. I guess I can't be that popular.'

'I don't believe that,' he said. 'You're popular with me.'

And he put a consoling arm round her shoulder, just as she'd anticipated he would. It was no small comfort.

Chapter Six

Carl was not enjoying his trip to Northern Ireland. He knew he was a fish out of water. Every word he spoke marked him out as a man travelling in a foreign country.

Manchester was Carl's turf and anywhere away from the north-west of England felt like an insult to the blood of Lancashire running through his veins. Of his fellow citizens of the United Kingdom, soft-as-shit southerners incurred his wrath on a daily basis but he reserved a special contempt for the Micks of Northern Ireland. Pig-headed bastards incapable of forgetting their tribal past. Pasty-faced idiots who were still fighting some arsy battle that had finished three hundred years ago. Carl could think of many good reasons for beating a man's brains out but they didn't include which church their mum went to.

But for all their stupidity about history and stuff, he couldn't deny the Ulster Irish were hard bastards. You had to respect that, especially when you were playing away from home and, in some respects, playing by their rules.

'When our man arrives, I'll come in with you,' Sharkey said. He was sitting in the back of the car. 'Smurf will wait here for us.'

The driver turned to Carl and grinned. Like a kid happy to get a name check from his teacher. Only he was a middle-aged mound of pork, twenty stone at least – had to be. Carl couldn't imagine he was quick on his toes so it was just as well he was staying where he was.

'Is that OK, Mr Harris?'

Carl had told him his Christian name but Sharkey didn't seem keen to use it. Carl didn't care, he liked to be treated with respect. Although it was yet another thing that served to emphasise that he was different from them. And on this kind of operation – the kind where you couldn't predict exactly what would go down – he'd have preferred to feel part of a team. Would Sharkey be as keen to look out for some Brit called Mr Harris as he would for his new mate Carl?

Benny had assured him Sharkey was OK and that he owed him a few favours on account of their business relationship. Carl could guess what that relationship entailed – most of these paramilitary types were now into drugs, weren't they? As was Carl himself, naturally, but he didn't deal with the Irish end of Benny's operation.

'Won't be long now, Mr Harris. He gets home about this time.'

Smurf's voice was soft but the accent still rattled around Carl's head. Did they all have to sound like Ian Paisley?

'How do you know?' he asked.

'We've been keeping an eye on him for a couple of days.'

Since Benny had made the call, no doubt. Carl almost felt sorry for Des Monaghan. He'd done nothing to Benny, they'd never even clapped eyes on one another, yet Benny had picked up the phone and Des was in for some grief.

But Des, whether he knew it or not, had missed his chance. Carl had visited his shop that afternoon. A nice old-fashioned bakery with the sweet smell of fresh bread in the air and rows of tempting-looking sticky cakes beneath the glass front of the counter. He'd had a cuppa and a scone in the tea room attached and admired the norks on the freckle-faced waitress. It had been the high point of his trip so far.

But his real interest had been in the small but stocky old feller with wire-rimmed spectacles who was in and out of the door to the kitchen, lending a hand when the queue built up at the counter and keeping an eye on the customer traffic.

The waitress confirmed the man's identity. Carl had known it had to be the O'Brien girl's uncle but it was as well to be sure.

'Excuse me, Mr Monaghan.'

'Yes?' Sharp black eyes had perused him. Took in his shaven head and English accent. This old fart probably didn't miss much.

'I just wanted to say hello. I believe I know your niece Tara. She said if I was ever in Belfast I should come in here for a cup of tea. Best bakery in town, she told me.'

The mention of Tara worked a charm. Monaghan's face wrinkled into a broad smile and the eyes softened.

'Tara's a grand girl, all right. So you're a friend of hers?'

'That's right. From Manchester. We knew each other at uni.'

'I see.'

Carl wasn't sure the old man did see. Maybe his student persona wasn't that convincing after all.

'So, how's she getting on now she's back home?' he said.

'Back where?'

'Here in Belfast. She left Manchester a couple of weeks ago.'

Monaghan cocked his head on one side, his face puzzled. 'Indeed. I'm surprised to hear it.'

The old bugger must be a good liar.

'The thing is, I was hoping to see her now I'm over. I was wondering if you might put me in touch.'

'Now, how could I do that, if I don't know where she is?'

'Aren't there friends she might stay with?'

The glint was back in the black eyes. Monaghan was suspicious now. 'I didn't catch your name.'

'Charlie.' He gave the old geezer his most disarming grin. 'And I'm sorry to come barging up like this.' He dropped the grin and his voice, stepped closer. 'Look, I'm worried about her. She's sold her car, left her flat and upped sticks. Not a word to any of her mates. I just hope she's not in trouble.'

The old man absorbed the information without reacting. 'She'll be fine. She's a smart girl.'

'You're sure she's not around? Is there anyone else who might know? Another relative maybe?'

'There are no other relatives here apart from me now her mother's gone. But if you'd like to leave a message I'll give it to her.'

'So you will be seeing her?' He'd said it too quickly. Monaghan's face froze and he simply produced a notepad from behind the counter and indicated that Carl should write down his details. Carl left a fictitious number – no point in writing anything incriminating – and said a polite goodbye as he left.

But if Des Monaghan thought he'd seen the last of him he was in for a nasty surprise.

'Here he comes,' muttered Sharkey from the back seat of the car. 'Told you so.'

It was less than a year since Rick had lived in Lambourn but it felt like ten. At his last yard here, the one he'd fled to after Kirsty's death, he'd been sharing a room in a hostel, surrounded by other lads. It hadn't been ideal for the lost soul he was at the time, though he'd never been short of drinking companions and friendly faces with whom he could waste time. And now, if he wanted, he could walk down the road to the pub and be guaranteed to find many of those same faces still there. The thought didn't appeal.

This time he was in digs that Christine had arranged for him, though after he'd moved in he found the idea had really come from Patsy. His landlady, Mrs Turner, must have mentioned Patsy's name a dozen times as she'd shown him round. Apart from his room – big enough to take a small sofa and an easy chair as well as a bed – she assured him he was always welcome to a place on the living-room sofa of an evening should he desire it. 'Though,' she added, 'if you can't stand kids' mess I shan't be offended if you barricade yourself in upstairs.' She and her husband, a haulier, had two boys, one not yet of school age, who followed Rick around with frank curiosity as his mother made sure he was comfortable. She said, 'Freddy wants to know if you like football. Patsy always used to have a kick around with him when he stayed here.' Which was, of course, an unavoidable invitation to take the lad out into the back yard with a ball. And why not?

So far the arrangement had worked out pretty well. Of an evening he kicked a football around in the dimly lit yard with the two lads before sharing the family supper and then made for his room. His new life at Latchmere, with early riding out and a handful of races under his belt already, didn't leave him much energy for anything else.

He was on the sofa, hunched over the form book with his mind on the next day's card at Haydock where both Treacle Toffee and Gingerbread were to have their maiden hurdle races, when a visitor appeared in his doorway.

'Rick, my man.' Patsy's broad-shouldered bulk made his room seem small. 'I've come to see how you're settling in.'

The Irishman sprawled in the easy chair and stretched his legs out in front of him, his booted heels coming to rest in the grate of the fireplace. 'I can see you've put your mark on the place already.'

In truth Rick had done nothing more than install his computer and place a few photos round the room, but he took it as a compliment. Patsy was the kind of fellow who could put any man at ease. Just as, Rick knew, he could as simply accomplish the opposite. Ever since Rick's ride on Rock Solid, the Irishman had singled him out for friendly interest.

'That's your father, isn't it?' Patsy pointed to a photo at the far end of the mantelpiece.

Rick was surprised. It was his favourite photo of his dad, sitting in his garden at home on the occasion of his sixtieth birthday. The camera had caught him in mid-laugh and the light in his eyes belied the lack of hair in his head – he looked boyish and happy. It had been taken just three months before his daughter's death.

'You've met my dad?'

'He came to the yard once.'

Rick remembered. Dad had gone to Latchmere to collect Kirsty's belongings shortly after Kirsty's funeral. That had been after he had travelled to the Caribbean to bring Kirsty's body back. Rick had stayed at home with his mother whose chronic arthritis prevented her making the journey. His job, the family had decided, was to lend support on the home front.

At the time he'd been relieved not to have to go with his father. He'd been in denial about Kirsty's death. She'd always been reckless. She threw herself into situations without fear – 'You only live once,' she'd say – and he could imagine how she'd managed to put herself in danger's way. He'd been with Kirsty on mountains, by the sea and, of course, on horses. She was always the one who strode closest to the edge, who was the last out of the water, who attempted the craziest jump when she rode with the hunt. He could imagine that she'd gone off dancing till the small hours, wearing her flashiest jewellery, smiling at the wrong men – taking one damn risk too many. So he'd let his dad go on his own and he'd stayed at home with his mum. She'd been glad enough of his company but he knew now that it had been a cowardly decision. He should have been by his father's side. He had left him on his own to undertake one of the most unpleasant duties that can fall to a man.

Rick had often thought about that when lying awake in the small hours on Hugh's farm. Had the situations been reversed, Kirsty would never have let their father go through it by himself. If he'd been the one to die, his sister would have borne as much of the burden as she possibly could.

His father had not returned the same man. And when he'd told Rick the facts, Rick had been choked with remorse. Kirsty had not been out dancing or flirting or flashing money around. She'd just been walking back from a beach bar to her holiday chalet, less than a quarter of a mile, at around seven in the evening. She'd suffered a heavy blow on the back of the head. The pathologist said she had a thin skull and death must have come instantly. Dad had said that was a consolation and Rick had agreed, though in reality it was no consolation at all. Beyond the wound, she'd not been assaulted or robbed. The murder weapon had not been found, though; from the nature of the wound, it was assumed to be one of the many volcanic stones that littered the headland on the seaward side of the cliff path.

The police had told his father lots of things, notably that another visitor must have committed the crime, as the locals would never dream of hurting a tourist. Rick could imagine the frustration his dad must have felt at discovering that island politics were undermining the murder inquiry. The investigation, such as it was, had led nowhere, but it had not been for want of effort on his father's part. And, through it all, Rick had remained in England.

Patsy was watching him closely. 'Your father's a fine man,' he said. 'I'm sorry we met the way we did.'

Rick shrugged. There was nothing to say to that.

'I hope,' Patsy continued, 'he doesn't think too badly of us all. Because of what happened in Amana.'

'Well, he won't think badly of you, you weren't even there. Anyway, my father's a fair man. He appreciates that every-one suffered a terrible ordeal.'

Patsy nodded. 'All the same, if I'd been him I'd have been after some bastard's head on a platter.'

'Dad's not like that. He wouldn't want some senseless revenge.'

'Like you, eh?' Patsy was grinning. 'You're a pretty laid-back customer.'

He supposed he was. Laid-back as in 'I don't mind', 'over to you' and 'you go first'.

'Except on a horse,' Patsy added. 'Are you coming for a drink with me then?'

How could he refuse?

As he followed the Irishman downstairs, the train of thought played out in his head and he realised he didn't feel the way he used to. The old Rick would not have returned to race-riding or shown up at the yard haunted by his sister's ghost – or stood up to the champion jockey in the changing room.

It was as if some of Kirsty's fearless spirit had been passed on to him. About time too – he was glad of it.

It was only nine o'clock but Christine said goodnight to Stephanie and left her in front of the television. She wondered if she should stay up longer to keep her daughter company; it seemed wrong somehow for a single girl in her early twenties to be on her own on a Friday night. But Stephanie was cheerful enough as she announced that she was going to watch a movie.

Though she was tired and tomorrow was a big day with runners at two meetings, Christine did not head straight for her bedroom but walked past her door down the corridor to Adrian's study. She went in without knocking. Adrian was sitting at his desk and music – some kind of jazz – reverberated loudly around the room.

He lifted a remote control and the music softened to a murmur. The room was tooled up with computers and high-definition screens and a sound system that probably cost as much as a half-decent yearling. Adrian's study was a boy's-toy dream. Christine had no interest and no objection – it was his money.

He looked surprised to see her – she didn't often venture into his haven. But there was something she wanted to discuss that she'd not been able to bring up over dinner in Stephanie's presence.

'Drink?' he said. He kept a cabinet in this room, well stocked with expensive liquor. In the early days of their marriage this had bothered her, having already lost one husband to the bottle. But she'd soon realised that Adrian was a different kind of drinker. One glass of vintage cognac could keep Adrian happy for the evening. A bucket of gut-rot had never been enough for poor Steve.

She rejected his offer. A glass of champagne with a happy owner after a good win was about her limit.

'So?' he said as the leather sofa opposite his desk squeaked under her weight. As ever, the noise irritated her but she ignored it.

'It's about Tara,' she said.

'I understand you've got her helping in the office now.'

She nodded. 'Jean's disappeared. She's probably at her mother's but I'm not sure I want her back.'

'And Tara is filling in?'

'She's a bit of a godsend, to be honest. She knows nothing about racing but you've only got to tell her something once. She's neat and well organised. Jean was good but Tara will be better.'

'She's not going to carry on, though, is she?'

Christine pondered. 'She seems willing enough but I can't get much out of her. I can well believe she's virtually a qualified solicitor but she tells me nothing about her work experience or why she left her last job or what she hopes to do next.'

'I thought she'd abandoned her career for Danny.'

Christine didn't know how to respond to that. She'd thought so too, that was the implication of Tara's sudden arrival and Danny's obvious passion. But there was no reciprocal passion that Christine could discern. She'd spent the best part of a week with Tara now, working for some part of every day with just the two of them in the tiny yard office, and the girl had not given the impression of a woman in love. She rarely offered a smile or an unsolicited comment and kept her responses to questions short and vague. Maybe Christine, quasi-employer, prospective mother-in-law, intimidated her. But Tara didn't seem the kind of young woman who was easily intimidated.

'I wondered,' Christine said, 'if there was any way you could check her out.'

Adrian's glance was sharp. 'You mean ask some questions?'

'I think we're entitled to know something about her.'

'I thought Stephanie had sussed her out.'

Christine grinned. 'Tara likes animals and has put a love-struck smile on Danny's face – that's good enough for Stephanie.'

'But not for you?

'Or you. You were the one who was complaining she'd appeared out of nowhere.'

He nodded, took a sip from his brandy glass. 'I know a discreet private detective.'

'No!' Christine was horrified. 'Danny would never forgive us if it came out. You do it – you're resourceful.'

And you did it with Kirsty, she thought to herself. Found out about her parents and schooling and jobs. That was all that was required.

'I suppose it's justified,' he said. 'Given that she's working here now.'

'And living with Danny. I don't want anything going wrong – not after, you know.'

He nodded. He did know. 'Leave it to me,' he said.

Des Monaghan lived in a cramped two-storey terrace in a suburb a few miles north of Belfast city centre. His freshly painted house, white with a navy blue door, stood out on the shabby street. Carl had wondered why the owner of a successful business hadn't done a bit better for himself but Sharkey said he had always lived there. 'Do you know him then?' Carl said and Sharkey just grunted, which Carl took to mean yes, stupid question. Everybody knew everyone here, Carl reckoned, and half of them wanted to kill the other lot. Talk about a primitive society. He couldn't wait to get back to civilisation.

Monaghan's front door opened almost directly on to the street and Carl was out of the car and at the old man's elbow just as he turned the key in the lock.

'Hello again, Mr Monaghan.'

The baker didn't look pleased to see him, his jaw jutted in irritation. 'What do you want?'

'Just a few minutes of your time.'

'You've had them already. I told you. I don't know where my niece is. Goodnight.' He stepped through the open door and turned to shut it. Carl blocked it with his body.

'Get out. You're not coming in my house.'

Carl was about to shove the old fool down the hall when Sharkey's voice sounded from behind him.

'We're coming in. Don't try and stop us.'

Monaghan froze, the defiance gone from his face. He said nothing and, with weary resignation, turned his back on them and trudged down the dark hallway. Carl followed him. Behind him the door closed. A light came on in a room at the end of the short corridor. He found the old man standing in the kitchen, facing them across a table laid with a blue and white cloth. He held himself stiffly, his hands behind his back.

Carl relaxed. This was better. He hated having to pretend.

'Sit down, Mr Monaghan.'

'I'd rather stand.'

'Now then,' Sharkey was in the room too, 'don't be difficult.'

'You're scum. You're both scum. Whatever you want, I can't help you.'

The old guy had balls, Carl gave him credit for that. 'Take a look around,' he said to Sharkey. 'See if she's here. Or if there's anything that looks like it could be her stuff.'

Sharkey grunted in his usual fashion and left the room. A moment later Carl heard the other man's heavy tread on the creaking stairs.

'I knew you were no friend of Tara's when I saw you in the shop,' said Monaghan. 'She's got more taste.'

'No need to be rude, Mr Monaghan. Your Tara's in a bit of trouble. If I can find her I can help her. Smooth over her problems with a friend of mine.'

The old man said nothing but Carl could tell he wasn't

convinced. Well, there were ways of convincing him and the sooner he began the sooner he could clear out of this dump. He moved round the table to get right in his face.

Monaghan stood his ground, which was a bit daft of him in the circumstances. Carl loomed over him.

He heard Sharkey coming downstairs. 'Any luck?' he called over his shoulder.

But he didn't hear the answer because something slammed into the side of his head like a brick. He staggered and fell against the table. Smack, he took another blow in the face. Blood fountained over the tablecloth. His blood.

Patsy took Rick to a pub that wasn't frequented by lads from the yards. Rick didn't mind. He guessed it was done deliberately.

Rick ordered a sugarless, flavourless – pointless – soft drink. With the two races at Haydock tomorrow – rides he was looking forward to with more intensity than he'd ever mustered before – he was determined to take no chances. Patsy knew he was watching his weight and his head and made no comment beyond a nod of approval.

'So, how are you coping so far?' he said.

'Pretty good. I'm enjoying racing again.'

'I didn't mean that. I was referring to you coming back after what happened to your sister. In your shoes, not many would have done that.'

Rick was taken off guard. Apart from Christine, no one had mentioned Kirsty at all since his return. But Patsy wasn't known for pulling his punches.

'I've come back for the horses,' he said. 'To see if I can make a proper living at it. Kirsty wouldn't have wanted me to give up on her account.'

Patsy raised an eyebrow. 'There's plenty of other places you could have gone.'

'Not as good as here. Christine's promised me some proper rides ahead of Cheltenham.'

Patsy ignored the remark. 'And it doesn't get up your nose that young Tara's now shacked up with your mate Danny? Just moved right into Kirsty's house. A straight replacement.' Patsy was grinning, being deliberately provocative. Rick was determined not to take the bait.

'I thought you liked Tara,' he said.

'Oh, I do. She's smart, sexy and Irish. What's not to like? Except maybe from your point of view.'

Rick put down his glass. 'Are you deliberately trying to stir things up?' he asked.

'Sure. It makes life more interesting.'

Rick laughed.

'You think that's funny?' Patsy said.

'I think,' and it struck Rick forcibly, 'that's exactly what Kirsty would have said.'

'Right enough.' Patsy raised his glass. 'Here's to your sister. God bless her.'

Rick joined in the toast, though he was surprised by the other man's action. 'What went on between you two?'

'How do you mean?'

'You weren't top of her Christmas card list, were you? I hope you didn't make a pass at her.'

Patsy shook his head, his mane of blond hair rippling across his shoulders. 'What, try and put the moves on the boss's daughter-in-law to-be? I don't know what kind of fool you take me for.'

It was not a conversation Rick could ever have envisaged having with the big man but he was having it all the same, and he found himself not afraid to push it further.

'I'm just thinking of your reputation with the girls, Patsy. There's this Jean business at the moment, isn't there?' Jean the yard secretary, who'd walked out last week and was rumoured not to be returning after things had turned sour with the Irishman. 'You can't blame me for joining the dots.'

Patsy shook his head. 'Me and your sister are the wrong dots. We had an argument over a horse, if you want to know. She objected to me giving some useless lump a whack when he needed it.' He drained his pint. 'You're a horseman. You understand.'

Rick understood that Kirsty would have objected to what she saw as mistreatment of an animal. And he understood that a man like Patsy might belong to the cruel-to-be-kind school of horse management.

'Another?' Patsy said. 'And we can move on to *your* love life.'

'That'll be a short conversation.'

'I thought it might be. So while I'm getting them in you can chew on the fact that there's a young woman at Latchmere who'd go a long way to keep you happy.'

'Sorry, Patsy, I'm not taking the bait.'

'More fool you then.' And he disappeared to the bar.

Rick shook his head. He had no interest in playing Patsy's games. No interest at all.

For a second Carl lost touch with the world. There were no more blows, just the sound of scuffling on the lino floor and the rattle of a key in the lock. Then Sharkey's voice.

'Stop there, Des, or I'll put one in you. You know I will.'

The rattling stopped. Carl could hear heavy breathing – his own. He blinked across the room. Monaghan was at the back door, his hand on the key in the lock. In his other hand he held what looked like a large wooden mallet. The old bastard had hit him with one of those things cooks use to tenderise meat. He must have grabbed it when he came in the room and hidden it behind his back.

Sharkey was at his side, holding a pistol in his hand. He

was pointing the weapon at Monaghan but his eyes were on Carl. 'You all right?' he asked. Was that a hint of a smile on his doughy face?

'Yeah, sure.' Carl straightened up.

With his free hand Sharkey lifted a tea towel off the back of a chair and held it out. Carl grabbed it and pressed it to the side of his face. It came away wet and red. Jesus Christ, the crafty old geezer. His instinct was to take that mallet and smash Monaghan's head open like a coconut.

But Benny paid him to think as well as thump. And he had a job to do.

'Where's Tara?' he said to the old man.

'I told you, I have no idea.'

'She's left Manchester to come back to her family in Belfast. That means you. I want a name, a number. An address where she hangs out. Or it's going to be a very long and painful night. Do you understand?'

The old man stared past him at Sharkey. 'Tell him he's wasting his time. I don't care what he does to me.'

Sharkey looked quizzically at Carl. He was probably enjoying the pig's ear Carl was making of this.

They tied Monaghan to a kitchen chair with electric flex they found in a kitchen drawer. In the same drawer, Carl found some household tools. He selected a pair of pliers and a hammer and placed them on the table directly in front of the old man. Let him think about the mischief that could be done with them.

'You've got ten minutes,' he said to the baker. 'I'm going to have a thorough look around this place, see if I can come up with anything that points me towards your girl. If I don't find anything then I'm going to use those.' He nodded towards the table. 'I tell you, you won't be making too many fairy cakes by the time I've finished with your fingers.'

The old man said nothing, just stared at him with undisguised venom. Really, the old bastard should have more sense. All he was doing was pissing Carl off.

There was eff-all to help him around the house. Sharkey hadn't found any signs of the girl and neither did Carl. The best he could come up with was a red book by the phone full of numbers, some of them obviously going back years. Tara was listed under O'Brien, a succession of places in Manchester with lines through them. The last address and number was one he was familiar with, her most recent, but that was no good.

He took the book with him back into the kitchen. There was another O'Brien.

'Who's this Kathleen?' he asked.

Monaghan glared at him.

'Who is she?'

'My sister.'

Aha. 'Tara's mother?'

'Yes.'

'See? That wasn't so hard.' He turned to Sharkey. 'We'd better get round there sharpish.'

Monaghan laughed, a bitter cough of a noise. 'She's got a more recent address. St Patrick's cemetery.'

Of course, he'd been told the girl's uncle was her last relative in Belfast. He had a stinking headache – no wonder he couldn't think straight.

'Pull his fingernails out,' he said to Sharkey. 'I want to see this stupid old fart weep.'

Sharkey was unmoved. 'Do your own dirty work,' he said.

Monaghan laughed again. This time the sound was full of contempt.

It had gone on long enough. Carl took the gun from his pocket and pointed it at the old man. 'I'm warning you,' he said.

'Call yourself a human being?' said Monaghan. 'You're a disgrace.'

Just my luck to come across such a stubborn old fool, Carl thought. Doesn't he care? He aimed at Monaghan's left knee.

The pistol shot in the room was deafening. The old man's body convulsed and the chair toppled over, a puddle of blood pooling on the lino of the kitchen floor.

Carl bent over him and looked into those currant-black eyes. 'Right, Mr Monaghan, are you ready to answer a few questions now?'

The eyes stared right back at him. The old man's lips did not move. Not even to take a breath.

Carl stared at the figure on the ground in disbelief.

For the first time in their short acquaintance, Sharkey looked uncertain. 'You've killed him.'

There was nothing for it but to clear off. Carl pulled the stained tablecloth off the table and bundled it under his arm. He took the tea towel too. He couldn't guarantee there weren't other traces of his presence in the house but all he wanted to do was to get out.

God knows what Benny would say about this. There had to be some way of putting it so it didn't appear like a complete fiasco. But coming up with something would probably be a bigger headache than the one he already had.

As they drove away, Smurf stared at him curiously.

'Just keep your eyes on the road, will you?' Carl snapped.

'Yes, sir,' the fat man murmured.

From the back seat Carl was convinced he heard a soft chuckle. The bloody Micks were all in it together.

Chapter Seven

Adrian waited till everyone had left for Haydock before he set off to find Tara. Christine had told him the girl had declined to go racing this weekend, despite Danny's cajoling. Her decision might have put his stepson's nose out of joint but it suited Adrian well enough. It was time for a heart to heart.

Last night's conversation with his wife was fresh in his mind. She was right to shine a searchlight on this new-comer, especially since Tara seemed to have made herself at home in the office. The girl might be shacked up with his stepson and living on his land, but did he want her on his payroll too? Because that was the logical next step.

Privately Adrian blamed Patsy for creating the secretarial vacancy. Jean hadn't been all that long out of sixth-form college, this had been her first job, and she'd hardly been equipped to maintain the Irishman's interest once he'd bedded her a few times. He had half a mind to have a quiet word with Patsy, tell him to keep it zipped around Latchmere. Except that trespassing on a man's fancies was a delicate affair. Adrian had made a fool of himself over Kirsty and Patsy had not said a word. He and Patsy knew too much about each other's business to fall out.

There was no sign of Tara in the yard. The office looked more organised than it usually did. Christine's desk was clear of paper and there was an ordered mosaic of blue Post-It notes arranged across the computer screen – phone messages, Adrian could see at a glance. There were no tea-stained mugs in the sink, the waste-paper basket was empty and even the ailing cyclamen on the window sill appeared to have been given a drink. If competence was the criterion, it looked like Tara was a shoo-in for Jean's job.

Adrian turned out of the yard on to the footpath which led through the woods to Danny's cottage. It had been a while since he'd taken this direction. Once it had been a fixture in his running route, back when the cottage was being done up. He used to check on the builders' progress before resuming his constitutional. Later, when the workmen had left and Kirsty was sorting the place to her satisfaction, his run would finish at the cottage itself. He still thought of it as Kirsty's place. Part of him hoped he wouldn't find Tara at home. It would be easier, probably, to talk to her in the office or up at the farmhouse. The cottage, he thought as he crossed the lane and turned through the garden gate, has too many memories.

He rang the bell and waited, tempted to turn and leave. But from within he could hear the faint drone of a voice, then a burst of music – a radio jingle. He rang again.

Keys turned in the lock, a bolt slid back and then the door opened.

She didn't look surprised to see him because, he guessed, she'd already checked out her visitor through the door spy-hole. That was a new feature, as was the bolt. He said as much.

'I asked Danny to put them in,' she said as she walked ahead of him down the hall. 'City-girl paranoia, I suppose.'

He hadn't stood in the kitchen for well over a year. For a year and five months to be exact, two days before the whole family had flown to the West Indies for a long-awaited – and ill-fated – holiday.

Kirsty had handed him a can of Coke from the fridge. 'And that's all you're getting, you old perv,' she'd said.

He could taste the sweet metallic liquid on his tongue now as Tara turned to him. 'How about some tea? Or would you like something stronger?'

'Tea would be fine, thanks.'

She put the kettle on, turned the radio off, took a carton of milk from the fridge. As she busied herself she praised the cottage, this room in particular with its top-of-the-range fancy equipment that Kirsty had made him put in, for all that she was strictly a microwave cook.

They embarked on awkward small talk, a mere repetition of the one conversation they'd already had.

She put the tea things on the big table in the centre of the room. It was strange to sit at this table once more – it featured often in his memories of Kirsty. Fashioned out of thick French oak, almost a metre in width, it had had to be delivered through the garden window as it couldn't be manoeuvred down the hall from the front door. Kirsty had summoned him to supervise its arrival because Danny was at Newbury that afternoon. It had been boiling and the delivery men had been in a sweat. Kirsty wore a candy-striped top, denim skirt, flip-flops and absolutely nothing else – or so she'd said.

She'd hoiked herself up to perch on the table – the new chairs were arriving separately – and the rough blue cloth had ridden up her lean suntanned thighs. She'd caught him looking, but that, of course, was the point. 'It's too hot,' she'd said. 'Too hot to wear knickers anyway.'

He'd said nothing. Dizzy with want and frustration.

Now he sat at the same table and stared at the grain of its polished surface.

Get a grip.

'Christine says you're a great help in the office.'

'Thanks. I'm enjoying it.'

'If Jean doesn't come back, how would you feel about taking over for a bit?'

She looked surprised though he couldn't believe the thought hadn't occurred to her.

'I mean, if you just want a break from the law. It might give you the chance to decide what you really want to do.'

'That's kind of you.'

'What was the name of the firm you worked for in Manchester?'

If her earlier look of surprise had been feigned, this sharp glance of suspicion was the real thing.

'It's just a small criminal practice, you wouldn't have heard of it.'

'We might need to get in touch.'

She looked aghast. 'You mean you're going to ask them for a reference?'

'That wasn't what I was thinking. We keep a file on all staff so it ought to be on record.'

'To be honest, Adrian, I'd rather you didn't contact them. It got a bit ugly when I quit. Anyhow, Jean could be back on Monday.'

'I doubt it.' He'd lay a fair amount of money that Patsy had scared her off for good. 'Have you got your P45?'

'Can't we,' she said, 'keep this arrangement informal? Call it work experience or something. I don't want to be paid.'

He studied her closely. Her small pointed chin was set firmly and those wide, mismatched eyes stared directly into his. In all his years of dealing with employees, he'd never met one who didn't wish to be rewarded for their labour. But Tara, it was plain, was in earnest.

He wondered why.

Tara was a mystery. Had she not given up her legal career – six months from qualification, he'd been told – to throw in her lot with his stepson? Thrown it all over for love. Yet in their conversations she'd hardly mentioned Danny. In Adrian's experience, smitten young women could never open their mouths without their lover's name tumbling out.

It seemed she preferred to spend Saturday hiding away behind lock and key rather than go racing with her partner. She was touchy about her previous employer – she wouldn't even tell him the name of the firm – and was volunteering for work well below her capability, for which she refused to be paid. He couldn't work her out.

'You're nothing like Kirsty,' he said.

'I know. Chalk and cheese. That's what we always said.'

'You shared a flat with her?'

'When we were students and after she started working. Then I got a separate place round the corner.'

'Why was that?' He was curious.

'We both needed a bit more space. I couldn't keep up with her social life, to be honest.'

'I can imagine,' he said. A little knot of jealousy twisted in his stomach. How inappropriate to be jealous of the dead. But no woman had ever had an effect on him like Kirsty had.

He was aware of being under scrutiny.

'You were very fond of Kirsty, weren't you?' she said.

'Yes,' he said simply. More than fond.

She suddenly pushed away her cup and leaned forward across the table to take his hand. 'I want to be straight with you, Adrian. Kirsty told me how you felt about her.'

'Told you what exactly?'

'That you had a special relationship. A bit more than father and daughter.'

So she knew about his obsession. But why was she bringing it into the open?

Her hand on his was small but her grip was firm. 'She told

me in strictest confidence and I've always respected that. And I've every intention of keeping that confidence.'

She was expressing herself carefully. He reminded himself that this was a woman who had been legally trained.

'I'd like to ask you something in return,' she said.

'Go on then.'

'It's very simple. Please don't quiz me about my former employer in Manchester or try to track down where I worked. I don't want them to know where I am.'

'Why not?'

'I can't tell you. Not now anyway. If things work out for me here then I promise I'll tell you everything.'

Her gaze was intense. She wanted an answer.

'OK,' he said. 'No more questions about your mysterious past. You have my word.'

'And this conversation is just between us?' Her fingers on his were still insistent.

'I promise.'

'Thank you, Adrian.' She withdrew her hand.

After he'd gone, Tara re-bolted the door and returned to the kitchen. She turned the radio back on as she cleared away their tea cups.

Had she done the right thing? She'd never intended to reveal to Adrian that Kirsty had spoken of their intimacy. But she'd been in a panic. Suppose he'd called Gallagher Ferguson? He could try to get the name out of Danny as he knew where she used to work. She'd done all she could to persuade Danny not to mention it but there was a limit to how much pressure she could bring to bear. 'I don't want anything more to do with them,' she'd said. 'If Tom knows where I am he'll start hassling me.' But she'd drawn the line at telling Danny the truth. If he knew that he would begin to doubt her reasons for being in his bed at night. And if Adrian asked for information, saying it was essential for employment purposes, might Danny not tell him?

Well, what was done was done. She'd driven a bargain with Adrian, though he might not think the better of her for it once he had time to reflect on what it amounted to. Don't ask about my past and I won't tell anyone – Danny, for example – that you were desperate to get his fiancée into bed.

The news bulletin interrupted her thoughts. Old loyalties died hard – the word 'Belfast' always captured her attention.

'The murder in Belfast of a local businessman has raised fears that sectarian violence has returned to the city. Desmond Monaghan, the owner of a successful bakery and tea shop in the city centre, was found dead in his home this morning. Police say it is likely his death was caused by a heart attack brought on by shock after suffering a gunshot wound to his leg.

'Mr Monaghan was a popular figure in the community who built his bakery into a city institution despite the upheavals of the Troubles. Monaghan's was still open for business today and the manager, Andrew Collins, spoke to our reporter.

' "This is an atrocity. I've worked for Des Monaghan for thirty years, throughout all the terrible times in this city, and he swore no gunman would ever close his shop. That's why we're open today. Des Monaghan was a great man, who never preached politics or took sides or did anyone any harm. Whoever did this should be ashamed to their soul. I hope they rot in hell." '

The bulletin moved on to other news, then sports headlines and music. Tara heard not a word nor a note as she stood by the sink.

Uncle Des. Her mother's beloved brother who'd been as

139

good as a father to her after her dad died. He was a star in her firmament, always there in his bakery, where she'd often helped out in holidays. She could hear his voice. 'I ought to pay you in doughnuts,' he'd say, 'you're such a skinny lass.'

And now he was dead.

Surely not because of her?

As he travelled up to Haydock in Danny's car, Rick couldn't help musing on his conversation with Patsy the night before. On his return from the bar, the Irishman had switched the topic from women to horses, a subject with which Rick was much more comfortable. He'd rather talk about anything but his non-existent love life. All the same he couldn't help wondering which girl at the yard was supposed to fancy him. There was Lucy, the stable lass who looked after Rock Solid and who'd led him up at Wincanton, but she was by all accounts deeply smitten with the assistant trainer. And he was too young for Sara, the head girl, who was on her second husband.

He'd like a woman in his life, of course he would. But right now he wanted winners more. And friends. One reason he was looking forward to the Haydock meeting was that Hugh and his family would be there. He'd missed the easy-going warmth of life in their farmhouse, where he could say honestly how he felt and there weren't any awkward silences.

Silences such as the one that now reigned in Danny's car. The other passenger was Stephanie, who had torn herself away from the stud for the afternoon to lend her support and clearly felt that fact should be more vocally appreciated by her brother. Danny, on the other hand, made it plain that the support he wanted came from another quarter – and Tara had opted not to offer it.

Personally, Rick was pleased Tara wasn't making up the fourth spot in the car. He didn't know where he stood with her and it was as much his fault as hers. They'd first met nearly five years ago, when he'd spent a weekend in Manchester with Kirsty. It had been in the spring of her first year at uni – her only year as it turned out. He was sixteen, and about to leave school for a life in racing, a decision that did not have the backing of his parents. After six months of argument, in which he'd made little effort to apply himself to his school subjects and every effort to put in time at the local stables, his mum and dad had almost given up hope. In one last attempt to get him to see the sense of staying on at school they'd suggested a visit to his sister at university.

The idea had been totally counter-productive. Almost the first thing Kirsty told him when he arrived was that she had no hope of passing her exams and would be packing in the student life at the end of term. Rick had found that hilarious and they'd sworn a united front against their parents. Then Kirsty had set about showing him a good time, whisking him from bar to club to party and introducing him to a whirl of people, all of whom, so Rick thought, considered talking to Kirsty's bumpkin little brother a major social chore. And somewhere in the blur of his only Saturday night in Manchester, Kirsty disappeared to shag her man of the moment and others were left holding the baby – namely, him.

He'd got horribly drunk, misinterpreted the concern of a fantastic-looking girl and tried to romance her – and then vomited over the pair of them. It had been the most embarrassing night of his life up to that point. In fact, it still was. And the fantastic girl, of course, had been Tara. He remembered the occasion vividly, as he was sure she did too.

'I give up, Danny.' Stephanie had been quizzing her

brother about his upcoming ride in the afternoon's best race, the three-mile chase, in which he was partnering Superstition, one of Christine's Gold Cup contenders. But Danny had not been forthcoming. 'If all you can tell me is that he's a nice ride,' Stephanie continued, 'I'm not going to waste my money on you. I'd much rather back Rick's horses.'

'I'm not sure that's wise.' Rick knew Stephanie had a bit of a reckless streak. He'd been with her at a racecourse years ago, when she'd confessed to Adrian that she'd put fifty pounds to win on the biggest outsiders in every race on the card. She'd lost over three hundred pounds and her stepfather had been appalled. 'But think how much I'd have won if just one of them had come in,' she'd protested.

'Ginger and Treacle have never raced over hurdles before,' Rick continued. 'Anything could happen.'

'Precisely. They could win. And I know you'll get the very best out of them because you're such a brilliant rider. Much better than Danny.'

Rick glanced across at her brother. She was trying to get a rise out of him, which as a rule she could easily accomplish. But on this occasion Danny did not appear to be rattled. He simply rolled his eyes and kept his mouth shut.

Rick couldn't let it pass. 'That's bollocks, Steph. You don't mean it.'

'It's good of you to stick up for him, Rick. I hope he appreciates what a loyal friend you are.'

Rick sighed. He liked Stephanie well enough but she was hard to predict. 'Don't put me in the middle of some brother/sister thing, please.'

He turned to look at her in the back seat, expecting to see a familiar scowl. She could be fierce.

'Sorry, Rick.' She was smiling. 'But it's not just me. Patsy also thinks you're a brilliant rider. He told me so.' And her

smile turned from one of smug satisfaction to . . .
something else.

In an instant Rick put two and two together. Over at the
stud, Patsy and Stephanie saw a lot of one another, and
obviously they'd been discussing him.

There had been a night, just before the Caribbean trip,
when he had taken Stephanie to a party at another yard.
They'd gone together as the only representatives from
Latchmere Park and Rick had seen no significance in that.
In fact, he'd had his eye on a red-headed stable lass but she'd
been whisked away by a jockey from Tim Appleby's after
Rick had spent the best part of an hour trying to make an
impression. Stephanie had found him in the paddock
behind the barn where the revellers were getting drunk. He
was pretty tipsy himself by that stage and Stephanie, who'd
made an effort for once to glam herself up, had looked
alluring in the moonlight. They'd only kissed and it had
been pleasant enough at the time but, in the light of day,
plainly a mistake.

However, he now knew which girl Patsy had been
referring to last night.

Danny dumped his stuff in the changing room and then
returned to the car to make his phone call. He needed
privacy to talk to Tara.

There was no reply on the cottage phone. He rang off and
tried again a few minutes later. Still no reply.

He rang her mobile. She might be out, up the hill where
there was reception. She'd taken to walking since her
arrival and that pleased him, although so far she'd refused
to get on a horse. He was determined to get her to ride out
with him. The way he saw it, it made sense for a girl who'd
been cooped up in the city to get some fresh air into her
lungs. It was one of the arguments he'd used, he remem-

bered, when he was persuading her to come and live with him. Not that she'd needed much persuading. None at all, now he thought about it.

So why had she agreed to live with him?

He'd been in a dream when he'd whisked her out of Manchester and installed her in his cottage. After suffering a blow to his spirit which he'd felt would blight his life for ever – losing Kirsty – to suddenly find himself in the middle of a new romance had seemed a miracle. Like emerging from a dark, cold tunnel into summer sunshine. It had been a complete transformation of his miserable world, made legitimate by the months of grieving that he'd shared with Tara. To be with Kirsty's best friend felt right. He couldn't have scripted it better.

But the euphoria of bringing Tara home was thinning like morning mist. He could see now that, though close at hand, his new love was remote from him. And the camaraderie of their old bond had gone. He'd swapped a close friend for a distant lover and he wasn't sure that was such a good bargain. It certainly wasn't in the script.

The pity of it was that he had so much to give her. He frequently held back from laying himself at her feet. He'd bitten off the L word more times than he could count, almost for fear of trespassing on her true feelings. In some circumstances, to tell a woman you love her is like holding a gun to her head. Well, he wasn't going to force Tara to tell him she loved him back. She'd tell him of her own free will or not at all.

All the same, there were times when he couldn't help forcing the issue. He found himself proposing plans for the future. Even just a small commitment would feel like a victory. Yesterday he'd suggested a week away in Spain after Cheltenham. She'd put him off gently. 'Can't we wait? Do you mind?' Of course he minded but he couldn't say so. The fact was that he couldn't get Tara to join him at the races, let alone leave the country with him for a week.

He gave up on the phone calls. She was out of reach. Just for a change, he thought, giving in to a sudden bitterness.

And yet, she came to bed with him every night. They were as intimate as a man and woman could be and yet, somehow, they weren't close at all.

Three nights ago, lying there in the dark, he'd said to her, 'Are you sure you want to be here?'

'Absolutely.'

'Only, you seem a bit low. If it's not working out for you, you've got to say. I can take you back to Manchester if you want.'

'No.' To his surprise, she'd hugged him fiercely. 'I'm sorry if I'm not what you expected. Are you saying you'd like me to go?'

'Don't be stupid.' He'd kissed her and she'd responded, clinging to him with that same fierceness, which had thrilled him. He'd thought that those moments in the dark marked a turning point but, in the morning, she'd announced she wasn't coming to Haydock and the wall between them was once more in place.

He wasn't experienced with women. There'd been casual girlfriends and some embarrassing one-night stands. And then Kirsty, who'd revolutionised his sensual life. In bed, she'd been earthy and direct, she took as much as she gave and she told him exactly how she felt. So Danny always knew where he stood with her. With Tara, he didn't have a clue. He had a feeling she operated on a different level, somewhere deep and mysterious, out of his reach.

Or else there was a more prosaic explanation. He turned it over in his head as he walked back to the weighing room. It had been eating at him ever since he'd caught her out making those phone calls to 'a friend'.

Tara had told him she wanted Tom Ferguson out of her life for good. But maybe she'd changed her mind.

There were so many entries for the opening juvenile novices hurdle race on the Haydock card that it was split into two divisions. Rick was pleased for Hugh because it meant that Treacle Toffee and Gingerbread did not have to compete against each other. Treacle was in the first division which, according to Christine, was the weaker of the two contests. Hugh agreed.

'I've had my head in the form book,' he announced as they stood in the centre of the parade ring. 'I reckon we've got a real chance with him.' His red cheeks shone like little apples as he surveyed the group.

Rick wondered what had happened to the man who'd mucked out by his side in the mornings and cursed the rain that fell, daily it seemed, on his yard. Hugh the small-time trainer was a gritty realist. But Hugh the racehorse owner, with his two adoring daughters on his arm, was already drinking at the fountain of optimism. To listen to him the race was already in the bag.

Christine was looking on with amused tolerance but no doubt she thought it wasn't politic to pour cold water on the dreams of her new owner. She'd seen the sticky clay soil of Haydock Park do that enough times; it didn't need her cupful as well.

It was left to Gwen to speak up. 'For God's sake, don't be putting the pressure on Rick. That horse has never gone two miles before, let alone over hurdles. We'll be doing well to see him finish at all.'

'Oh Mum!' protested her eldest daughter, unhappy to have the bubble burst.

'Well, it's true. So let's not get carried away, eh, Christine?'

The trainer nodded, a twinkle in her eye.

Hugh shrugged and appealed to Rick. 'They're ganging up on me. You've got to help me out, mate.'

Rick was relieved to be legged up and away out on the course. He was determined to do his best but, in the race itself, events conspired to make that best not quite good enough.

For all Hugh's talk of poor form, the competition was stiff, as Rick had anticipated. Haydock is a top track, attracting the best horses and the most ambitious trainers. It doesn't host any soft contests.

It was ironic, Rick thought, that with a name like Treacle Toffee, the horse hated the sticky going from the moment they set off. In years gone by you could tell just by cantering to the start if a horse liked the ground or not, but nowadays the all-weather track on the inside took you to the starting point and you had to wait until the tapes went up before knowing your fate. Treacle Toffee just couldn't handle it. He struggled for the entire two miles and was beaten over twenty lengths by the winner.

The only good thing Rick was able to tell Hugh was that the horse had jumped like an old hand. Even so, he knew his friend was disappointed with the result.

Tara ignored the phone, let it ring and ring and was relieved when it stopped. Only for it to start up again a few minutes later.

Had they tracked her down? If they'd found Uncle Des, they could find her too. Or had Des told them – after they'd shot him?

That was impossible. He didn't know where she was.

It was the shock. She wasn't thinking straight.

As the phone stopped, she realised it must be Danny calling. He'd arrived at the racecourse and was ringing to see if she was all right. Danny her protector – though he didn't know it. He was a sweet, sweet man and she wasn't treating him as he deserved.

There was just so much to think about and poor Danny was not at the top of her list.

She took a deep breath. Put the kettle on for more tea then said out loud, 'Sod it.' She had a brandy instead. She'd wash the glass before Danny came back or else he'd worry. After that conversation the other night she'd half expected a suggestion she make an appointment with the local GP to check if she was depressed.

After all, she had good reason to be.

Calmer now, she tried to think about her uncle's death – God rest his soul. There might be peace in Northern Ireland these days but there were still punishment shootings, murders and all sorts of crime, like a bloody big hangover from the Troubles. Des's death might be nothing to do with her at all.

Except that, what on earth would a 69-year-old baker have to do with paramilitaries or criminals of any sort? He'd survived through the bad times by being an honest tradesman, espousing no causes, making no enemies. Both sides of the community patronised Des's bakery and respected him. It was hard to see why he would fall foul of the gunmen now.

She supposed it was possible he could have become the victim of a burglar or some other local criminal. She didn't know enough about the circumstances of his death, though she could try to find out.

Outside, it was wet and windy. She'd not come to the country prepared for weather like this but Danny had told her to use his Barbour which hung in the hall. It was a bit big for her but it did the job. She pulled on her old trainers – they'd get mucky but who cared? – and slipped her mobile into her pocket.

She didn't like disturbing Duncan on a Saturday afternoon but this was an emergency. She didn't know what else to do.

To Rick's surprise, Stephanie came into the paddock for Gingerbread's race.

'I'm here to bring you luck,' she said. 'Our horses always run well when I'm here, don't they, Mum?' Stephanie flashed Rick a triumphant grin.

Rick tried to ignore the interchange. He wasn't averse to benefiting from whatever luck might be going but he'd prefer to concentrate on the contest ahead. Christine's instructions were straightforward. 'Do the same as on Treacle Toffee, only finish twenty lengths closer.' She added, 'But you know him better than me. Do what you feel is right.'

That was good to hear. In his early days as a rider Rick had sometimes felt weighed down with advice – hold him up here, don't hit the front too early, give him a reminder two fences out. Too many instructions could drag a young rider down as much as an extra couple of pounds in the saddle cloth. The more experienced jockeys, of course, took the essential information and let the rest go over their heads. He liked to think he would soon reach that stage.

Rain had been falling since they'd arrived, lightly at first but now with more intent. Officially the going was soft but it was now almost heavy. Would Gingerbread mind the conditions? He'd know soon enough. Unlike some animals, though, Gingerbread was a trier. And he'd need to be if he was going to win today.

As the starter let them go, three runners set off at a gallop that Rick knew would be impossible to maintain and Ginger would have followed but Rick didn't think that was such a great idea. The horse might be game but there was no point in letting him run himself into the ground.

Ginger took no notice of the first hurdle and crashed straight through it. All he was interested in was galloping. He wasn't much better at the second flight either but at the third the penny dropped and he was looking for the obstacle from some way out. Now that he was concentrating, Rick knew that his jumping would improve. Gingerbread pricked his ears, lengthened his stride and powered over it just as he'd done when schooling. As they rounded the bend for home, when he might have been forgiven for beginning to tire, Ginger slogged on. The wind lashed rain into their faces. Conditions were at their wildest. It was just like that day with Hugh in the shadow of the Cambrian Mountains. Ginger hadn't minded that either.

The leading group were coming back to them fast and it occurred to Rick that a finish in the top three might just be on, provided Ginger didn't falter. But there was no sign of that. One-paced he may be and without much finesse, but Ginger had found something he was good at, like an also-ran 1500-metre athlete suddenly discovering he was a world-class cross-country runner.

He scrambled over the third last and dug in, passing the horse in fourth place who was treading water. The next two horses were just ahead, neck and neck it seemed, locked in what looked like a private duel.

Rick steered Gingerbread to the right of them, on the stand side, and gave him a slap on the shoulder. The horse didn't respond in any noticeable way, just continued to grind on relentlessly, cleaving a passage through the wet air and over the soggy turf.

Ginger crashed through the top of the next hurdle but it didn't slow him down. He was past his two nearest rivals now and had the leader in his sights, some half a dozen lengths ahead. Rick could see the jockey working hard in the saddle as he drove the animal into the final jump. To his credit the horse put in an enormous leap but stumbled on landing, losing momentum.

Then Ginger was clearing the last with his best jump of the race. They were only two lengths down and there was plenty of time to make that up on the long run-in.

Rick didn't use his whip – what was the point? Ginger had no change of gear. But he worked hard with his body, crouching low over the horse's shoulders, trying to make himself as much a part of the animal as possible.

If he were honest, Rick would have expected the other horse to have gone away from him – he was reckoned to be the better animal, one Hugh had singled out as being a particular threat – but Ginger was running him down remorselessly, barrelling past the favourite twenty-five yards from the line.

The way Gingerbread finished, Rick reckoned they could have gone round again.

There was someone different handling the police station calls this time and Tara was put straight through to Duncan's extension without comment. The phone was picked up after two rings but it wasn't Duncan. There would be no reassuring Scots burr to soothe her fears today.

'He won't be in till Monday. Is this an urgent matter? Can I help you?'

He sounded nice. A southerner's voice, confident and capable. But the temptation to unburden herself was momentary.

'No, that's all right.'

'Let me take a message for him then. What's your name, please?'

'I'll call on Monday, thanks.' She killed the connection.

She had another number for Duncan, a mobile. She tried it but there was no reply.

Damn. What was she going to do?

Nothing. There was nothing she could do, except keep her head down and play the part of Danny's girlfriend. Was that so difficult?

Actually, it was. Pretending to be head over heels in love with someone when she didn't feel that way was hard, especially when that person was by her side so much of the time, scrutinising her every word and facial expression. She knew what Danny wanted – the kind of spontaneous passion that Kirsty had been able to dole out to her lovers. Tara wasn't like that. She'd never been much of an actress, especially when it came to affairs of the heart. Once, she'd chucked a boyfriend the day before he was due to take her down to London for the weekend. Kirsty had disapproved. 'Are you mad? Always dump a guy *after* you've been away on a jolly, not before.' But Tara couldn't do that.

All the same, she had to try harder with Danny. There was no need to make him unhappy just because she was. The next time he asked her to the races with him she'd say yes. He'd been disappointed about Haydock but, once she'd looked at the map, its proximity to Manchester had put her off. There was no telling how far Tom's connections spread and half an hour's drive up the motorway was too close for comfort. Besides, she'd selfishly leapt at the chance of an afternoon by herself. She wouldn't make that mistake again.

In any case, what did her feelings matter in the shadow of Uncle Des's death? If she were the cause, what a vile creature she was.

But one who, despite her revulsion, was determined to see justice done. More than ever, she had to keep herself safe to testify against Tom. She owed it to her uncle now.

*

Danny walked stiffly back to the car to try and reach Tara once more. It hurt to put weight on his left leg but he tried not to show it, just in case anyone was watching. It had taken some play-acting to get himself out of the medical room without the doctor scratching him from his remaining ride on the card.

So far it had been a pretty disastrous afternoon, and he wasn't expecting to get hold of Tara. But this time she answered on the second ring.

'How are you doing?' she asked.

She might at least have been watching, he thought. Then he banished the reproach. There was no reason why she had to sit in front of the TV because of him.

'Not great,' he said. 'Superstition fell at the last. Just when I thought I might have a chance he went down like a sack of spuds.'

'Are you all right?'

There was concern in her voice. It made the pain in his leg a sight more bearable.

'Yeah, I'll be fine. They've given me the all-clear to ride in the last.'

'Oh Danny.' She sounded tearful. 'I'm sorry. I really am.'

'It's not your fault, sweetheart.'

He didn't entirely believe that. She should have been here and just her presence would have made it all better. She could have been at his side right now and he could have read in her face the anguish she evidently felt.

It was as if she could read his mind. 'I wish I'd been there. I will be next time, Danny, I promise. If you want me, that is.'

'Darling, I always want you with me. But I don't expect you to spend all your time coming racing with me.'

'I can't anyway. Adrian was here – he offered me Jean's job. On the assumption she doesn't come back.'

It was no more than Danny expected. Christine had sounded him out already and he'd said he was all in favour. And he was. There were lots of advantages to Tara working in the yard. Apart from having something useful to do with her time, she'd be learning the racing game and contributing to the family business. What's more, she'd be working under his nose. He'd know where she was almost every moment of the day.

Not that he wanted to be her gaoler.

Tom was standing on the touchline amongst a knot of other parents when his phone began to vibrate inside his overcoat. He glanced at the number, hoping he could shut it off – couldn't a man watch his son play rugby on a Saturday afternoon without being hassled? Of course it might be Carol and it would not be wise to ignore his wife at this delicate point in their family life.

It was worse than that. He moved away from the parent next to him with an embarrassed smile and retreated until he was sure he was out of earshot.

His caller got straight to it. 'You know the Mandrake Hotel in the centre?'

'I know where it is.'

'The bar downstairs. Be there at nine thirty.'

'What, tonight? Can't do it.'

'You'll do it.'

'Look, I'm committed this evening. Any time tomorrow is OK.'

'No, it's not. Don't you keep up with the news? This can't wait.'

And that was the end of the conversation. Tom stared in anger at the phone as if the inanimate piece of plastic were to blame. Hoots of parental encouragement caused him to lift his head. On the field, a swarm of adolescent youths in black and yellow striped shirts were charging up the far touchline, led by a tall dark-haired boy with the ball in his hands. He chipped the ball over the advancing full back and beat him to the touch down in the corner. A small but enthusiastic cheer went up from the parents with whom Tom had been spectating. The man who'd been by his side turned in Tom's direction and gave him the thumbs-up.

Tom cursed his bloody awful existence. He'd just seen his son, Cosmo, score a brilliant try for his school and the moment was ruined by a call on behalf of the man who now ruled his life. And he did not relish the argument with his wife that would follow when he announced that he would not be accompanying her that evening. They were due at some neighbours for dinner, along with other parent couples from Sophie's school. With the possibility of soon being married to a jailbird, Carol was bonding hard. In the circumstances it might be good practice for her to go on her own.

So, what was it that Benny wanted? They'd agreed to meet as little as possible before Tom's case came to court. Something must have happened.

It had been Jason on the phone, a slimy little prick, twice as deadly as Benny's bruisers. 'Don't you keep up with the news?' What had he meant by that?

He glanced at his watch. His car was two minutes away, behind the cricket pavilion. He could catch the news on the half hour and still have ten minutes before he'd have to do the proud dad bit, having tea and biscuits with the other parents while their sons changed. With luck, Cosmo wouldn't even notice he'd gone.

Rick couldn't have been happier. Gingerbread's courageous victory had made this the best day he'd had since returning to Latchmere. The smile on Hugh's face alone justified the decision to send the horses to Christine. He didn't even resent the fact that he had no more rides for the afternoon. After he'd changed, he joined Hugh and Gwen in the bar. They were drinking champagne.

'That's the first prize money I've ever earned from a jumps race,' Hugh announced. 'And I'm going to drink it all here.'

'No, you're not,' said his wife.

Hugh shrugged. He seemed happy either way.

He put his arm round Rick. 'As for Treacle, I know you always thought he's the better horse and, technically, he might be but he's not got the stomach for a race. Not enough bottle. Ginger's got the bottle.'

Rick didn't contradict him. It was what they'd always said. If they could blend the talent of one animal with the guts of the other they'd have a champion. But right now he was just content to bask in the glow of victory.

Gwen shot him a sharp glance. He knew that look of concern. 'How are you getting on back in Lambourn?'

'As you can see, things are going OK.'

'I don't mean horses, Rick.'

'Well . . .' He wasn't sure exactly what he was going to say, certainly not the truth – that he was lonely and haunted by memories of Kirsty – when he was saved from saying anything at all.

Stephanie appeared through the crush, cheeks flushed and black curls flying, and threw her arms round him. 'Fantastic!' she cried, enveloping him in a cloud of flowery perfume. 'I told you I would bring you luck!'

Rick had forgotten about her.

'And look,' she thrust her hand into the pocket of her jeans and pulled out a bundle of notes. She fanned them open in her hand like a card sharp preparing to perform a trick. 'Two thousand smackers – what do you say?'

'Good Lord, Steph, how much did you put on?'

'Lots, there's no point otherwise, is there? And you told me not to bet. Thank God I didn't listen to you.' She slipped her arm round Rick's waist and smiled happily at Hugh and Gwen. 'My hero,' she added with satisfaction.

Gwen's concern had been replaced by something like amusement. She raised her glass and smiled at the pair of them. 'Congratulations, Rick. I can see you're settling in just fine.'

Tom was disturbed by the sound of the car boot opening and the thump of a bag being tossed inside with some force. Then the passenger door was flung wide and Cosmo, in school trousers and blazer – the school insisted, even on Saturdays – threw himself into the passenger seat.

'Jesus, Dad, where were you? You left twenty minutes before the end – you didn't see my try.'

'Yes, I did. It was a smart kick. Well done.'

'No, not that try. I scored another at the end. I got it on the twenty-two and ran through half their team. They couldn't lay a finger on me.'

The murder had been the third item on the news bulletin, behind the latest government cock-up and a Premier League sacking but ahead of a continuing genocide in central Africa. These days, Northern Ireland was rarely top of the news agenda, though sectarian killing was sufficiently unusual to rate as more than a footnote. The death of Des Monaghan, a popular Belfast baker, had aroused indignation and disgust on both sides of the divide. The hunt was on for the perpetrators and the police were keeping an open mind about the motives behind the attack.

'Mr Curtis said it was the best try he'd seen scored for the school in five years. Especially considering it won us the game in the last minute. Everybody was talking about it. And my own father bloody well missed it!'

'Sorry, son.' He was too. But he was a damn sight sorrier about a lot of other things.

Chapter Eight

Tom wasn't in the mood to make conversation, which was as well because the two men in the front of the car made no attempt to talk. On the occasions he'd been required to endure Jason's company, he'd found him hostile beyond mere rudeness. And the driver next to him, bull-necked and unshaven, was plainly not employed for his social graces.

Jason had appeared at Tom's elbow in the hotel bar the second after he'd ordered a large Scotch.

'Get you something?' Tom had offered.

Jason rejected the suggestion with a shake of the head. 'Let's go.'

'Not yet.'

Tom's son wasn't speaking to him. The argument with his wife had been as rancorous as he'd expected and his daughter, having overheard, had been in tears when he left. And the truly shitty part of the evening was still ahead. Tom needed the drink he'd just ordered.

He added a cube of ice to his glass and a dash of water, mixing it slowly with a plastic stirrer.

Jason's sigh of impatience was music to Tom's ears. As he raised the glass to his lips, he reflected that this would doubtless be the high point of his day. The whisky hit the back of his throat in a moment of peaty magic. He swallowed thirstily. All gone. He'd have had another except he still had sufficient wits about him to know that blurring his intellectual capabilities before a meeting with Benny Bridges would be foolhardy.

Now he sat in the back of an unfamiliar car being driven into the dark hinterland north of the city. He had no idea of his destination and frankly he didn't much care. Buoyed by the whisky, he felt bullish and resentful. Someone had screwed up and it wasn't him. A man was dead – an innocent pensioner, a pillar of his community. How the hell had that happened?

He needed some answers.

On second thoughts, as the big car purred silently through the night, the less he knew about the whole sordid business the better.

All he'd done was give Benny a name. He didn't know this would be the result.

Maybe it was a coincidence.

By the time the car turned off the road to travel fifty yards up a wooded drive to a pair of tall security gates, the effect of the whisky was wearing off. Ahead he could make out the shape of a looming mansion whose high windows on the ground floor blazed with light. The building was constructed on an imposing scale, which Tom appreciated as the car followed the drive round to a rear entrance. He doubted it belonged to Benny but who could say? He'd certainly never met Benny here before.

'C'mon, out you get.' Jason spoke with his customary contempt, an unnecessary shot since Tom had already opened the car door.

As he felt the wet wind in his face and the gravel of the drive beneath his feet, all his whisky bravado vanished. He'd represented men accused of murder many times. But there had always been a barrier between him and them.

Now, he couldn't help reflecting, he was on the other side of the fence.

The last thing Tara felt like was a jolly night out but Adrian had decreed that there should be a celebratory dinner for the returning Haydock party and had booked a local restaurant. Given her resolve to try harder with Danny, Tara did not see how she could refuse to accompany him. The irony was that he didn't even want to go.

'I'd much rather spend the evening here with you,' he'd said, 'but Adrian won't be happy if we duck it.'

Tara could have argued for rebellion but she had no intention of rocking the boat. It was plain that Adrian's invitations had the authority of a three-line whip.

So here they were at a large table at the back of a pretty green and white dining room busy with hungry diners and bustling staff. The place was a cheerful haven from the damp January night and obviously popular. Tara wondered if Adrian had had difficulty in making his last-minute booking. From the way he was greeted by the owner she concluded he could have had every table in the place had he so desired.

Patsy, typically, arrived late and greeted everyone at the table with individual enthusiasm. He threw an arm round Rick's shoulder as he shook his hand.

'Next time,' he growled, 'tell me you're going to win and I'll get some money down.'

Rick smiled happily in the face of this treatment. 'I was a bit lucky.'

'Oh, bollocks.' Stephanie had poached the seat by Rick's side. 'He was brilliant, Patsy. Pity you didn't have faith in your own judgement like me.'

Tara had heard of Stephanie's successful wager from Danny. He'd taken her behaviour as some kind of personal affront.

'Be careful, Stephanie, I'm thinking of making you pay for this meal,' said Adrian from the other end of the table. 'I hear you can afford it for once.'

Stephanie pouted at her stepfather. 'I hope you're not suggesting I'm too mean. I'll pay for the champagne and we can all toast Rick.' And she waved at the wine waiter.

Through all this Tara kept an eye on Rick. She remembered meeting him in her first year at Manchester. He'd been a handsome boy, though too shy to realise it and thoroughly intimidated by being thrust into a crowd of strange students on a night out. She'd felt sorry for him, particularly when Kirsty had abandoned him and he'd got horribly drunk. She'd felt ashamed that none of them had looked after him better. He'd looked at her so fiercely the other day – obviously he remembered that weekend and still resented her for it. And she'd been too bound up in her own problems since she'd arrived at Latchmere to try to build bridges.

She watched the way Stephanie was fussing over him. Rick must know her well, having worked at the yard before. Maybe they were an item. The thought pleased her. Rick had obviously overcome his shyness with girls.

As she reflected on this, he lifted his head and caught her eye. She smiled and, to her surprise, his cheeks flushed pink and he looked away.

How strange. Maybe his problem was no longer with girls in general but just with her.

The sounds of music and laughter came from far off, muffled by the thick walls of the house. Tom was conscious of having been admitted through a back entrance, down a flight of poky stairs into a room that was barely furnished: a table, two chairs and, incongruously, a vase of lilies which filled the small space with a suffocating scent, beneath which Tom could detect a musty note of damp. A threadbare rug covered the stone floor and a baseball bat was propped against the wall. He reckoned he'd been in friendlier police interview rooms.

It was ten minutes before Benny arrived. Time enough for Tom to speculate on the nature of the black stains on the wall and for the chill to seep through his clothes.

At last came the sound of doors opening and footsteps descending and Benny Bridges swept into the room.

'Jesus, it's parky,' he exclaimed as he extended a hand to Tom. 'Bring us a heater, will you?' he shouted over his shoulder. 'We've got Manchester's top lawyer freezing his bloody balls off in here.'

The handshake was warm and the smile was wide. Benny Bridges, in his tailored suit and open-neck blue check shirt, his long hair fashionably groomed, his teeth polished and his skin tanned, looked like a stylish young businessman on the way up. This wasn't far off the mark, though his business was drug-trafficking, money-laundering and murder.

The driver who'd transported Tom from Manchester came into the room with an electric fan heater and plugged it in.

'Thanks, mate,' said Benny and the man departed. He adjusted the heater so it directed a warm breath of air in Tom's direction. 'Is that better?' he asked.

Tom had long ago concluded that Benny had acquired his manners and concern for others along with his cars and expensive clothes, not to mention the yachts, an estate on Majorca and, it was rumoured, a fortified island off the east coast of Africa. Benny presented himself as a nice guy because he could afford to do so. These days he employed others to get their hands dirty on his behalf.

Benny took the chair on the other side of the table. 'Sorry, but I can't stay long. Got a bit of a do on.' On cue from above came the muffled shriek of a woman's laughter. Tom could imagine the occasion – he had been to one or two of Benny's 'dos' in the past. 'I don't think it's a good idea you show your face,' Benny added. 'In the circs.'

Tom couldn't have agreed more.

Benny leaned forward. 'So you've heard about the baker?'

Tom's heart sank. Though the truth had been plain ever since he'd heard the news that afternoon, a small part of him had harboured a hope that Monaghan's death had nothing to do with him or Benny. People got killed in Belfast all the time, didn't they? It could have been coincidence.

'I heard,' he said. 'What on earth happened?' He regretted the words the moment they were out – it was surely healthier to remain in ignorance. But it was plain Benny was going to tell him anyway.

The other man pulled a face. 'I put Carl in touch with some friends of mine in Belfast. Between them they made a mess of it.'

'They killed an old-age pensioner. That's some mess.'

Benny shrugged. 'He was a tough old bird. Sounds like he had it coming.'

'What do you mean?'

To Tom's surprise, Benny grinned. 'He whacked Carl over the head with a wooden mallet. Looked like he'd fallen out with Mike Tyson.'

'And that's why he killed him?'

'Not exactly. The way Carl tells it, Monaghan admitted he knew your girl but swore blind she wasn't in Belfast – as far as he knew anyway. They put a bullet in his leg to loosen his tongue and the old fellow had a heart attack. Game over.'

'Why on earth did he shoot him?'

'I know. Some people have got no finesse. You're better off making an old bloke like that *think* you're going to shoot

164

him. Carl knows that but I reckon the smack on the napper scrambled his brain. He wasn't in good shape when he got back here.'

Tom couldn't care less about Carl.

'So he didn't find out anything about Tara?'

'No.' Benny wasn't smiling any more. 'The whole thing was a cock-up. We've just got to hope that the Paddy police are as thick as the rest of them or we're in the shite. I've got Carl out of the way but he lives with a bird and they've got two kids, so I've got to keep her sweet. It's getting expensive. I'm not running a welfare service.'

It was plain the unnecessary expenditure touched a nerve.

'Sending Carl to Belfast was a mistake,' Benny continued. 'Maybe you should have gone.'

'Me?' The notion was outrageous.

'Don't get on your high horse. I'm just pointing out that maybe a bit more elbow grease from your end is what's needed. After all, you promised to smooth her over in the first place.'

Tom knew Benny would bring that up. It was a sore point. He'd been certain he could keep Tara quiet but the girl had turned out to have some idealistic commitment to justice, as she'd put it. 'You're committing professional suicide,' he'd told her. 'I'll make sure no one ever employs you.'

'I'll take that chance,' she'd said in a superior fashion.

Then he'd turned her over to Benny. He'd done his best.

'I gave you the uncle's name, didn't I?' he said.

'And a fat load of use it turned out to be. It might not be your fault but it's like football, isn't it? We're in the results business and if those results don't come, someone gets sacked.'

Silence fell for a moment. The chill had been banished and Tom could feel himself beginning to sweat. But he refrained from asking Benny to turn off the heater.

'The bottom line, Tom, my friend, is that you were in the knickers of this girl Tara and as a result she knows things she shouldn't about my affairs. What's more, as far as we're aware, she is prepared to go to court and say so. Which she is well capable of doing considering she is a trained-up solicitor like yourself.'

Tom thought better of correcting Benny's grasp of Tara's legal standing.

Benny sighed. 'I don't know. A bright bloke like you, university educated, capable of dancing round the coppers and the CPS all day long, but when it comes to picking a bit on the side you haven't a clue. Mouth shut and legs open, that's what you want, mate. You should have asked me. There's half a dozen of 'em upstairs right now.'

Tom let the diatribe wash over him. It was always the same with Benny. You started off in thrall to what looked like charm and within a quarter of an hour your stomach was churning with disgust.

'I hope you understand what I'm saying, Tom. If she brings you down then I'm smack in the middle of the frame. Which is precisely the place I cannot afford to be. I'm running a major business here. It might not be quoted on the stock exchange but I've got customers to think of, employees with dependents, like Carl's girl and her kids. So, no offence and nothing personal, but I can't go to the wall. It can't be allowed. Do you get me?'

Tom did get him. Loud and clear. Benny was saying that if Tom couldn't find Tara and shut her up, then it would be safer for him if Tom himself were out of the picture.

Nothing personal, of course.

Tara found the evening overwhelming. Laughter and well-honed family banter swirled around her. She felt excluded, trapped in a bubble of silence where lurked some nasty demons. So she pasted a smile on her face and sipped her champagne.

Drinking was probably a bad idea. How much had she had? Three glasses or four? And there'd been the brandy earlier. She'd hardly touched alcohol recently and it was having an effect. The people around her became larger than life, their gestures exaggerated, caricatures of themselves.

None more so than Stephanie. She'd made an effort tonight. She wore a tight red leather skirt and well-cut cream lace blouse, unbuttoned just far enough to give a hint of cleavage. She'd tamed her wild curls into an elaborate coiffure piled high on her head, showing off her long white neck and, on this rare occasion, she'd even applied some eye make-up.

Tara assumed she'd made the effort for Rick. She was flirting with him in an obvious fashion, involving much mutual food sampling and laying on of hands. But Rick, now she observed him more closely – or was the drink fooling her? – seemed less a participant in this mating ritual than a victim.

Something else occurred to her, a memory of a conversation she'd had with Kirsty a few weeks before her death. Kirsty could be deliciously indiscreet with those she trusted. Early on in their friendship Tara had made a note never to tell her anything she badly needed to keep secret. She couldn't have borne to be discussed the way Kirsty gaily dissected the foibles of others. Stephanie for example.

'You know Steph would love to shag Adrian, don't you?' Kirsty had said one evening as they were discussing her prospective in-laws.

Tara had laughed – she'd been a bit tipsy that night too. 'Oh, for God's sake, he's her stepfather.'

'So? I'm not saying it's a conscious urge. Steph doesn't analyse what she does or why she does it. She's all instinct.'

'And her instinct is to bed her stepfather?'

'Right. She's in competition with her mother. Always has been.'

'Very Freudian.'

'Don't make fun of me, Tara. I know what I'm on about.' Kirsty had grown serious. 'Stephanie has always seen herself in a fight with her mother for Adrian. Danny told me. When Christine married him there was none of that "you'll never take the place of my real dad". Stephanie was dead keen for her mum to hook up with Adrian. She was all over him right from the start.'

'But she was just a child.'

'Ten or eleven. A sweet little bridesmaid at the ceremony. But within a couple of years she was a proper teenager. All budding boobs and a big curvy bottom apparently.'

'You've got a lurid imagination, Kirsty.'

'It's fact. I've spoken to Adrian about it too. Stephanie used to come downstairs in the evening to say goodnight in little T-shirts and knickers and wriggle around on his knee right in front of Christine.'

Tara had reached for her wine glass at that point. 'You're saying Stephanie was trying to seduce him in front of her mother?'

'More like making a point. Like I said, I don't think it was conscious on her part. It was bloody tricky for Adrian though. After all, you're supposed to bond with your new stepkids. He could hardly shove her away.'

'You're not saying he encouraged her, are you?'

Kirsty had thought that was funny. 'No fear. She terrified him – I think she still does. Luckily Christine cottoned on fast and forbade her to walk around the house unless she was properly dressed. That saved his blushes.'

Adrian wasn't blushing now, Tara thought, though he could scarcely be unaware of his stepdaughter pawing Rick right in front of him. But maybe both he and Christine would be keen on such a match. She wondered what Rick himself made of it.

Dessert wine had appeared on the table and a variety of sticky puddings. She toyed with the gooey confection of cream and chocolate that she appeared to have ordered and settled for the wine instead.

It was a mistake. The sweet, heavy alcohol made her head spin. The conversation had taken another horsey turn – no one could expect her to contribute.

'I won't be a moment,' she murmured to Danny and got up from the table. She headed for the door which led to the toilets but walked past them, out into the night air.

That felt better.

Rick had said no to a pudding but Stephanie had insisted he have one 'to share'.

'Why don't you get your own, then,' he'd suggested but she'd told him that would look like she was being greedy and he had to order the treacle tart and clotted cream. He'd gone along with her – it was easier.

He'd only eaten one spoonful – it was delicious – and left the rest to her. What he craved was a cigarette. He wasn't a full-time smoker but, on occasions like this, it dulled his appetite. As a jockey, he could never permit himself to eat all that was placed in front of him.

He headed out of the back door, his hand already on the packet in his pocket. He hoped the rain had eased off though just a few puffs should do it.

He was standing on the terrace overlooking the shadowy garden when he became aware he was not alone. Tara was leaning against the wall a couple of yards to his left.

'Caught you,' she said.

'Sorry.' Though why should he apologise? He held up the cigarette. 'It's this or treacle tart.'

'Can I have one?'

'Sure.' He fumbled in his pocket. 'I didn't think you smoked.'

'So you do remember me?'

She was right up close now, taking the small white tube from him. Of course he remembered her. The little gap between her teeth and those full lips – which he'd kissed clumsily until she'd stopped him.

'The hair's a bit drastic,' he said. 'You have such lovely hair, why did you cut it off?'

She shrugged and dragged uncertainly on the cigarette. He could see she wasn't a practised smoker.

He felt awkward, which was stupid of him. He was no longer an adolescent overawed by the presence of an attractive woman. 'I'm sorry about throwing up on your dress that night,' he said. 'Not a very good first impression, I'm afraid.'

'Nor is letting you get drunk. It wasn't your fault. We didn't look out for you like we should.'

She coughed and crushed the cigarette against the wall, half smoked.

'That was a mistake,' she said. 'I came out here to get some air.'

He saw she was shivering.

'You're cold. We ought to get back inside.'

'I'm OK.' She put a hand on his arm. 'Let's leave them to talk about horses for a bit longer.'

Rick was puzzled. She wasn't as he remembered her, though that evening was a long time ago and he'd been young and drunk. But all the same, there'd been something serene about her then. She'd been the kind of girl who hadn't been fazed by his oafish behaviour, who had cleared up his sick and put him to bed with the calm of a mother looking after a poorly child. Now she was a jumpy bag of nerves.

He put his jacket round her shoulders. Her whole body was trembling.

'So you've given up the solicitor's life?'

'For now. I might go back sometime.'

'To Manchester?'

'No.' The word shot from her lips like a bullet. She caught the surprise in his face and added, 'I meant I could finish my training somewhere else.'

'You should. Kirsty always said you were brilliant.'

'That's only because I wrote her essays for her in the first year.'

'That sounds like Kirsty.'

'You must think it odd me being here in her place.'

He'd not thought of it like that. 'You and Danny know each other because of Kirsty, don't you? I mean, friends fall in love all the time. You're not some kind of substitute.'

She didn't reply.

'Anyhow,' he added, 'Danny's nuts about you. Kirsty's his past and you're his future.'

'Don't say that.'

'Why not? Kirsty's gone and we've all got to get on with our lives.' He believed it to be true but it was hard to say with conviction.

'And some are doing it more successfully than others.' She looked at him, her face pale and severe in the dim light. 'Doesn't it seem spooky to you that half the people at our table were there when Kirsty was killed?'

Her words touched a nerve. The laughter and jollity at the table and Kirsty long gone. She'd had her head bashed in and yet all the others at the scene were safe and well and happy. Sure, it spooked him too, but wasn't that just part of the never-ending pain of losing someone you loved?

But he didn't have a chance to say these things because the restaurant door suddenly flew open and a voice rang out. 'What on earth are you two doing out there?'

Stephanie had found them.

Tara sat in bed in a daze. On her side. She and Danny were like an old married couple already. She wondered if her side had been Kirsty's side too.

It had been a long day. When she'd made the decision to run from Manchester and into Danny's arms, she'd thought somehow that she could put her life on hold until it came time for Tom's trial. She'd thought about getting away and covering her tracks. And she'd thought about the courage she would need to stand up in court and testify against him. But she'd not thought about the months in between, keeping her head down, pretending to be a different person – just *being*.

If all the days were as endless as this she didn't know how she would cope without having some kind of crack-up. She'd felt on the edge of it tonight. She was living on her nerves, with all her true feelings bottled up inside her.

She could come clean to Danny. Tell him about her role as a witness in Tom's trial and how she had to hide for her own protection. But how would he take it? Badly, she knew instinctively. She'd allowed him to believe she cared for him – maybe not to the degree he cared for her but deeply all the same. Enough to move in with him and see if they could make a serious go of a life together.

Things had gone too far now. She should have been honest with him right at the start. Kept him out of her bed but thrown herself on his mercy, as a friend. Maybe then she'd be able to pour out her heart to him as she'd once done. To talk to him about Uncle Des's death and how it might be – must be – her fault and how terrible she felt about it. And how she wasn't even going to the funeral because she was too scared.

But she hadn't been honest with him. She'd been too scared of rejection. So she'd sealed the deal the best way she knew how at the time – with her body. Like a tart. Poor Danny was sleeping with a woman who, for all her principles and commitment to justice, had behaved just like a whore.

Her self-loathing lay heavy in her stomach.

She'd made a new commitment to Danny just that afternoon and she would stick to it. She would prove herself an honest woman to him yet.

Where was he? He'd been a long time in the bathroom.

'Danny? Are you OK?'

His reply was muffled and she couldn't catch his words but she could hear a note of fatigue – and pain.

She got out of bed fast, dazed no longer, and found him sitting naked on the chair by the side of the bath. His left leg was stretched out in front of him and she gasped when she saw the state of it. From groin to knee, his thigh was a puffy pink mass.

'Oh, Danny, that looks horrible.'

He looked at her ruefully. 'I've had worse. Lots worse, actually.'

She was filled with remorse. He'd told her about his fall when they'd spoken on the phone in the afternoon but she'd scarcely given it a thought since then. And when he got home, he'd made no mention of it.

'Stay right there,' she commanded.

'OK.' There was exhaustion in his eyes. He didn't look as if he could move even if he wanted to.

She fetched a thin towel and a large bag of frozen peas.

'That's going to look pretty spectacular in a day or two,' she said, as she wrapped the peas in the towel and placed the bundle carefully on his thigh. 'We shouldn't have gone out – you should have said something.'

'You've got to fly the flag sometimes. Anyhow, it was Rick's night. It wouldn't have been right if I'd not been there.'

'But weren't you in pain?'

'I took some pills. I thought I was going to have trouble getting up from the table though.'

'Why didn't you tell me?'

'You're with a jockey now, babe. We're iron men.'

She could see he was joking, but there was an element of truth in what he said.

'Well, man of iron, are you tough enough to get yourself next door and into bed?'

He grinned. 'I'd have to lose a leg not to make it into a bed beside you.'

She smiled awkwardly and helped him to his feet.

'You give good TLC,' he said as she drew his arm round her shoulder and helped take his weight. 'I'll be sure to fall off more often.'

'Don't you dare.'

He looked as happy as she'd ever seen him as she settled him on the bed and fussed around him, resting his wounded leg on some pillows and fetching paracetamol.

She was good at playing nurse but all the same she was acutely conscious of being a fraud.

It was late when Tom got home. He'd been driven back to Manchester – the same driver but no Jason, which was an improvement – and he'd made straight for the hotel bar. He'd downed his first drink fast but made the second last as he chewed a sandwich which may have been beef; he hardly tasted it. All he could think of at first was that he was damned glad to have got out of that foul little room with the baseball bat standing in the corner.

By the time he got home the family were all in bed. That was a relief. So, too, in a funny way was the fact that Carol had locked the bedroom door. She'd put his pyjamas and dressing gown on the spare room bed and placed his alarm clock radio on the bedside table. It gave his exclusion an air of permanence. Right now, he didn't give a monkey's.

The bottom line was not the state of his marriage or even the prospect of remaining at liberty, it was simply staying alive.

To ensure that he did, he would have to find where Tara was hiding and then turn the location over to Benny.

Fortunately he had not exhausted his resources. A solicitor didn't spend fifteen years in criminal practice without encountering all sorts of people, some legit and some not. So far he'd shrunk from seeking help from his regular criminal clientele. He'd trusted Benny to come up with a solution. But Benny's men had screwed up and he had to get more involved, take more risks.

He'd met a few of Tara's friends. One ran a catering business – he could look her up in Yellow Pages. Tomorrow he'd make a few calls.

Chapter Nine

As Tara walked with Danny to the yard, she tried again to get him to change his mind.

'Look, you're limping. I really don't think you're fit to ride.'

'That's why I've got a horse. I just sit on him and he does all the work.'

'Don't be feeble, Danny.'

He grinned at her happily. He'd been basking in her attention ever since Saturday night and loving every second.

'Feeble is what I'd be if I let a bruised thigh keep me at home when I've got a job to do at Ludlow.'

It was like talking to a brick wall. As they emerged from the wood, with the stable buildings just ahead, Tara made a final attempt to get him to at least acknowledge that he was injured and should see a doctor.

'Are you sure you don't want me to drive you?'

He'd rejected the suggestion the night before.

'No need. I texted Clive this morning and he's giving me a lift.' Tara knew that Clive was the stable jockey of another Lambourn yard. 'See, I was listening to what you said.'

'I don't think that four or five hours sitting in a car is good for you either,' she grumbled.

What on earth was she playing at? Being a good girlfriend

was one thing but now she was sounding like his mother. And the irony was that his real mother didn't appear in the least concerned.

Christine was waiting for them as they crossed the yard. 'Hurry up, Clive's waiting for you,' she said to Danny before turning to Tara. 'I was hoping you were on the way. Jean's resigned.'

Tara hadn't given much thought about Adrian's offer for her to replace the office secretary.

'I was wondering,' Christine said, for once looking a little uncertain, 'would you mind standing in for her again? You've been such a help.'

How much had Adrian relayed to his wife of their conversation on Saturday? Not all of it, she could be certain.

'Yes, of course. I'm happy to make myself useful.'

The trainer smiled with relief and Tara found herself smiling in return. Danny hugged her goodbye and she headed for the office with lightness in her step. There was something to be said for being wanted.

She noticed at once that the cyclamen had gone from the window sill and the mug with the Thelwell pony was missing from the draining board.

Christine saw the direction of her glance. 'Jean reclaimed a few things.'

'She's been here?'

'First thing. She scurried in and out. I don't know whether she was more scared of me biting her head off or of Patsy turning up.'

'And did you bite her head off?'

Christine sighed. 'I didn't have the heart. She was always putting herself out for me. I just felt relieved she'd brought back some paperwork she'd taken home. I'd have been looking for it.'

Tara spotted a carrier bag which had been jammed in the

gap between the sink and a filing cabinet. From the top spilled what looked like a paint-stained sweater.

'Are you sure there's papers in there? It looks like clothes.'

Christine smiled. 'A few of Patsy's things. She asked if we would return them for her.'

Poor Jean, thought Tara. Most girls would have simply chucked his belongings in the bin.

Tara sat back in the secretary's seat, which looked like it was hers for the taking in more ways than one.

She thought of Uncle Des, as she'd been doing ever since she'd heard the news of his murder. The funny thing was that thinking of him made him more alive in her head than he'd been for years.

Uncle Des's sons, Kenny and Raymond, were twenty years older than Tara and had left Belfast before she could toddle. She barely knew them. Des, her mother's elder brother, had loved her as if she were one of the grand-children that he so rarely saw.

What would he want her to do now?

She knew he'd want her to make herself safe. To keep her head down in this feathery little nest she'd lucked into. And not to venture to Belfast for the funeral because they would surely be looking for her there.

Her dead uncle's wish would be to get herself to court in one piece to tell the truth about Tom Ferguson.

She turned her attention back to the mess of papers on the desk and began to open the remainder of the day's post.

'Do me a favour?' The voice came from the door of Gingerbread's stall where Rick was bending down, checking the horse's legs for signs of a reaction to his winning run at Haydock.

He looked up to see Sara, the head girl, leaning on the door.

'Patsy says you've got a knack with awkward sods.' Sara spoke in a tone that implied she didn't believe a word of it.

Rick stood up. Ginger seemed fine, in great shape happily.

'Which awkward sod did you have in mind?'

'Wing Wang Woo. Stupid bloody name. Stupid bloody animal. We can't risk him out with the string or he'll upset the lot.'

Rick knew the horse she meant, a big handsome chestnut with a gleaming coat and a grand head. Unfortunately there didn't appear to be much in it. He spooked at the wind in the trees or raindrops spattering into a puddle. The kind of horse whose irrational fears could spark off a mass panic attack amongst a group of horses.

'Sure, I'll ride him out.' He was pleased to be asked, albeit grudgingly. He didn't take Sara's attitude personally. He guessed the chip on her shoulder was a defence against the kind of sexist banter often directed at attractive young females in positions of authority in racing yards. Though, to be honest, he'd not observed it at Latchmere and couldn't imagine Christine putting up with that kind of behaviour.

He added, 'Doesn't he normally go out with Miller's Tale?' He'd noticed Wing being exercised as one of a pair with a docile grey.

'Yes, but we're short today. I can't spare anyone to take him out. But considering your advance press, that shouldn't present a problem, should it?' And she marched off.

Rick resigned himself to the task, not that it was an unwelcome chore. He had no rides today, worse luck, and the prospect of riding out on any animal was pleasing. He walked over to Wing's box to begin the process of getting acquainted.

The horse looked on with considerable suspicion as Rick

began to sort out some tack. He wickered unhappily and shuffled his feet. Across the yard, the big grey shape of Miller's Tale considered them placidly from his box. He'd enjoy a trot up on the gallops, Rick could tell. It was a pity there was no one available to bring his calming presence along.

Rick considered calling Stephanie at the stud. If she wasn't too busy, she might be interested in riding out. In fact, after her behaviour the other night, he had a feeling she'd jump at the chance.

He'd given her a lift back to Latchmere from the restaurant at her insistence, though frankly it would have been more convenient for her to go with Adrian and Christine since she was still living in the main house. She would also have been considerably more comfortable in a BMW than his ten-year-old Fiesta. But there had been no shaking her off.

When he'd parked, she'd put her hand on his arm and said, 'You've not seen my little palace, have you?'

Since he'd last been in the house, Stephanie had been granted more space, as befitted her status as assistant manager of the stud. She'd taken over Danny's old room next door and had even annexed a handy backstairs entrance for her exclusive use. She could now come and go without her mother clocking her in and out, so she'd told Danny.

'Not tonight, thanks,' he'd said. 'I'm a bit bushed.'

'Well, I'm not,' she said.

'Sorry, Steph. Another time, eh?'

'What makes you think there'll be another time?' And she'd flounced out of the car. Danny had waited till she'd unlocked the side door before driving off but she'd not turned round to acknowledge him.

So inviting her to ride out might be a prudent move. He

pulled out his mobile then remembered there was no reception. He'd have to use the phone in the office.

As he walked across the courtyard that separated the stables from the row of utility buildings where the yard office was situated, he saw Tara's blonde urchin crop in the window.

The thought flashed into his head at once – a much more satisfactory plan. Maybe he had no need to call Stephanie after all.

Rick's sudden appearance took Tara by surprise.

'Busy?' he asked.

She wasn't particularly. She'd sorted out the post and the Monday morning chaos of jumbled messages, some of which she'd returned and the rest she'd listed for Christine. She'd washed up a sink of dirty mugs and fetched a new jar of coffee from the store in the barn. She was now contemplating unjamming the shredder into which someone had tried to feed a plastic folder. Mundane though it was, she had enjoyed her morning. The succession of little jobs had stopped the thought loop that ran remorselessly through her head.

'Hi, Rick,' she said. She was pleased they'd reconnected the other night. It was good to see him. 'Is this a lunch invitation?'

'Later maybe. Stand up and let me see what you're wearing.'

She laughed but he didn't. He appeared to be serious as he rounded the desk and peered at her legs.

'That's OK,' he announced.

'Are you the fashion police or something?'

'I just want to see if you're dressed for riding. But jeans are fine. So if you're not busy, how about it?'

Suddenly she understood. He wanted her to get on a horse.

'You do ride, don't you?' he said, as if the thought she might not had only just occurred to him.

It had been a few years since she'd sat on a horse and even then she'd only ridden docile riding school animals with school friends. The thought of riding out with a proper jockey like Rick was daunting.

'I've never been on a racehorse,' she said, 'if that's what you're suggesting. I've only hacked around a bit.'

'Don't worry. Miller's Tale will look after you. Come and have a look at him and I'll sort you out some gear.'

She should have objected. After all, she'd squashed every suggestion of Danny's that she go riding with him and here she was meekly following Rick across the yard to the stall of a handsome grey horse who had already caught her eye. There weren't many of his colouring in the yard and she'd noticed him frequently.

'He's fantastic,' she said, 'but he's enormous. I'm really not sure it would be a good idea.'

Rick was unconcerned. 'Rubbish. You're in for a treat. If you've only been on riding school nags it'll be like changing a Mini for a Roller.'

That's what was worrying her.

He caught the anxiety in her face. 'Relax. All you have to do is sit on him and keep me company. I'm on that silly bugger Wing over there who's inclined to play up. But he won't if Miller's Tale comes along.'

She helped to saddle up the grey and, under Rick's instructions, she selected a hat and boots from the tack room. As she did so she tried to analyse her feelings. Why had she been so resistant to Danny's requests and yet she was seemingly prepared to go along with Rick?

'You're not going to shout at me, are you?' she asked. Memories of painful riding lessons in the past were sharp in her mind. Maybe that's how she feared Danny might treat her – keeping an eye on her every move and bombarding her with instructions. In which case a gentle hack around would be like getting driving lessons from a family member. Tense and not much fun. 'I mean,' she continued as he looked at her with a degree of puzzlement, 'you're not going to keep saying I've got my legs in the wrong place and telling me what to do with my seat, are you?'

He held her gaze. 'So you don't want me to tell you what to do with your seat?' She realised he was holding back laughter.

'Don't make fun of me, you bastard. I'm nervous.'

He laughed out loud this time and she made herself join in. All the same, she was aware she was blushing. Girl-shy Rick had turned the tables on her.

'Look, Tara,' he wasn't laughing any more, 'don't let me force you. You'd be doing me a favour and I thought it might be fun. But if you're really worried I'll go out on my own.'

'No.' That was not what she wanted. 'I'll give it a try.'

Tom had done nothing all morning. Nothing of conse-quence in the service of Gallagher Ferguson, that is. Instead he'd shuffled bits of paper around his desk and consulted his computer screen earnestly, to give the impression of endeavour. But even the odds for the afternoon's racing on the betting sites could not hold his attention.

How the hell was he going to find Tara?

He'd tried her catering friend. It had been a one-sided conversation. Judy had given full vent to her concerns for Tara – there had been no word from her for weeks, she'd just packed up and gone, none of her friends had a clue what had happened. It was like she'd vanished into a hole. What did Tom think they should do? Should they talk to the police? After five minutes of this, Tom just wanted to get her off the line. He had no doubt of her sincerity, or that Tara's Manchester friends had no idea where she'd gone.

He'd made other calls. In his line of work he knew a lot of policemen and not all of them were hostile to his cause. That is, a select few were not averse to taking money. If he could at least discover whether Tara was part of a witness protection programme, it would be helpful. Though in theory that should make it harder to track her down, in practice – expensive though it might be – it could be a whole lot easier. What worried Tom most was that she had found some means of dropping off the radar altogether. She was a resourceful young woman. If she had organised her own hiding place she might well prove more difficult to find.

He also called some regular clients who had provided him with useful information in the past. Who knew what kind of titbit he might pick up? At this point anything was better than nothing. He had a feeling, however, that all he was doing was boosting his own morale.

A perfunctory knock was followed by the opening of the door. Jack's morning visit. It was later than usual and the older man looked even more shrouded in gloom. He did not sit down, just dropped a copy of the *Daily Telegraph* on Tom's desk, folded open to page five.

'What do you make of that?' he said.

Tom looked at the headline: 'Belfast shocked by the murder of a favourite son.' Beneath a photograph of a grinning bespectacled man in an apron, the caption read: 'Des Monaghan outside his baker's shop – friends say he had no enemies.'

'That's terrible.' Tom shook his head. 'I thought there was meant to be peace in Northern Ireland these days.'

'Yes, but look at the name.' Jack's podgy finger prodded the newspaper page. 'Des Monaghan.'

'Yes?' Tom could act pretty well when he had to. And he had to now.

'He's the baker we were talking about last week. When we were wondering where Tara could have gone.'

'My God.' Tom's mouth opened wide in surprise. 'It's the same man? That's a heck of a coincidence.'

Jack sank heavily into a chair. 'You're not bloody kidding. I couldn't believe it when I opened the paper this morning.' He shook his head. 'He was a great fellow, you know. Everyone loved him.'

'Not everyone, Jack. It looks like he fell out with the paramilitaries somewhere down the line.'

Jack shook his head. 'Impossible.'

'But he ran a successful business right in the heart of Belfast. He must have had to deal with the paramilitaries, pay protection or whatever. They're like the mafia, aren't they? It looks like they were putting the frighteners on him and overdid it.'

Jack's eyes narrowed. 'So you do know about this?'

'I heard something on the news the other day but I didn't make the connection.' Tom quickly scanned the newspaper in front of him and pointed to the page. 'Look, it says here that he suffered a heart attack after being shot in the leg.'

Jack shook his head unhappily. 'I don't know how it is, Tom, but even doing what we do every day, dealing with some of the most brutal and senseless of crimes, something can still come along and shock you to the core.'

'Maybe that's a good thing. It shows that we're not just cynical agents of the system. You've got heart, Jack. That's what makes you such a fine solicitor.'

The funny thing was that, as Tom said it, he believed it.

Jack managed half a smile at the compliment. 'You're not too bad yourself, Tom. We'll get you over this stupid mess of yours, you'll see.' He hoisted himself to his feet and made for the door. 'I tell you what,' he added. 'Old Des will have a hell of a turnout at his funeral.'

Tom pondered on that parting thought as Jack left him to his own devices.

Tara wasn't as bad on a horse as she made out, Rick thought, as they made their way up the bridle path to the gallops. If she was nervous at least she managed not to convey it to her mount who ambled along serenely. The presence of Miller's Tale was undeniably helpful in calming his own jittery animal. So, he reflected, he was fully vindicated in twisting her arm to accompany him.

They rode in silence until they emerged on to the broad expanse on top of the incline. If he'd been riding with Stephanie, she'd have probably burned his ears off every step of the way.

Even at the end of January, the gallops sparkled in the watery winter sunshine.

'Are you up for a bit of a canter?' he called.

To his surprise, she simply nodded and kicked Miller's Tale into action. The next thing he knew, the pair of them had gone flying past him, taking him off guard. He hadn't expected such an instant response.

Wing, in typical fashion, was distracted by the roar of a motorbike from down in the valley and skittered sideways. It took some effort on Rick's part to haul him back into line and set off after Tara who was now six lengths ahead of him and crouching low over the horse's shoulders.

'Hey!' he yelled after her. 'Slow down.'

But she didn't – or else she couldn't. He'd made light of her inexperience once he'd satisfied himself she knew how to sit on a horse. People often underplayed their capabilities – people like Tara, that is. Intelligent and modest – he knew the type. He'd reckoned right from the start that she was protesting too much about her ability as a rider. But was that because he really wanted her beside him up on the gallops instead of Stephanie?

And maybe, because he'd pushed her into it, she was way out of her depth on a horse she couldn't control.

'Tara!' he roared and dug his heels into his horse's flanks.

Wing Wang Woo might be an odd customer with the kind of temperamental quirks that drove his handlers mad, but he was quick. It was the only reason people put up with him. At Rick's urging he lengthened his stride and bolted after the horse in front.

They made up ground fast, with Rick still yelling after Tara and all sorts of nightmares flashing through his head. Suppose she fell off? Got trampled and broke a bone? Or worse?

Suddenly Miller's Tale slowed and Tara whipped her head round to look at him, her face beneath the riding hat split by a happy grin.

In a second he was alongside her.

'I won,' she said, her eyes sparkling.

'You daft woman, what were you playing at?'

'Racing,' she said. 'I wanted to see what it felt like.'

He was at a loss to know what to say. She had given him a real fright.

'Tara, please don't ever do that again. You could have broken your neck.'

'Sorry.' But she didn't look it at all. In fact she looked happier than he'd ever seen her.

After, when they'd returned and settled the horses, he drove her to the pub. They just made the end of lunchtime service and baked potato was all that was left on the menu.

'It's not very grand,' he said as he laid the plates on their table.

'Who cares?' she said and tucked in with more enthusiasm than she'd shown in the restaurant on Saturday night.

'Can I ask you a question?' he said when they'd finished eating.

'You just did.'

He pulled a face. This was serious, something that had been worrying him.

'What are you doing here?' That wiped the smile off her face. 'I mean, why have you packed in your job? I thought a career in the law was all you ever wanted to do.'

She looked at him shrewdly. 'Did Kirsty tell you that?'

'Actually, you did. That evening when I was sick over you. We had a long conversation before I got pissed. There's no reason you should remember.'

'I suppose I told you I was passionate about working in a small criminal practice, down on the front line, making a difference.'

'Something like that.'

She laughed, though there wasn't much joy in the sound. 'I was a first-year student, Rick. I was still idealistic. Working in the real world was entirely different to what I expected.'

He thought about that but he wasn't satisfied. It didn't explain everything.

'What about your father, though? You told me you were going to specialise in criminal law because of him.'

'You've got a good memory.'

Rick didn't necessarily agree with her. But he did know he had a good memory for anything that involved her. And she'd told him that night, as she'd babysat him in the corner of a student house where a party raged, about her father. Jerry O'Brien was a Belfast detective who had spent the final six years of his life paralysed from the neck down as the result of a shooting. A drug dealer's revenge.

Tara had told him that night that her father's lingering death had inspired her to learn about a legal system that pursued the kind of men who had crippled her dad. The way she told it, studying law was not simply an academic option but a vocation. So why had she abandoned it?

'You don't strike me as the giving-up type,' he said. 'Kirsty told me you loved your job. She said you were thrilled with your trainee placement. What went wrong?'

For a moment he thought she was going to tell him to mind his own business.

'You've got to realise,' she said, 'that I've been working as a defence solicitor. Most of my clients are pathetic or stupid, though I never minded that. They are people who find life difficult. Without help the system would chew them up. But I've also found myself working with the kind of people who my dad used to go up against. Being on their side is not so easy.'

'Didn't you think it would be like that?'

'Of course. In theory. And it's important that all sides have fair representation. But the practice is a bit different.'

'So why don't you get a different kind of job in the law? Conveyancing or divorce. Or you could work for the Crown Prosecution Service, couldn't you?'

'Maybe I will. Right now I want a break. You know, time out.'

He grinned. 'Danny time, you mean.'

She shot him a look that was defensive – suspicious. Had he said something wrong?

'Sorry,' he said. 'But I thought that was part of it. You and Danny getting it together.'

'I suppose so,' she said.

The lack of conviction in her voice threw him.

'It's the talk of the yard,' he said. 'There's a few wondering what kind of bridesmaid's dress they'll be forced to wear.'

She looked appalled. 'Surely not.'

No, but he could hardly come straight out and ask her if she was in love with Danny. Though that was the question he really wanted to ask.

Danny would have preferred to go straight home after Clive returned him to the yard but instead he made his way to the farmhouse. His stepfather had called earlier and asked if he'd drop in. Danny had long ago concluded that Adrian ran the family like a business. He liked to pop up unannounced to see if his workers were functioning as required and administer words of encouragement or a bollocking, as he deemed appropriate. The invitation to his study at the farm was the equivalent of a summons to the managing director's office and not to be avoided.

Adrian had a pot of tea sitting on a side table. He knew his stepson's preference at this time of day though he himself was sipping what looked like gin and tonic.

'Well done, Danny,' were Adrian's opening words. So he knew about Danny's winner at Ludlow that afternoon – and so he should. 'Tell me about the race.'

Danny was happy to oblige. It had been a good afternoon, with a couple of the yard's horses running above expectation, capped by a victory in the penultimate race, a two-mile four-furlong novice chase. The horse's owner was a former colleague of Adrian's from the world of advertising. It seemed he'd been on the phone singing Danny's praises – which made Adrian's congratulations even heartier.

'And how's your leg?'

'It was bloody sore to start with but it got a lot better after I won.'

'Tara was rather concerned, so Christine says.'

'Well, you know how women are.' He regretted the words the moment they were out. Tara deserved better. 'Actually, she's been brilliant. Nursed me all through yesterday. It's thanks to her I was able to get out of bed this morning.'

'You like her, don't you?'

Like her? Of course he liked her. He'd brought her to Latchmere to live with him and it was a darn sight more than like. He'd have thought it was obvious how he felt.

Adrian must have read the irritation in his face. He smiled slyly. 'I mean, you're serious about her, aren't you?'

'Yes. Really serious.'

'And how does she feel about you?'

That was the question. One Danny couldn't answer with certainty. He'd not had the nerve to come straight out and ask Tara how she felt about their relationship. He might not like the reply she came up with. Though, to be fair, things were going pretty well at the moment.

Adrian was studying him, waiting for a reply.

'I think she feels the same. But we're just seeing how we rub along together for now. It's a whole new life for her.'

'And she's taking to it rather well. I'm impressed with the way she's stepped into the breach in the office.' Adrian added the remains of the tonic bottle to his glass. 'I expect she'll soon get bored with sorting the post though. It hardly compares to sharpening your wits in a solicitor's practice.'

Danny nodded and said nothing. He knew his stepfather was building up to something.

'Where was it Tara worked before?'

'At a solicitor's in Manchester.'

'I realise that but I'd like the name of the firm. You must know surely.'

He did indeed, but Tara had asked him not to tell anyone, even members of his family. And for his part he was quite happy to obscure any possible connection with Tara's former lover, Tom Ferguson.

192

'I do know, Adrian, but she's sensitive about it. I'm sworn to secrecy.'

Adrian put his glass down with a heavy hand. 'What's all the mystery? I just think if she's here with us, working for the business, for God's sake, I'm entitled to know something about her past. Like where she was working until a few weeks ago.'

'Why don't you ask her?'

Adrian looked sheepish. 'I have and she won't tell me.'

Danny wasn't surprised. Tara knew how to retain her secrets, as he well knew.

'I don't see why it matters,' he said. 'If she's doing a good job, why not leave it at that?'

Adrian gave him a long, cool look. 'It's not just the job. Your mother's worried and so am I. As far as we're concerned, the girl's appeared out of nowhere. We don't want to see you get hurt.'

So it was down to him, was it? Danny resented being made a scapegoat for Adrian acting like a control freak.

He stood up. 'For once in your life,' he said, 'why don't you mind your own damn business?'

Up on the gallops, where the reception could be relied on, Tara tried Duncan for the second time that day. He'd not been in the office earlier but the woman who'd answered said she'd thought he'd be available at the end of the day. She'd offered to take a message but Tara had refused. That's all right, love, the woman had said. They'd had several conversations of this sort by now.

This time she got hold of him.

'Tara.' It was good to hear his voice. 'How are you?'

'I'm safe, if that's what you mean. But there's something you ought to know. My uncle has just been killed in Belfast.'

There was a pause. 'Killed?'

'His name was Des Monaghan. It's been all over the news.'

'The baker?'

'Yes. My Uncle Des.' She found the words were sticking in her throat. 'He was fantastic to me and my mum. My dad was ill for years and he—' She gulped in air and forced herself to get a grip on her emotions. This was the first chance she'd had to talk about Uncle Des and it was like trying to hold that horse today – almost impossible.

'Take your time, Tara. Breathe slowly.'

'I'm sorry.'

'There's no need to be. Just take it slowly.'

'It's just that I'm terrified it's my fault.'

'How can it be your fault?'

'Because . . .' Did she have to spell it out? 'Maybe someone thought he knew where I was. And they shot him to make him say and he had a heart attack.'

'That's putting two and two together and making five.'

'Why else would anyone shoot him? He lived all his life in Belfast without making enemies. He was an elderly man, no threat to anyone, what other reason could there be?'

Duncan thought for a moment before replying. 'Listen to me, Tara. I don't know the details of this case and neither do you, I imagine, beyond what's been reported. There could be many reasons why this unfortunate event befell your uncle. A burglary gone wrong. Maybe someone assumed your uncle kept money hidden in the house and tried to force him to say where. It might have nothing to do with you.'

'And it might.'

'Yes, it might. Let me see what I can find out. I imagine the guys who are investigating the murder will be interested to hear about this.'

'Tell them Des's brother-in-law was a detective in the RUC

for fifteen years.' She didn't know why she said it but it seemed relevant.

'And that would be?'

'Jerry O'Brien. My father.' The tears were back.

'Tara,' he said softly, 'have you got anyone to talk to wherever you are?'

No, she didn't have.

'I'll call again soon, Duncan.' And she broke the connection.

Chapter Ten

Danny wondered where Tara was. The lights were on in the front room and, from the aroma wafting from the kitchen, there was a meal in the oven but the cottage was empty. He chucked his bag into the corner of the bedroom and kicked off his shoes. His leg hurt and he was beat. The bed invited him but he ignored it and trudged back down the stairs.

He sat glumly on the bottom step, all the good humour of his successful afternoon banished by his interview with Adrian and by Tara's absence.

Maybe Adrian was right. Maybe he did need to be protected from this woman who had taken over his life. Tom Ferguson nagged at his mind. What had gone on between him and Tara to send her running to him? Perhaps Tara had only jumped into his arms in an attempt to wipe Ferguson from her mind. It would explain the wall that divided them. She'd been in deep with the solicitor and when it had gone wrong she'd looked for someone else as a replacement. And, though she'd chosen him, it could have been anybody.

A key scraped in the lock and the front door opened to reveal Tara in his old Barbour jacket. Her face was drawn and preoccupied and, for a few seconds, she didn't register him sitting on the stairs.

'Where have you been?' he asked. He didn't mean it to

sound the way it did, as if he wanted her to account for her movements, but that's the way it came out.

'I just went out for some fresh air.'

He knew at once what she had been up to. It was a dark winter's evening, hardly the kind of time you'd choose to go for a walk unless you had a purpose. He'd bet Tara had been up the hill calling Tom Ferguson on her mobile.

'I hear you had a winner,' she said, smiling now and holding out her hand. 'Come and tell me about it.'

He forced himself to keep his jealousy bottled inside as she led him into the kitchen. The table was laid and the smell of roasting chicken was intense. He took the glass of wine she offered him and drank half of it in one go, for once uncaring of the consequences. As she served the food, he answered her questions about the day's racing, feeling himself mellow as he did so, though discontent still gnawed at him.

The irony was that this kind of scene – Tara tending to his needs, happy to see him, looking like she really belonged in the cottage – was exactly what he had imagined when he'd invited her into his home.

Perhaps he'd got it wrong about ringing Tom. She could have been calling Sharon or some other friend and she was quite entitled to do so. Not every woman lived with one man and schemed with another, did they? Would Tara?

'Adrian's been asking about you,' he blurted out. 'He wanted me to tell him where you used to work.'

Her fork stopped halfway to her mouth. Then she put it down. 'When was this?'

'Just now, back at the yard. I got hauled into the headmaster's study.'

Her good humour was gone and the soft light in her eyes had dimmed. 'What did you tell him?' Her voice was chilly.

'I told him to ask you. He said he had and you wouldn't tell him.'

'That's true.'

'Anyhow, I told him to mind his own business.'

She smiled and put her hand over his. 'Did you really? Thanks, Danny.'

A glow of pleasure bloomed in his chest and gave him courage to say, 'You did finish with Tom, didn't you?'

'Tom?' She sounded surprised, as if Danny bringing his name up was the last thing she had expected. 'God, yes. It finished all right.' She squeezed his fingers. 'You don't think I'm still involved with Tom, do you?'

'Of course not.' But that's exactly what he had been thinking. He regretted it instantly.

He grinned happily. His mother and Adrian had got it all wrong about Tara. She really did love him.

Adrian had no intention of letting the mystery of Tara drop. He'd just have to be more devious about it. The fact was, he believed in checking people out. Especially someone who appeared to be setting herself up as his daughter-in-law.

He scribbled down what he knew about Tara. She'd read law at university, starting in 2002, which was when she'd met Kirsty. So she would have graduated in summer 05. Then she'd done some other course for a year, which was obligatory to becoming a trainee solicitor, and finally she'd joined this firm whose identity she was so keen to obscure. All of these things she'd undertaken in Manchester. Surely it wouldn't be that hard to track down someone who knew precisely where she'd ended up.

He started the ball rolling by calling Simon Molloy, the former colleague whose horse Danny had ridden to victory at Ludlow that afternoon. It was a natural extension of their earlier conversation and Adrian knew he was bound to get a good reception.

'I meant to ask you earlier,' he began. 'Do you know anyone connected with the Law School at Manchester University?'

'Not off the top of my head. I know plenty of lawyers though. And I use a couple of directors who started out at Granada TV. Why do you want to know?'

This was the important bit. The story behind the request. It was funny how people went out of their way when they thought they were doing a good turn.

'I don't know if you remember, but Danny's fiancée was killed when they were on holiday in the West Indies about eighteen months ago.'

'Yes, of course I do. A terrible thing.'

'Kirsty, his fiancée, started off doing law at Manchester and made a great friend of a girl called Tara O'Brien. Tara went on and graduated and she's now training to be a solicitor somewhere in the city.'

'And you want to get in touch with her?'

'One of my lads here is selling a property in the Manchester area – his great-aunt passed away – and he asked me if I knew a local lawyer. It's a sort of sentimental gesture but I'd like to put the work Tara's way.'

'OK, I understand. I'll call a couple of people.'

'Don't get anyone to go out of their way, Simon. It's not a big deal.'

Adrian put the phone down with a sense of satisfaction. If this didn't work, he'd think of something else. He'd promised Christine.

Danny had spent enough time mollycoddling himself. He'd got up early to ride out and was now driving himself to Plumpton where he had three rides. The leg felt fine – the painkillers in his system were doing their job. In any case his thoughts were buzzing too much to have room to worry about a few bodily aches.

He'd put yesterday's irritation with Adrian out of his head. Resenting his stepfather would do him no good. Might as well resent the clouds in the sky or the rain that was lashing down. Why beat your head against something you cannot change?

It was a conversation he'd had with his sister just before he left that was upsetting him. She'd told him she'd seen Tara riding on the gallops with Rick.

He felt sick. Each time he thought the way ahead with Tara was plain sailing, something came up to blow him off course. Like this. Every day, it seemed, he had tried to persuade Tara to come out with him and she'd always fobbed him off. So what the hell was she doing riding out with Rick?

Stephanie had given him every detail: Tara had been on Miller's Tale and Rick on Wing.

Tara had not said a word to him about it last night. Had just played the demure little wife and he'd sucked it up. More fool him.

'How do you know so much about what Tara got up to?' he asked.

She'd flushed pink at that. 'I wasn't spying on her if that's what you mean. I happened to be up there myself on Mitzy. And Sara told me that afterwards Rick took her to the pub.'

He'd said nothing, just explored his damaged feelings, as he had done throughout the drive to the racecourse. He parked up and remained sitting in the car in the rain.

Tara had cared for him so sweetly last night. Her concern for his injury, her pleasure at his Ludlow success – those things couldn't have been put on, could they? And the way she'd talked about her old lover, Tom, as if the memory of him repelled her – that couldn't have been assumed. Could it?

And now came this revelation about her going riding with Rick after resisting all his entreaties to do the same. What's more, she'd never mentioned it, as if she'd deliberately gone behind his back and kept it a secret from him.

He was discovering there were many mysteries about Tara and it robbed him of certainty. He'd always sworn to himself that he'd make sure he knew where he stood with his girlfriends, but with Tara he didn't have a clue.

The rain was easing slightly. Time to get changed and focus on the afternoon's first ride. He was confident that his mount, The Optimist, would not let him down. It was funny to think that he had more faith in a half-ton horse with a three-inch brain than he did in a human being.

'Lunch?'

Tara looked up from the papers spread over her desks. She'd been so absorbed she'd not heard Rick open the office door. It had been satisfying to immerse herself in paperwork to the exclusion of all else. Like the old days, she thought. Except that assembling a paper trail of horse-feed consumption hardly compared with crime casework.

'If we get along to the pub now,' Rick added, 'we might get something better than a baked potato.'

She suddenly realised she was hungry. And that it wasn't hunger alone that tempted her to get up and grab her coat.

'Best not,' she said.

He sprawled in the chair opposite her and smiled. He didn't often smile, she realised, which was a shame. It lit up his face. 'And why's that?'

Tara was tempted but their tête à tête had been noticed. Already that morning Sara had gone out of her way to let

Tara know they'd been seen yesterday and immediately she'd felt guilty about it, which was ridiculous. However, she realised she'd forgotten to tell Danny and, given his sensitivity, she mustn't let anything rock the boat. And a second 'secret' lunch would be bound to get back to him. 'Just because,' she said.

'Just because you've gone off me?'

'I've never been on you,' she replied with a little too much snap in her voice, irritated that he was trying to flirt. It was entirely inappropriate. 'Anyway,' she put her hand on the papers on the desk, 'I'm in the middle of something.'

'Looks riveting.' He picked up a bill from the feed merchants, one of many.

'It is, sort of. Christine's worried that there's a discrepancy between the amount of feed we're using and what we've been billed for. Or else some of it is going walkabout. It's a job Jean was doing for her at home.'

'And what's this?' Rick was pointing at a separate pile of documents weighted down by a can of shaving foam. 'You investigating the lads' beard growth too?'

She glared at him, or tried to. He was obviously not intending to leave her in peace.

'Those things belong to Patsy,' she said. 'Jean shoved them all in a carrier bag along with the office stuff. I'll give him a call so he can pick them up.'

Rick picked up the shaving foam, gave it a shake. 'I don't think he'll be bothered about getting this back. It's empty.'

'Rick, I don't want to be rude but I'd like to finish what I'm doing.'

He ignored her, picking something else out of the pile. 'He might need this though.'

That got her attention. Rick was holding up a small maroon-coloured booklet. A passport.

'Don't be nosy, Rick,' she said sharply. 'Put it back.'

'Keep your hair on. It's expired – see, the corner's been clipped.'

'It's still a private document.'

'Oh, come on, don't you want to see what Patsy looked like ten years ago? Bet he's got short back and sides.'

'Rick . . .' She could see it was hopeless telling him to put it down. Anyway, why should she care? She was quite curious to see what Patsy looked like in his youth herself.

Rick was flicking through the pages.

'So,' she said, 'what *did* he look like?'

But Rick said nothing, just stared at the page. He wasn't smiling now.

'Rick?' She was thrown by his abrupt change of mood. 'What is it?'

'Look for yourself.'

He held the passport out to her, open not to the back page photograph but to what appeared to be a visa stamp. She took the booklet and looked at it closely. It was an entry stamp for the British Virgin Islands, dated 12 September 2006.

For a second she thought he was simply undermined by this sudden reminder of his dead sister.

'I'm sorry, Rick. It's always going to be hard, isn't it?'

He glared at her, plainly she'd misunderstood. 'Look'. He jabbed a finger at the passport. 'He was there! He was on the island two days before she was killed!'

Then she got it. As far as she knew – as far as anyone knew – Patsy had not been part of the holiday group in Amana at the time of Kirsty's murder. He'd not been involved in the investigation. He'd been here at Latchmere, minding business at the stud.

But she was holding the proof in her hands that that had not been the case at all.

It didn't make sense.

She stared at Rick. 'Are you sure Patsy didn't go on that holiday too?'

'I know he didn't. I was rather hoping I might get an invitation myself. Kirsty tried to swing it with Adrian but he said there wasn't another room available.'

'Maybe Patsy had the last one.'

He shook his head. 'I'm sure that wasn't it. None of the others ever mentioned Patsy being there. I'll check with Dad. He flew out the moment he got the news. He'll know.'

'There could be a simple explanation.'

'Such as?'

'Well, it could be a coincidence. Suppose he wanted a holiday in the Caribbean too?'

'That's a big coincidence, Tara. And no one's ever mentioned him going there.'

'But he could have been miles away. Amana's just a little island, isn't it?'

'Yes. You fly to the main island, Tortola, and catch a ferry over.'

'So this just proves he was in Tortola, not Amana.'

Rick shook his head. 'It's still weird.'

'He could have gone out there in secret to talk business with Adrian – I bet that's the kind of thing Adrian gets up to. Patsy could have stayed somewhere else. Maybe he just flew in and out for a meeting. And that's why no one else saw him.'

'So suddenly you're defending him?'

'I'm simply looking for an explanation.'

He didn't reply for a moment. 'It was a bit of a holiday week at the yard. Since I hadn't been asked to swan off to the West Indies with Kirsty, I tagged on to a golfing trip to Scotland with a couple of lads. It poured with rain. But it wasn't all bad because that's where I met my mate Hugh.

His wife had let him off for a few days. He was with me when Dad rang to tell me about Kirsty.'

His face was a mask with no trace remaining of his earlier merriment. Tara wanted to reach out and touch it.

Jesus, hadn't she been through this already with Danny?

'Look, why don't we just ask Patsy?' she said. 'I'll do it, if you like. His passport's right here on my desk and I'll tell him, sorry, I'm just a nosy cow. I'm used to asking people awkward questions.'

The mask slipped and he grinned. 'Are you sure you're not defending him?'

'I'm simply trying to establish an innocent explanation.'

'And suppose there's a guilty one?'

'What are you suggesting, Rick?'

He hesitated. 'I'm just saying I want to talk to my father before we mention this to anyone else. He knows all the details of the investigation. After that we can put our heads together.'

'If you like.'

'In the meantime, would it be possible to forget to tell Patsy his stuff is here? Obviously he's not too bothered when he gets it back.'

'OK, but how about a bit of insurance?' She took the passport over to the photocopier and began to scan the pages. 'Just in case Christine has already told him.'

'Good idea.'

In the small room the machine whirred and clattered. She looked out of the window, across the courtyard, seeking out a tall broad figure with a blond head of hair. What would Patsy say if he came in at that moment and found her copying his passport?

She was amazed at herself for even caring.

*

Later, in mid-afternoon, Tara phoned Duncan. His voice was urgent.

'Thank God you've called. I'm putting you in a witness protection programme as of now.'

'No, Duncan.'

'I insist.'

'You can't make me. I suppose this means you've discovered what happened to Uncle Des.'

'I've had a word with the PSNI – the police in Belfast.'

'And?'

'They want to talk to you.'

'So I'm right? Uncle Des was killed because of me?'

'I'm not saying that. But it wasn't a random attack. Your uncle appears to have been targeted. And he had a suspicious visitor at his shop the day he died.'

'Oh God.' Her hand was shaking as she pushed the little phone hard against her ear, desperate to catch every word. 'Go on, tell me what happened.'

'An Englishman came in, had something to eat, asked the waitress to point your uncle out and then spoke to him. They only talked for a couple of minutes but Mr Monaghan looked a bit upset after he left. The waitress asked him if he was OK and he said he'd had a bit of worrying news but didn't elaborate. Apparently he spent the next half an hour on the phone and was a bit grumpy for the rest of the afternoon. That's what the waitress said.'

'He could be grumpy. If he had something on his mind. He didn't mean anything by it.'

'Yes, well, apparently the staff in the shop are devastated by his death. The girl who made the statement was distressed but she was able to describe the Englishman. A bruiser with a shaved head and a northern accent.'

'That should narrow it down,' she said bitterly. She could imagine just the kind of street scum who'd put a bullet in her uncle. She'd defended dozens of them at Gallagher Ferguson.

Maybe even this one.

'There's something else you should know. In the office by the phone was a notepad with a phone number written on it, apparently not in Mr Monaghan's writing. Next to it was your name.'

'What?'

'It just said "Tara", underlined. And that, according to the shop staff, was in your uncle's hand. The investigating team didn't think it had any significance till I mentioned your name. And now, as I said, they're dead keen to talk to you.'

'I can't. Not at the moment.'

'They've got an artist's impression of the English visitor. They'd like your opinion of it. Why don't I set up a meeting? You call the time and place. Everything to suit you.'

She felt terrible. There was nothing she'd like better than to help the Belfast detectives. But, much as she trusted Duncan, she was not convinced it was safe. It wasn't just Tom she was up against. Tom wouldn't have the resources or know-how to send an assassin to Belfast. But Benny Bridges would.

None of this, her sacrifice in abandoning her career, Danny's loving hospitality, Uncle Des's death, would be worth it unless she survived to take the stand in June.

'Sorry, Duncan. I can't risk it.'

He sighed. 'I tried, I suppose.'

'Yes, you did. Do they know I'm in touch with you?'

He hesitated. 'I don't believe I mentioned that.'

'Thanks, Duncan. It's not you that I don't trust, you know that, don't you?'

'Huh.' He didn't sound mollified.

'What did they tell you about what happened at my

uncle's house? They didn't torture him, did they?' It had been preying on her mind. There had been no mention in the news reports of any other injury apart from the gunshot but that might have been just to protect the squeamish. She knew how brutal Benny Bridges' people could be.

'No. There was no indication that he'd suffered beyond the wound to his leg. But there's no telling what they would have done had he not had a heart attack.'

Quite.

'They found a significant amount of blood in the kitchen,' he added. 'Not your uncle's. They think it must have come from whoever killed him.'

'How did that happen?'

'They also found a wooden kitchen mallet, the kind you use to tenderise meat. From the state of it, it looks like your uncle got the first blow in.'

Knowing her uncle, Tara wasn't surprised.

'Hey, Dad.' As usual, it was gone midnight when Rick called his father. 'How's Mum?'

'Doing pretty well. Always busy.'

Rick knew that's how she coped with the loss of her daughter, cramming her days with work and social events, always planning something new, while her recently retired husband sat at home and brooded on what he could not change. Rick and his father had talked about it often enough, though he never raised this disparity in their behaviour with his mother. Kirsty had been her confidante and he was aware he could never fill that breach.

Right now his mother would be tucked up in her bedroom in a medically assisted slumber, the bedside phone turned off. These days she and her husband followed a separate schedule.

'Dad, do you mind talking about the case?'

The case was how his father referred to Kirsty's murder. It was less painful that way, offering the pretence that the slaughter of his daughter could be analysed objectively. That, of course, was the way the schoolmaster had always taught his subject.

'What about it?'

'The couple who found the body –' he chose the word carefully; 'body' was suitably neutral – 'you spoke to them, didn't you?'

'Ron and Maureen Benson,' his father said. 'Very nice people from Chicago. They were on a trip to celebrate their wedding anniversary. I don't think being mixed up in a murder was part of their plans.'

Rick didn't suppose so either. Finding a dead body would ruin any party – though it would help to make the anniversary memorable. He pictured the unknown Bensons recounting their experiences to their friends back home for years to come.

'What did they tell you about the man they saw running away?'

'Just what they said in their statement to the police. I don't think I got anything new out of them. Let me just have a look.'

Rick pictured his father shuffling through the folders he kept on his desk. He had taken notes of all his interviews, which he had then typed up on his Mac and printed out. They formed part of a large file of documentation which he kept in meticulous order, in the manner of the geography projects he'd once demanded from his pupils.

His father found what he was looking for. 'They were very eager to help. Mrs Benson was in tears half the time. Bloody nuisance.'

Rick could imagine how much harder the show of

emotion would have made the conversation for his dad. Though he couldn't help liking Maureen Benson for it.

'They said they were leaving Cliff Tops – that's the bar – to go for dinner in town. Not that it's much of a town, just a street of restaurants and clubs. It was their anniversary night and so they were in a merry mood. I didn't ask but I guess they were a couple of rum punches to the good at that stage. As they came round the bend in the path they saw a man crouching by the sea wall about thirty metres ahead. Well, they didn't say thirty metres but I've measured the distance between the bend and where the body was lying, so I know it was. Almost the moment they registered somebody was there, he saw them, straightened up and walked away very fast. They didn't realise the significance till they got to where Kirsty was lying. They didn't see the body till they were almost on top of it and by then this man was gone.'

'How did they describe him?'

'They said he was a white man and looked like a holiday-maker, not a local. He still had beach clothes on. Shorts and a sun hat. And, of course, a loose shirt, dark blue with a horizontal yellow stripe running round the chest.'

'That's the shirt that was similar to the one the Texan was wearing.'

'Indeed. It was probably exactly the same shirt. They sell them all over the island. They're very common, those are the colours of the island flag.'

'What else did they say?'

'Not much. They hardly saw his face, just for a fraction when he glanced their way. Ron said he was clean-shaven and Maureen agreed though I have a feeling she simply went along with everything her husband said.'

'What do you mean?'

'Well, when I met her she was wearing spectacles. I bet you anything you like that a woman going out on the town for a celebration will leave her glasses at home. She'll want to look her best.'

Rick laughed. The remark was typical of his dad. It had the ring of truth about it though.

'Did they say anything else? Age? Size?'

'Only that he was an energetic-looking fellow. I tried to get them to guess his age but Ron said he could have been anything from twenty to forty-five.'

'That doesn't narrow it down much.'

'No. But they did say he was well-built. Over six foot and athletic. Which made it all the more stupid that the police locked up poor old Larry Gresham.'

'You mean the Texan?'

'Yes. He was only five foot nine with a beer belly. You'd never call him athletic.'

'I see.' Rick reflected for a moment. None of what his father had said had ruled out his suspicions, only confirmed them.

'I told you all this before, son. What's up?'

His father had always known when Rick had something on his mind.

So he told him about the entry stamp in Patsy Walsh's passport.

Chapter Eleven

Gareth Jordan sat patiently in the departure lounge of the airport in Antigua. The moment Rick had told him about Patsy he had decided to go. Maybe it was foolhardy but the thought of doing something had seized him. At last here was something he could do. He had been travelling since the early hours, by train from Shrewsbury, across London to Gatwick and then by air, some nine hours of flying time, and he still had another hour by plane to Tortola. He'd catch the boat to Amana tomorrow.

It was a punishing day's travel, not alleviated by any kind of distraction. He communicated to his fellow travellers as infrequently as he could, this side of rudeness. He read no books or newspapers and ignored the in-flight entertainment. Once, the enforced idleness of this travelling would have maddened him. Now he simply sat and thought.

He thought of the two most important women in his life, his daughter and his wife, one of them dead, the other as good as, in so many ways. Margaret had changed profoundly since the news of Kirsty's murder, as he had too, and these changes had pushed them far apart. Margaret now submerged herself in pointless activity and he did just the opposite, not that this would matter if they had managed to preserve the connection that had held them together for nearly thirty years.

He tried to talk to her as he once had but, unusually for a woman, she was not interested in revealing her feelings. He suspected he knew what they were, however. Unlike him, she'd always been a church-goer but now he doubted if she drew any comfort from religion. Kirsty's murder had demonstrated to her in the most painful way possible that there was no God, that the world was ordained by an impersonal Nature, subject to acts of random cruelty that fell on deserving and undeserving alike. At least, that's how he would have expressed it – and would have liked to express it to Margaret, given the opportunity. But she shut him out whenever he tried to talk about it.

At first he had thought that this change of belief would bring them together in their mutual distress. But the opposite had turned out to be the case. Margaret was a woman who liked to apportion blame and her husband was nearest to hand. He had spent weeks in the West Indies trying to find the truth of their daughter's murder but had come up empty-handed. Worse, he had been instrumental in clearing the name of the chief suspect, an American tourist, and she blamed him for that. She blamed him for giving up his job and indulging himself in fruitless, non-productive speculation on Kirsty's fate. At least if he'd kept on teaching he would have been doing something useful with his days, for the time allotted to you before death was there to be filled with deeds not thought.

As for her disenchantment with her faith, he imagined she blamed him for that too. Though he'd tried hard to respect her devotion, she resented the way, as she no doubt saw it, he had patronised her beliefs and indulged her superstitions. And now, it seemed, she resented him most of all for proving he'd been right all along. And the proof lay in Kirsty's random, Godless murder.

When he'd told Margaret he was making another trip to

the West Indies, she'd scarcely looked up from changing into her heavy-duty shoes preparatory to walking Mrs Elmhurst's dogs. All she'd wanted to know were the details of his schedule. 'Let me know when you're coming back,' were her parting words. So she could adjust the household catering, no doubt.

Gareth took the silent blame his wife levelled at him. He had let her down. How could he have lived with someone for thirty years, formed a successful social partnership with her and brought up two children, and then allowed her to slip beyond his reach when disaster struck? Whatever the arbitrary and unlucky nature of Kirsty's death, the break-down of his relationship with his wife could be laid at his door and he accepted it.

'Cheer up, buddy,' said a man in a floral shirt who'd subsided on to the seat next to him. 'It might never happen.'

Gareth managed a thin smile. As far as he was concerned, it already had.

Tom was immersed in thought when the motorbike cut him up at the lights so he simply put his foot down and prepared to overtake. But the bike refused to pull over. The rider, the usual hulk in leathers, was making some kind of hand signal and looking over his shoulder at Tom. Stupid bastard was going to end up under his wheels which, deserved though it may be, would be a hassle he could do without. He sounded the horn angrily.

The bike swung over into the outside lane, still pointing. Tom was preparing to overtake on the inside when the rider swerved in till he was level with the driver's door, mouthing something – some kind of obscenity, Tom assumed. He jabbed the window button and lowered the glass, about to give this yob the earful he deserved, when he realised the yob was familiar to him. It was Carl.

'Take the next left,' Carl screamed, 'and follow me.'

The bike hovered upside of him till Tom raised his hand in acknowledgement.

He could ignore the instruction but what would be the point of that? He signalled left and obediently turned off the dual carriageway, with Carl's bike leading the way.

The road led through a new housing estate, neatly laid out dwellings of red brick with postage-stamp gardens, every one identical. Then they left the fringe of housing behind and followed a country road. Tom began to worry. If Carl wanted to talk – run a post-mortem on his ill-fated Belfast trip, for example – why on earth didn't he just pull over?

The built-up area was far behind them now and they were heading into the wilds, off the road and up an unpaved track. Tom was becoming increasingly nervous. It didn't look as if anyone ever came along here.

Then they crested a hill and through the trees he glimpsed a road ahead with a stream of traffic flowing along at a fast clip. Two minutes later they were pulling into a gravelled area with a parked-up lorry at the far end and a moss-covered brick building with the word Toilet painted over a rusty metal door. Carl had led him the back way into a lay-by off the main road.

Carl gave him a thumbs-up and parked his bike. Tom ground to a halt by his side and climbed out.

'What on earth is going on?' he began then stopped, the words dying in his throat as Carl removed his helmet.

Tom knew that Carl had suffered an injury at the hands of Des Monaghan but had assumed it was relatively trivial – how much damage could an elderly baker inflict on a hulk like Carl? Plenty, it appeared. His bony skull was puffed up like a melon, a black and purple melon with an angry row of stitching from above his right ear to his cheekbone. Tom wondered how on earth he could bear to wear his helmet.

'Don't say a word,' muttered Carl, catching the look of horror on Tom's face. He pulled a black beanie from his pocket and pulled it over his scalp. It improved his appearance but not by much.

'Why are we here?' Tom asked.

'We wait.'

'What for?'

Carl did not reply. The bang on the head had plainly not improved his mood or his manners.

'I thought you were . . .' Tom reached for the right expression, 'having a break.'

Carl glared at him. 'Two days off, that's all I got. I got mouths to feed.'

So much for Benny's generosity, Tom thought as he got back into his car. He resigned himself to a wait, switched on the radio and tried to pretend he was cool about the situation. He wasn't.

Eventually – it was probably only ten minutes but it felt like twenty – a navy blue Mercedes with tinted windows nosed into the lay-by from the road entrance. Tom knew at once who was inside.

Carl rapped on the window. 'He wants a word,' he said but Tom was already on his way to the other car. Let's get this over with, he thought.

He'd had plenty of meetings with Benny in the past. Formal encounters, mostly, in the early years of their association, followed by happy back-slapping social ones in which, in Tom's eyes anyway, they'd bonded over meals and games of golf and the occasional sunshine weekend at Benny's villa in Majorca. By then they were having certain other meetings, surreptitious ones like this, and Tom could remember the feelings of excitement they'd engendered. Their dealings had appealed to the gambler in him and, with Benny, it seemed he was on a winner every time.

And now here he was stepping into the back seat of a limousine across from his client-cum-friend not to discuss some money-making proposition but the murder of a former colleague and ex-lover. He did not feel like a winner any more.

Benny looked weary, barely able to raise the pretence of charm.

'Got any news for me?' he began.

There was no need for him to spell out exactly what kind of news.

'Not yet,' Tom said. None of the feelers he'd put out had yielded any results. Neither his snitch in the witness protection programme nor his contact at the CPS had been able to point the way to Tara.

'Why doesn't that surprise me?' Benny muttered. He looked straight ahead, at the partition that had been pulled across to seal off the front of the car. Tom had a pretty good idea who'd be sitting on the other side of it, listening to every word no doubt. However, he wasn't sorry not to be looking at Jason's weaselly face.

'Well,' said Benny, turning his pale blue eyes in Tom's direction, 'I've got some news for you, though it's not the sort that's going to cheer anybody up. Your baker friend in Belfast was buried this morning. Lovely do. They dug up a horse-drawn carriage, paraded the coffin on it past his old shop – the way they used to distribute the loaves back in the old days. The Irish, they've got heart, haven't they? Quite chokes you up.'

Tom said nothing. Only silence was required.

'I had a few friends keeping an eye on proceedings. As you can imagine. I'm owed a favour or two after the balls-up they made of it in the first place. Anyhow, guess what they saw?'

'I can't guess.'

'Typical bloody lawyer, won't commit yourself till you know which way the wind's blowing. Well, I'll tell you. Amongst the hundreds of people who stood outside his shop and walked behind the carriage to the church and sang their heads off in the service, there was no one who corresponded to the description of your wandering lady love. No cute little blonde honey with a sexy arse and a two-faced smile. No Tara O'Brien, got me? Sweet Fanny Adams, that's all.'

Tom wasn't surprised to hear it. He'd not seriously expected Tara to show her face, but it was a blow all the same. He could see it was a blow to Benny too.

'Unless we've got extremely lucky, she's out there somewhere, just waiting to drop her little bomb on us. I suppose she could have walked under a bus, or emigrated for good or been struck by lightning, but I don't believe in that kind of luck. Do you?'

Tom didn't, though there was no need for him to say so. Benny was not a man you interrupted, even if you had something worth saying.

'So, my friend, I'd like to know exactly how you are going to find this girl because it's as plain as Dolly Parton's tits we're going to have to arrange the lightning strike ourselves.'

As soon as he'd finished his supper Rick headed for his room, making his excuses to the Turners. Young Freddy was angling for a bedtime story which Rick sometimes supplied. But not tonight.

His mind was on his father, flying out to the British Virgin Islands. Where was he now? Rick wondered. He was scheduled to arrive in Tortola at 9p.m. local time, which was four hours behind GMT. So he couldn't hope to hear from him much before two or three in the morning. His father wouldn't call him at that time, he knew. He'd have to wait until tomorrow.

He felt restless. He could go down to the pub, look up some of the old faces he used to carouse with. But that didn't appeal. Individually, he liked those lads but to go out drinking with them as he used to seemed like taking a step back in time.

But he didn't have to go out in a group. He could call Stephanie. Apologise to her for being a bit stand-offish and buy her a few drinks. If he was lucky, she'd appreciate that. If he wasn't, she'd see it as more than an attempt to rekindle their old friendship. He'd always liked Stephanie, but not in the way she liked him. To take her out just because he was bored and restless might set a few hares running. What was the point in asking for trouble?

He could try Patsy. The Irishman had been friendly enough last week. But how could he face him across a pub table, knowing his father was heading off to the West Indies specifically to check on his movements? He'd be tempted to ask questions he shouldn't, such as, why have you got a BVI entry stamp in your passport for the time of my sister's murder?

And why had he? Rick had been turning it over in his mind ever since he'd got his father excited about the discovery. On reflection, he was inclined to think there had to be an innocent explanation and the way to discover it was to ask the Irishman to his face. Instead, he'd managed to send his father four thousand miles, armed only with a couple of emailed photographs of Patsy and some half-baked suspicions. He should have known his father would jump at the chance. Once he'd thought of the idea, there would be no deflecting him.

Rick was feeling bad about the whole thing. His mother wouldn't approve of his father playing detective and the expedition wouldn't be cheap. He'd send Dad a cheque to help towards the cost, but that was hardly the point. Knowing his father, he'd refuse to bank it.

But it was too late to air his reservations now. It was the only thing on his mind and there was no one to share it with. Except Tara. That was who he really wanted to see. He'd call her right now if he could. But she was at home with Danny.

Out of his reach.

Gareth spent the night near the airport and caught the first boat in the morning. To his surprise he'd slept like the dead, six hours of uninterrupted, dreamless slumber, probably the longest period of rest he'd enjoyed since the loss of his daughter. It felt like a gift and he was grateful for it. Now he stood at the rail of the ferry and looked ahead to his destination, rounded hills of olive green rising from a sea of piercing aquamarine. The fantasy island of Amana. As they drew closer he could make out the ribbon of beach that joined sea and land, almost white under the subtropical sun. He could understand why Adrian Spring had chosen to bring his family on holiday here year after year. It was a paradise location created to an adman's specification.

A young couple stood next to him along the rail, their arms around each other's waists, plainly thrilled by the prospect ahead. He'd noticed them on the flight from London to Antigua. He felt like saying to them, 'It's not as idyllic as it looks,' but he edged away and held his tongue. He wasn't here to spoil anyone else's dreams.

Kirsty had been impressed with Amana, as any first-time visitor would be, yet he knew she'd not been entirely seduced. Their last conversation had taken place shortly after her arrival on the island. He'd waited his turn to talk to her across the kitchen table from Margaret, picking up clues from one side of their conversation. 'So,' he'd said when his wife had passed him the phone, 'it's paradise on earth, is it?'

'Oh God, Dad, you wouldn't believe it – well, you would. You'd be out there taking soil samples and noting plant species.'

'I wish I was there to do it.'

'I wish you were too because I need someone like you to tell me it's real.'

'What do you mean?'

'It's too perfect. Like it's a film set. You're the only one who'll understand this, Dad, but it's just a teeny bit creepy.'

He thought of that conversation now as the boat nosed its way to the jetty through the placid blue water. He wished he could have it over again, just to savour the sound of his daughter's husky, mischievous voice. But it was gone, now a fragment of memory that he hung on to and replayed as a souvenir of their last contact.

Kirsty had not been an easy girl to bring up, and she'd pushed every boundary she could. In some respects he and Margaret had been far too conventional for a rebellious young lady like her. There had been many scenes of conflict and many nights of tears and door-slamming. Margaret had been distraught, had demanded discipline and curfews and, above all, that Gareth back her up with a heavy hand. But Gareth had trusted his judgement, had bent and swayed and relied on negotiation. He had taken the long view with Kirsty and he'd been proved right. They'd all come through stronger and better for the experience.

Then fate had stepped in and robbed Kirsty of her life.

So maybe Gareth had not been right after all. Suppose he'd driven all the mischief out of his daughter as Margaret had demanded, would she have ended up murdered on a paradise island? Until he'd spoken to Rick the other night he would have dismissed the idea as absurd. How could Kirsty's behaviour have been in any way responsible for her random butchery?

But he was here to discover if Patsy Walsh, Adrian Spring's right-hand man and well known to his daughter, was here secretly at the time of her death. He didn't want to speculate at this point. First he had to gather soil samples, as his daughter might have put it. But there was one other fact he knew which made it hard to curb his imagination. A fact which he had deliberately concealed so far because he hadn't seen how it could be relevant.

He hated to think how that knowledge would devastate his wife, for he knew the pain it caused him. It lay at the heart of his daily grief. He wondered how much longer he could in conscience keep Kirsty's last secret.

Adrian's call to Simon Molloy was returned just when he was thinking it had not paid fruit.

'Finally tracked your girl down,' said Simon Molloy. 'Sorry it took so long.'

'Three days isn't long. Anyhow, I'm most grateful. What's the story?'

'She's a trainee at some outfit called Gallagher Ferguson. A friend of somebody's junior used to share a flat with a Manchester law grad and he looked your Tara up on an alumni site.'

Adrian took the details down with relish.

'I owe you one, Simon.'

'No, you don't, I owed you and your clever missus, remember? But if you'd like to arrange another visit to the winner's enclosure next time I have a runner, I shan't complain.'

Adrian replaced the phone, well satisfied. It was tempting to call Gallagher Ferguson straightaway. But he had a better idea. He had a longstanding invitation to visit a stud outside Chester to look at a mare.

He could kill two birds.

It didn't take Gareth long to unpack. He had no clothes to speak of and his most significant items of luggage were papers and a laptop. Despite catching the early boat, it was now past midday, as Isaac, the proprietor of the Arcadia Beach Rooms, had insisted on sitting him down for a welcome cold beer. One beer had turned into two, accompanied by Isaac's famous – so he said – piri-piri omelette. It was the first food that might be recognised as such that Gareth had eaten for well over twenty-four hours.

The moment he had decided to return to Amana he had called Isaac to see if his old room was available. It wasn't. He had stayed in the Arcadia for ten weeks in the autumn of 2006 but now it was high season and packed. However, Isaac had promised to find a corner for him somewhere. The corner in question was barely big enough to hold a bed and a wardrobe but it had a magnificent sea view – but then all views of the sea on Amana were magnificent.

'Have you ever seen this man?' he'd said to Isaac when that gentleman had sat at his table. And he'd shown him the photographs of Patsy Walsh that Rick had emailed him and which he'd printed off before he'd left home. There were just two. One had been cropped from a recent shot of Patsy at Wincanton with a horse which, so he gathered, Rick had ridden to a second place; the other was taken from the website of the Latchmere Park stud. Gareth had higher hopes of a match from the second of these. The Wincanton photo showed a man with wild blond hair blowing in the wind, and a winter chill in his cheeks. It was hard to imagine him transported to these balmy surroundings. The other shot, however, was cropped in tight to his features, showing a broad brow and firm chin, an unembarrassed smile and wide-spaced glittering blue eyes. It was a good likeness and he hoped that someone might remember Patsy.

Unfortunately Isaac didn't. He looked long and hard and sucked his teeth. 'This is to do with your daughter, right?'

'It's been eighteen months since she was killed and no one has been charged. I'm still looking even if no one else is.'

Isaac nodded, then picked up the photographs. 'I assume you have more of these.'

'It's about all I packed.'

'Then I'll put them up behind the bar. Good-looking guy – some of the girls might remember him. And if you give me more I'll get them shown in other places, too.'

'Thanks, Isaac.'

'Don't thank me. Your daughter's death was a scar on the community. We feel it. Besides, if we've still got a killer on the loose, it's bad for business.'

But business didn't look like it was suffering, Gareth thought, as he surveyed the many boats in the bay, the hordes on the beach and the laughter from the bar. Tourists came and went and the probability was that Kirsty's murderer had long gone too. It no doubt accounted for the fact that no one had been charged with the crime. He gathered from his regular calls to Superintendent Edwards that there was little prospect of finding the person responsible at this late stage. What depressed Gareth was that no one was even looking. It was down to him.

He had considered hiring a private detective last time but the only candidate had not impressed him. 'Bit of a looker,' the man had said as he'd examined the photographs of Kirsty that Gareth had handed him. 'Did she like to party?'

It was an attitude that had reminded him of the police investigation, where it had been assumed that the murder was the result of a flirtation that had gone wrong.

'Girl like that cosies up to a guy, gets a few free drinks, then doesn't want to pay for them. Don't worry, we've got the guy.'

Only they hadn't. They'd simply got a guy who was wearing the same shirt.

Gareth booted up his computer. One of the reasons he had ended up at Isaac's in the first place was that it had an internet wireless connection. He logged on and, amongst the junk, found an email from Rick hoping he'd arrived safely. Gareth felt a stab of guilt. He'd not called as he'd promised.

He customarily felt guilty about his son. He'd tried hard not to favour one child over the other and thought he'd succeeded. But Kirsty's death had skewed the equation. He'd devoted so much mental energy to his dead daughter he permanently felt as if Rick had been neglected. But Rick was a grown man, not a boy, making his way in a tough world. He never forgot that he'd opposed Rick's riding ambitions and he'd been wrong. Now he thought about it, Rick had proved he had a mind of his own many years ago.

Gareth acknowledged the email and promised to call later, though he doubted his son would be looking at his computer before he spoke to him. It was late afternoon in England. He'd be riding or driving back from a meeting. Gareth hoped he'd had some luck.

There was one more message of note in his in-box. He'd emailed the Bensons, the unlucky tourists who had discovered Kirsty, and attached the photos of Patsy. Could this be the man you saw fleeing the body? he'd asked.

The answer was no, though Ron Benson had phrased his reply carefully. 'I'm sorry to tell you that neither Maureen nor I recognise the man whose pictures you have sent. But, as we have always maintained, the circumstances were such that it would be very hard for us to identify anybody.' In other words, it might be him but I couldn't say so.

Gareth had also emailed the photos to Larry Owens, the Texan tourist who had been initially charged with the murder, but there had been no response from him. Gareth was not much surprised.

Danny was an early bird, good at getting out of bed at first light, eager to get on with the day. He reckoned he'd inherited the knack from his mum. Whatever the reason, he'd always been grateful – it made being a jockey a darn sight easier. Today, however, he'd been reluctant to crawl out of bed. His leg was stiff and he resented the recumbent form of Tara, dozing beneath the duvet. She opened an eye and offered to make him some tea which, on reflection, was more than Kirsty had ever done first thing in the morning. She'd hated early starts but he'd never had hard feelings about that. He'd taken Kirsty just as she was, a force of nature whom he loved without reservation.

This feeling of discontent had hung around him all day, poisoning his early-morning work on the gallops and making for an ill-tempered drive to Newbury as he swore at every other motorist and seethed at the tiniest hold-up on the way. Today he had been riding for Tracy Evans, a local trainer and not one of his regular patrons but a friend of Christine's. He suspected that it was the connection to his mother rather than his own horsemanship that had earned him the job. This would not have mattered had his two rides gone better. But his runner in the novice chase had obstinately pulled to the right on the left-handed track, then he'd mistimed his finish on the other horse, finishing like a train in second. 'Another twenty yards and you'd have reeled him in,' Tracy said as he dismounted. He'd taken it as a justified criticism.

The fact was that his thoughts of Tara were eating away at him, putting him out of sorts. He had been waiting for her to tell him that she had been out riding with Rick – she'd had plenty of opportunity – but so far she'd not mentioned it. In fact she'd been particularly secretive. The evening before he'd quizzed her about her day in the office and she'd changed the subject quickly. She was getting on OK, the work was different enough for her to find the doing of it absorbing but it wasn't interesting enough to discuss over supper. How was his leg? And how had he managed at Plumpton on that horse he fancied for Cheltenham?

At first he'd been pleased she was interested in talking about racing and he'd happily answered her questions, dwelling in particular on the promising performance of The Optimist, who'd come in second without being ridden into the ground. Christine said he would have a chance at Aintree.

Now he thought about it, Danny reckoned Tara had only been talking in this way to humour him. He didn't like being patronised.

'Hi, Danny.'

A small figure, well wrapped in a bright yellow parka and a scarlet scarf, had appeared by his side as he made his way back to the weighing room. For a moment he didn't recognise her, though it was common for race-goers to claim familiarity with riders. Unlike some, Danny didn't mind. Then he realised who it was.

'Jean! What are you doing here?'

She pushed the scarf back from her face, releasing a wayward lock of auburn hair, and smiled at him. 'Gosh, it's so good to see you. Are you all missing me?'

He didn't really know what to say to that. Tara had

usurped her seamlessly, though it would hardly be tactful to say so.

'Of course,' he said. 'It's a shame we never got a chance to say a proper goodbye.'

Her full red lips turned down for a moment. 'I think I was a bit silly. My dad told me I was a baby for running away.'

Danny didn't want to get into any of that. 'So what are you up to now?'

'I did a couple of days in an estate agent's in Swindon but it was horrible so I packed it in. I'm here to see who I can chat up, to be honest. I want a job like I had with you.'

Danny felt a pang of sympathy for her. He'd go mad in an office too, without the chance to ride out.

'Well, if I come across anyone I'll put in a word for you. And I'll make sure Mum gives you a good reference.'

Her eyes glittered and she threw her arms round him in gratitude. As he carried on his way, he reflected that it would be nice if his girlfriend could give him a hug like that.

Chapter Twelve

It seemed an age since Adrian had been to Manchester – he'd not been back since Kirsty's death. Even the city centre seemed unfamiliar, though that could hardly be the case. He guessed it was just the way he looked at things in the light of then and now. In the rosy glow of 'before', when Kirsty had been in residence and he would drive over to lunch with her at the newest restaurants, the city had seemed awash with colour and teeming with life. But now it was drab and dull, decidedly 'after'.

The dreary urban landscape that surrounded the office of Gallagher Ferguson didn't help. It stood on the corner of two soulless shopping streets, three doors up from a bookmaker's. To Adrian's eye the white and red lettering on the glass frontage proclaimed estate agent or employment agency rather than a centre for legal advice. He wondered how Tara had felt turning up here every day. Maybe nothing more complicated than aversion to urban blight had caused her to pack in working on this spot.

The furnishings in the reception area were new but cheap, already tarnished. The receptionist looked similarly careworn as she listened to a caller and deliberately, so it seemed, refused to register Adrian's presence. It was certainly a far cry from the kind of lawyer's office he was accustomed to. But maybe, he reflected, if he was a local kid on a charge for theft or vandalism or GBH it would be the sort of place he'd choose to go for representation. He'd bet most of their clients were on Legal Aid.

'Can I help you?' The phone call had ended and he had the receptionist's attention.

Adrian asked to speak to the senior partner. No, he did not have an appointment but he was prepared to wait. He handed over his card, which she regarded with distrust; plainly his name and reputation were not known in this sphere.

'May I ask what this is in connection with?'

He was tempted to say that he was thinking of bunging a million-quid brief their way just to see what reaction he got but instead said, 'It's regarding Tara O'Brien. I believe she used to work here.'

The woman kept a poker face but she couldn't hide the widening of her pupils as he mentioned the name.

'Perhaps you know her?' he added but she'd got her surprise under control and gave a nervous shake of her head as she asked him to wait a moment and headed through an adjoining door, where he could hear her engage in a muffled phone conversation. She returned to say that she was sorry but Mr Gallagher was in a meeting at present but the other partner, Mr Ferguson, was available for a short consultation. Her manner had softened considerably and Adrian wondered if perhaps Mr Ferguson had recognised his name.

A matter of seconds later, as Adrian was considering whether to have another go at the woman about Tara, a tall fellow with floppy dark hair appeared from the back of the building.

'Mr Spring.' He seemed delighted to see Adrian, offering a broad smile and a firm hand. 'Tom Ferguson. Please come through.'

Adrian followed Ferguson up the narrow stairs. He couldn't help noticing that the other man's suit was well-cut and pricey. Maybe the general appearance of this little firm was deceiving.

He took a seat across a chipped and well-worn desk and declined coffee. He was conscious that he was interrupting this affable solicitor's morning, not to mention intruding on time that was billable.

But Ferguson seemed in no great hurry to move him on.

'How can I help you, Mr Spring? Or have you appeared in my office to hand out some hot tips for Cheltenham?'

So he had been recognised and his host was a racing man – that explained a few things. He must have spotted Adrian's name in association with Latchmere. It was funny how often his racing connection, rather than his millionaire adman past, opened the doors he wanted to walk through.

Tom's day had turned from dark to light in a matter of moments. The last meeting with Benny had been grim. He'd come into the office that day simply out of habit. The work he had to do was of no significance – Jack had removed him from contact with clients and he was functioning simply as a clerk. He felt his days of freedom were slipping away in meaningless toil and domestic hassle. The call from Elaine in reception had interrupted the blackest mood of his life.

He'd nearly told her to get lost. He had no stomach for talking to some character off the street no matter how smooth an operator – Elaine's description – he appeared to be. What would be the point? He couldn't take on any new clients in his current situation. Then Elaine had told him that this Mr Spring was inquiring after Tara.

When he'd met him – about thirty seconds later, he was that eager – the penny had dropped. Adrian Spring, the

233

advertising guy who'd married his way into racing and was a big-wheel philanthropist, angling for a knighthood, so it was reported. In the days before his troubles it would have been a privilege to sit down with the bloke.

He'd thrown in the line about Cheltenham just to let Spring know he'd recognised him but the fellow had taken it as an invitation to bang on about his wife's horses. In days gone by, Tom would have been thrilled; now he listened with mounting impatience.

Eventually Spring said, 'But I mustn't take up your time. I've come to inquire about a young lady who used to be employed here. Tara O'Brien.'

At last. Tom did his best to hide his burning curiosity. 'Tara was a trainee here until recently. We're all very disappointed she left us.'

'Why did she decide to do that?'

Now they were getting down to it, the trading of inform-ation, and he was determined to get the better of the bargain.

Also, he had to bear in mind that Spring could well have a hidden agenda. Had Tara put him up to this? Was he wearing some kind of recording device in the hope that Tom was going to incriminate himself? No, that was ridiculous, surely.

'Before we continue, Mr Spring, I think it would be best if you told me your connection to Tara. I'm sure you understand that as a firm we have a duty of confidentiality towards our former employees.' That was pretty much bullshit in Tom's eyes but it sounded plausible. At any rate, Spring appeared to swallow it.

'Quite right. Well, Tara has come to work for us at my wife's yard and naturally I am wondering why she should exchange a promising career in the law for the humdrum duties of our office secretary.'

234

The news was astonishing. Could he take it at face value? He played for time.

'Is she doing a good job?'

'Absolutely excellent. She doesn't know the horseracing world, but she seems to be picking things up very fast.'

That was no surprise. Tara, as he knew to his cost, was nothing if not a quick study.

'So you just want to satisfy your curiosity about her?'

'Yes. It's customary for new employees to submit a reference from their last employment and she does not have one.'

Tom played it straight. 'She can come to us any time and we will be happy to supply one. She was a diligent and conscientious employee.'

Spring pulled a wry grin. 'She doesn't want to have any contact with you at all. I'll be frank, she wouldn't approve of me coming to see you, but I think I'm entitled to know why she left here in such a hurry. She could have been fiddling the books.'

Tom chuckled, his good humour almost genuine. Could it be that this man was telling him the truth? There had to be more to it.

'I can put your mind at rest. There is no suggestion that Tara behaved dishonestly while she was in employment here.'

'So why the mystery? Why did she pack in a good career? And why did she try and conceal from me the name of your firm? Off the record, Mr Ferguson, what went on?'

Tom considered his reply. It was time to give a bit and see what else came out into the open. In any case, he was fed up with playing it by the book.

'What went on, Mr Spring, was that she was having an office affair that came to a sticky end. The other party was married and when he refused to leave his wife she lost the plot. She accused the guy of unprofessional conduct and other unfounded slanders and quit the office. We haven't seen her since.'

Spring nodded, taking the information in, though not looking all that surprised. 'I see. Thank you for your candour.'

'I'd be interested to know how she comes to be at your yard.'

'My stepson arrived with her – almost out of the blue. She's his girlfriend.'

Tom was amazed at the weight of these words, as if he'd been punched over the heart. He'd been so busy hating Tara for her betrayal and the threat she posed that he'd forgotten how he'd once cared for her. The roots of their attachment must have grown deeper than he'd thought.

'Your stepson?'

'You might know of him. He's a jockey. Danny Clark.'

'Is it serious?' he asked.

'She's living in his cottage and working in the yard. It's been some weeks now. I'd have to say that the answer looks like yes.'

'So, Mr Spring –' maybe it was a cheek to come right out and say it but Tom reckoned he had now discovered his visitor's hidden agenda – 'you're not just checking out an employee but a possible new member of the family.'

Spring did not deny it.

So far Gareth had not had much luck. He'd spent his time trawling the shops and bars around Amana's three west-side beaches, places where, he calculated, Patsy must have shown his face – if he'd been there at all, of course. People had been pleasant and happy to accommodate him – dropping Isaac's name was a help – but a lot of tourists had passed through in eighteen months. Nobody had recognised the face in his photographs.

This hasty dash to the island, a spur-of-the-moment decision inspired by Rick's phone call, now seemed ill-judged.

But trying still counts, Gareth said to himself. Fruitless though his efforts may be, he owed it to Kirsty to do something.

He turned to his laptop. He had a message from Larry Owens.

'Dear Gareth,' it said, 'sorry it's taken a while to get back to you but I've been turning your email over in my mind. It brought back a heck of a lot of things I've been working hard to forget. My little vacation to Amana back in 2006 just about derailed my life and I'm only now getting back on track. I lost my job what with being away so long. Being locked up in a jailhouse on suspicion of murder didn't help either. Of course, some folks here still think I'm guilty. But I've always been conscious that I owe my liberty to you and not the police.

'Anyway, I was talking it over with my wife last night. That's right, my wife. We've been married for four months and ten days. I met her just after I got back from the BVI and I never would have met her if I hadn't been through hell and back because she came to interview me from the TV station about my experience on a so-called paradise island. When the show went out I got a lot of people ringing and being nice to me and one of them got me to try for a job at his pharmaceutical company and I've been working there ever since. So, me being accused of murder was the worst of times in my life but has led to the best of times. Talking to Marianne made me realise that.

'And when Marianne learned about your email she insisted I get back to you right away. All this stuff I've written here is to just to explain why I've been so long and where I'm coming from. But you're a good man and a sight wiser than me so you can figure it out.

'Anyhow, to get to it, I do recognise the picture you sent me. Me and Dave were sitting in a bar across from the beach just after lunch on the day your daughter was killed. I swear this character was in there too. He was wearing dark glasses and a sun hat – and the same shirt as me. Yeah, that shirt and I reckon he's the reason it caused me so much trouble. Dave thought me and him wearing the same shirt was funny and we tried to have a laugh with him. But he wasn't playing, he just hid behind a newspaper he must have read twice over.

'I'm sending your email on to Dave to see what he thinks and I'll get back to you with what he says.

'Finally, I've got to say that the last thing I want to do in the world is to think about any of this stuff or talk to any more police or, God forbid, go anywhere near the Caribbean ever again. But if it would help convict the man who killed your daughter I would get on the first plane to the BVI in the morning. Like I said before, I owe you and I haven't forgotten how much.

'Larry.'

Gareth read the message twice before he allowed himself to smile. Finally he'd got the confirmation he was seeking though the irony was that he'd had no need to fly four thousand miles to get it.

He began to pack. He should be able to get to Antigua in time for the night flight to London. Before he shut down the computer he sent a short message to Rick to say so. But the big news – Larry's mail – he'd save until he could talk to his son face to face.

Tom knew that the visit of Adrian Spring had been a lucky break. It was ironic that after all his dealings with Benny and his dismal cronies like Carl, the phone calls and promises of bribes to stooges and narks who sniffed around the police and the CPS, what had turned the tide in Tom's favour was a pillar of society like Spring. He'd walked in off the street and laid a gift at Tom's feet. A gift summarised on the little white rectangle lying on Tom's blotting pad – Adrian Spring's business card with all his contact numbers and the address of his equine estate at Latchmere Park where, with any luck, Tara O'Brien was hiding from her fate.

As Spring rose to leave, they both agreed not to take their exchange of information any further, given its sensitive nature. Tom had no need to put his official statement of Tara's suitability as an employee into writing, and Adrian would not be telling Tara about his visit to Gallagher Ferguson.

'Knowing Tara,' Tom added gratuitously, 'she'd be furious if she found out you'd gone behind her back.'

'Don't worry, I've no intention of looking like some control freak. The last thing I want to do is fall out with such a pretty young woman.' He eyed Tom closely and added, 'The fellow she was involved with, does he still work here?'

Did he suspect the fellow was Tom himself?

'He does. He was greatly wounded by her allegations of misconduct but he's come to terms with it now. I believe he wishes Tara all the best for the future – but you'd better not tell her that.'

'Understood.'

They shook hands and Spring's pale grey eyes bored into his. Tom had no doubt the other man took him for Tara's former lover. In which case they'd both come out of this meeting a lot wiser.

In fact, things couldn't have been better but for the last-minute arrival of Jack Gallagher. His chubby face was puffed as he burst into the room. He must have run down the stairs from his office.

'Sorry, I've been tied up but I couldn't resist the chance to say hello to such a distinguished visitor.' And he held out his hand. 'Jack Gallagher, senior partner.'

Naturally Jack wanted to know why Adrian had dropped in and Tom had to dance quickly to make sure Jack sang from the same hymn sheet. But Jack had no desire to go into the details of Tara's departure or to reveal that she was scheduled to be the chief witness in the trial of his partner for perverting the course of justice.

Together they saw the former advertising mogul off the premises.

'So he came all this way just to get a reference for Tara?' Jack was still a bit behind the play.

'In a sense. The real reason is that she's having a fling with his son. He's checking her out for the daughter-in-law stakes.'

'Really?' Jack looked shocked. 'She doesn't let the grass grow, does she?' He laid a meaty hand on Tom's shoulder. 'You're not upset about this, are you?'

'It's fine, Jack.'

'Well, at least we know where she is now. Perhaps in her new circumstances she might be less hell-bent on getting back at you. She may be more amenable to dropping those charges.'

'I'll get to work on it right now.'

'Good man.'

Tom had trouble getting past Jason to talk directly to Benny.

'What's his new number?' he asked. Benny regularly changed his phones.

'Not at liberty to divulge. At any rate, not to you.'

'I'm his solicitor, for God's sake.'

'Not any more, you're not. A solicitor who's up on a charge is not good for Benny's business image. If you want Benny you've got to go through me.'

'Jason, you're a prick.'

'I hear nice things about you too, Mr Ferguson. So, did you wish me to pass on a message?'

'Jesus.' For a few seconds he considered telling Jason where to stick it. But this was too important. 'Tell him I know where she is.' And he rang off.

Benny himself called back ten minutes later.

'Where is she?'

'She's working as a secretary in a racing yard in Lambourn.'

'What? Horseracing?'

'Yes. She's moved in with a jockey.'

Benny hooted unpleasantly. 'So she's swapped a long streak of piss for a short-arsed rider?'

Tom remained silent. Sometimes the man behaved like a child. A dangerous child.

'Go on, where is she then?'

'It's called Latchmere Park. Quite a large estate owned by Adrian Spring. There's a stud and the training yard. Tara is working in the yard office, apparently.'

'Apparently? You don't know for sure.'

'I'm pretty certain. My information comes from Spring himself.'

'He's the guy who made millions in advertising, isn't he?'

'Correct.'

'That's a good racket, if you ask me. There's more than one way to take people to the cleaners in this world. So what's the jockey's name?'

'Danny Clark. He's Spring's stepson.'

'Never heard of him. The first thing we'd better do is check that she's really there.'

'I know she is.' He'd called the Latchmere yard. He'd recognised her voice before he'd cut the connection.

'Well,' continued Benny, 'you'd better leave it with me for the moment.'

Tom broke off the call. He'd done it. With luck, he was now off the hook.

He ought to feel nothing but relief. Instead he just felt sick.

Rick drove into Lambourn feeling the effects of four rides at Newbury. He'd not had the chance to talk to his father since he'd flown in that morning from Antigua. Mrs Turner was putting him up for the night.

He found his father helping Tim, the elder Turner child, with his maths homework.

'If you've got any geography to do,' Rick said to Tim, 'he's not bad at that.'

After a quick supper with the Turners, Rick proposed a walk.

'What did you find out?' he asked as they stepped outside.

'To be honest,' Gareth said, 'it was a bit of a fruitless visit.'

'But you circulated the photos, didn't you?'

'I did. People were good to me. Isaac was a big help. I must have visited every bar and restaurant along the west coast. If your friend Patsy paid a visit he'd get a shock – his photograph is on display everywhere.'

'Did anyone recognise it?'

Gareth shook his head. 'There's still a chance. People come and go all the time. Isaac will be in touch if something comes up.'

Rick felt deflated. 'I suppose it's a lot to expect people to remember eighteen months back. I'm sorry, Dad, for wasting your time.'

To his surprise, his father smiled at him. 'Don't be sorry. I only said it was fruitless in some respects. Going back made me look again at a lot of things. One of them was you, Richard.'

'How do you mean?'

'I've been trying to protect you from what I found out on my first visit. I thought you weren't mature enough to handle it. And, as you've probably noticed, I've put my foot in it with your mother. I don't seem to get it right. I told her too much and you too little.'

Rick was alarmed. What did his father mean? He'd noticed that his parents lived separate lives these days but he'd put that down to the strain of living with the murder of their daughter.

'How have you upset Mum? And what is it you should have told me?'

His father sat down on a bench.

'Let me explain.'

Rick was silent as they walked back to Mrs Turner's. He had a lot to take in. His father had given him far more detail of his first visit to Amana after Kirsty's death, including his visit to the local jail to talk to Larry Owens and his subsequent interview with the British police which had ended with him arguing the case for Owens' innocence. And earning the disapproval of his mother. He had not realised that was the cause of the distance that had grown up between them.

His father had also recounted the frustrations of the past few days as he'd travelled the length of the happy holiday island on a trail that had long grown cold. 'They were kind to me,' Gareth said, 'but most of them put that photo up just to get me out of their hair. They pitied me.'

'Did you go back to the police?'

'The new assistant commissioner gave me ten minutes. He was very polite and apologised in a roundabout way for the failure of the investigation. He believes Kirsty was murdered by another tourist who has long gone and is out of their reach.'

'That's probably true.'

'Indeed. I asked him if it was possible to check the immigration records for the period of her death for Mr Walsh's name.'

'But we know Patsy flew to Tortola then, it says so in his passport.'

Gareth shrugged. 'True. Anyway, I haven't heard anything yet. This is old business for them. There've been other murders since then. Drug shootings, or so they think. There's a worm in every apple, son.'

Rick wasn't sure he wanted to agree with such a gloomy view but he pondered it all the same as they returned home.

Now, in the little room at the top of the house, Gareth started his computer. 'I want you to look at something.'

They watched the small screen flicker through its start-up sequence.

Gareth said, 'Though it was good for me to get off my backside and get out of the house, as it turns out I could have got the information we want if I'd never set foot out of doors. Read that.' He indicated that Rick should sit at the small table in front of the computer, which was now displaying the text of an email.

'It's from Larry Owens,' Gareth added unnecessarily.

'Good Lord,' Rick murmured as he read the message. It was what he had been hoping for, a positive sighting of Patsy on Amana at the time of Kirsty's death, but the implications were daunting.

'There's more. Larry heard back from his friend and forwarded it.'

His father changed the page to another email.

'Hi Larry. Bit of a shock to get this but tell Gareth Jordan I reckon I can ID the guy in the photo as the one in the Thunderclap bar on Amana. He was wearing the same stupid shirt as you and we kept bugging him because we were a bit merry – about the last time I was merry till Thanksgiving just gone, to tell the truth. I don't think he was shy or surly or anything but he just had other things on his mind. Given what happened later, I think we can guess what that might have been.

'As I remember, he hardly said a word. "No thanks" "I'm fine" – that kind of thing. But he didn't sound American. English maybe? Another thing, the Thunderclap is right across the road from the holiday village where Kirsty Jordan was staying. Maybe that guy was staking her out. Would make sense, wouldn't it? Take care of yourself. Dave.'

Rick turned to look at his father who was sitting on the bed behind him.

'Patsy killed her, didn't he?' he said.

'Possibly.'

'Come on, Dad. Why was he out there stalking Kirsty?'

'If he was. It's no more than circumstantial.'

'Sure, but he has to explain it, doesn't he?'

There was silence for a moment as they both considered the implications.

Eventually, Rick said, 'Suppose it was Patsy in that bar and suppose it was him getting away from Kirsty's body, what reason could there be for him to kill her?'

His father shrugged and began to close down the computer.

'What are you going to do, Dad?'

'Right now I'm going to bed.'

'But tomorrow you're going to call Superintendent Edwards, aren't you?'

'I've a feeling Edwards has come to the conclusion I'm a bit of a nuisance.'

'So what?'

'So I'd like to think about this more before going off half cock. These are serious allegations to make against a man.

If we call the police in and Patsy can explain himself then I doubt if you will be welcome at Latchmere any more.'

'That's not important. Justice for Kirsty is more important than a job for me.'

Gareth laid a hand on his arm and squeezed. 'I'm glad you feel that way, son.'

Adrian set the alarm for seven and forced himself out of bed at that ungodly hour. All the same he missed Christine who had already left the house. He'd been late back from his trip the day before and she'd been asleep by the time he got home. They were like figures in a weather clock – when she was in, he was out, and vice versa.

By the time he got to the yard she was up on the gallops with the first lot. He made himself a cup of instant coffee in the office and sat down to wait. Fortunately there was no sign of Tara yet – that would have put another obstacle in his way.

Despite his money and celebrity, Adrian was well aware who ran his life. These days he sought Christine's opinion on every one of his ventures. He was planning a move to buy into a stud in Kentucky but he would never have proceeded with the idea if Christine had not given her permission.

As time went on, he realised how much he needed his wife's approval. He'd made a fool of himself over Kirsty but she'd never reproached him for it, even before the poor girl had died. In retrospect, he was ashamed of the way he had behaved. His fallibility had led him way out of his depth. Christine would never have made such a mistake. He was determined now never to show such weakness again. He owed her, in many ways.

So he waited for her return. For all his customary impatience, he was happy to be at his wife's beck and call.

When she returned she was in a rush. This was a busy time for her.

'How was the mare?' she asked.

The mare he'd been to see up near Chester – he'd almost forgotten about that part of his trip.

'She looks nice enough. Small, though. I don't think I'll bother.'

'Told you.' She accepted the mug of tea he'd made her. She'd never been enthusiastic about the animal.

'On my way to Chester I stopped in Manchester. I dropped in on Tara's old firm.'

She put the mug down on the desk and fixed him with one of her cool stares. He had all of her attention now.

'I spoke to the two partners. They were full of praise for her capabilities. Said she was smart and honest. They were sorry she left.'

'Why did she?'

'Temperamental reasons, apparently. An affair with a colleague that went wrong. He wouldn't leave his wife so she did a runner.'

'So Danny's got her on the rebound?'

That was one way of putting it, he supposed.

'What are you going to do?' he asked. 'Get rid of her?'

'It's hardly grounds for dismissal, Adrian. Anyway, as far as the work goes, she's excellent. I just hope—' She stopped abruptly.

'Hope what?'

'That she doesn't break Danny's heart.'

Adrian put his arms round her and pulled her close. He hoped that too but the matter was out of their hands.

Carl brooded as Jason drove. They were nearly at Lambourn, which was a sight better than blundering around Belfast, but all the same not his preferred location.

Horsey people were not his type. Bookies and tipsters and spending the afternoon in the boozer watching racing on the box was OK, but the characters who owned and trained the nags were a breed apart. Jawing on the telly, accepting prizes at festivals, they were either officer types or bloody Micks. He'd had enough of officer types from his own short stint in the army. As for the Micks . . .

'We're almost there.' Jason opened his mouth for the first time in twenty minutes.

Carl didn't acknowledge the comment. Jason had been navigating by satnav but Carl had a map open on his lap so he knew just where they were. The army hadn't turned out like he'd wanted – for him or the service – but it had taught him to read a map. Latchmere Park covered a fair amount of ground and he reckoned the stone wall coming up on their left marked the beginning of the estate.

They drove on for a couple of hundred yards to a gateway marked with stone pillars and a handsome sign in gold leaf. Latchmere Park, their destination. Jason turned into the driveway and stopped the car.

'Out you get,' he said.

Carl disliked Jason heartily. The oily rat was far too tight with Benny, or at least gave the impression he was, and was always making sarky remarks at Carl's expense. But he was reliable on a job and never wasted time blowing his mouth off, like most of Benny's crew – when Benny wasn't on hand, of course.

The plan was that Jason would drive into the yard, bold as brass, and look for the girl. Carl was to check out the lie of the land. Their information was that Tara was shacked up with this jockey Danny Clark, who lived on the estate. It shouldn't be too difficult to find out where that was.

They checked their watches and agreed on a rendezvous

at the crossroads by the phone box at 3p.m. That should give Carl plenty of time for an initial recce.

He got out of the car and Jason drove on without a word, which was fine by Carl. He set off down the drive by foot. He had the largest scale Ordnance Survey and a pad for making notes. If anyone challenged him he was just a walker, a bit off the beaten track.

When Rick called his father from the yard to say Tara would be joining them for lunch, the response was uncertain. Their plan was to meet in the same pub as the night before, after which Gareth would return home to Shropshire. Rick explained that it was because of Tara that he had had the chance to look at Patsy's passport and, as Kirsty's best friend, it was appropriate she was part of their discussion.

'She's the lawyer, isn't she?' his father had said. He could have added 'and the girl who has replaced Kirsty in Danny's life', for Rick had told him about the new girlfriend.

When they met, it was apparent Gareth remembered Tara well. Fortunately Danny was riding at Hereford, so there was no chance of him gatecrashing the conversation.

Rick wondered whether it was simply the need for secrecy that made him think that way. He couldn't deny that the chance to have Tara to himself, even in such a grim context, lifted his spirits.

'So,' she said after they'd found a quiet corner where they couldn't be overheard, 'tell me.'

Gareth deferred to Rick who encapsulated events as briskly as he could, every now and then checking with his father that he'd got it right. They had printed off the emails from Larry and Dave and Tara read them slowly.

'What does your trained legal mind make of that?' said Gareth without, as far as Rick could tell, a hint of sarcasm.

'Just what anyone would make of it,' she said at last. 'It

looks as if Patsy was on Amana on the day Kirsty died, possibly keeping her under surveillance and dressed in a similar fashion to the person seen rushing away from her body. So, at the very least, he has questions to answer.'

Though she had no new insights, Rick found it reassuring to hear her state the case. At least he and his dad had not been fooling themselves.

She turned to Gareth. 'So this is it? There's nothing else you've discovered that's relevant?'

His father swallowed, looked quickly from Tara to Rick, and said, 'There's one more thing.'

Rick was not entirely surprised. The old schoolmaster knew how to organise his material for maximum impact. Rick felt a jolt of irritation, nonetheless. This was not a subject on which his father should be holding out on him.

It seemed his father could read his mind.

'I'm sorry, Richard, I've known for some time and I think you'll understand why I've never told you or your mother. I didn't think it had any bearing on Kirsty's death but it's a secret I've been carrying for long enough.'

'For God's sake, Dad, what is it?'

'When she died, your sister was four weeks pregnant.'

Jason followed the signs to 'Latchmere Stables'. If he drew a blank there he'd try the stud but it was thought the little filly was hiding in the yard. If she was, he'd find her, somehow or other. He parked up and walked towards the main huddle of buildings. He had his salesman's suit on and a big square leather briefcase which looked as if he meant business, which he did, of course.

Ahead was a row of redbrick stables with dark green painted doors, their top halves open. He could even see the odd horse inside. He strolled past, injecting confidence into his stride. Where the bloody hell were the people?

At last. A fellow in a short waterproof jacket and baggy cord trousers had appeared off to his right. Jason turned, his best salesman's smile in place.

'Can I help you?'

The fellow was young, early twenties, with pink cheeks.

'I'm looking for the office,' he said. 'Can you steer me in the right direction?'

The lad elected to show him, leading Jason into a courtyard and pointing to a door on the other side. As they approached, Jason could see through the window that the little room was empty.

'Where is everyone?' he asked.

'Lunchtime. None of the lads will be back until four. I've only just come over from the stud.'

Jason evaluated the information. Frankly he didn't give a monkey's where anyone was provided he found out about Tara.

'That's OK,' he said. 'I'm really just looking for the girl who runs your office.'

'Jean? She's left. No longer working here.'

Jason didn't like the sound of that. But maybe Tara was here under another name.

'Oh no,' he said. 'And I've come up from London.'

'Did you have an appointment?'

'No, but I was in the area. I'd heard she might be in the market for office equipment. We've got great offers at the moment.' And he lifted his bag as if to prove it. 'This Jean,' he added, 'is she blonde? Bit of a looker?'

'She isn't blonde,' the lad said.

This wasn't turning out how Jason had hoped. The fellow was plainly beginning to tire of being helpful and any moment now Jason would have to beat a retreat without achieving what he'd come for.

At that moment a girl appeared from another direction.

The lad hailed her loudly. 'Lucy, over here.'

Jason quickly explained his dilemma.

'Jean doesn't work here any more,' she said.

Thanks for nothing, Jason thought.

'You want to see Tara,' the girl added. 'She's taken over. But she's gone for lunch.'

Thank you, Lord.

As he made his excuses, explaining that he had another appointment and couldn't wait around, Jason's smile, fixed in place for the past five minutes, was tinged with authentic satisfaction.

Rick was in shock. So his sister had been going to have a baby. Even after eighteen months, that added a whole new dimension of anguish to her death. To think he'd have been an uncle by now, maybe to a little chap like Freddy Turner who, in a couple of years, would be nagging him to come and play football. He'd have liked that.

But it was even worse for his parents. A grandchild would have given a new meaning to their lives and a mutual interest to keep them together, in place of the hole in the family which was driving them apart.

'Mum doesn't know?'

'I've not had the heart to tell her, I'm afraid.'

Rick understood. Since his mother had found a way of blaming his dad for Kirsty's death, how much guiltier would he be in her eyes if she thought him responsible for depriving her of a grandchild?

Tara turned to his father. 'How do you know she was pregnant?'

'Ian Edwards told me. It didn't come up at the inquest, it was just an open-and-shut affair, but it was in the post-mortem report. I didn't tell anybody – things were bad enough already. The knowledge has weighed heavily with me.'

Tara covered his hand with hers. 'I imagine it would.'

Gareth smiled at her, acknowledging her gesture.

'You didn't tell anyone at all?' she said.

'No. Not even Danny. Of course, Kirsty might have told him but, if not, I didn't feel I should add to his loss.'

'Danny didn't know,' Tara said with certainty. 'He talked to me endlessly about Kirsty and the life they were going to spend together but he never once mentioned children. Besides,' she added quietly, 'he didn't expect to be a father. Ever.'

'What do you mean, my dear?' Gareth said.

Embarrassment flashed across her face but she said firmly, 'When we first started sleeping together he told me he'd been kicked by a horse when he was younger. It was quite serious but he recovered, only he couldn't have children.'

'Jesus,' said Rick. 'I didn't know that.'

'That rather changes the picture,' said his father.

'You mean, whose baby was it?'

Gareth nodded. 'Thank God I never told your mother.'

'I can imagine who was responsible,' said Tara. 'She always swore to me she'd never let it go too far but it looks like it did.'

'Who?' Gareth asked.

'Adrian,' said Tara. 'She told me she had this special relationship with him but it was harmless – she was just being a bit wicked but she knew how to keep him in line.'

'Adrian?' Gareth looked aghast. 'He's almost my age. He was going to be her father-in-law.'

'I'm sorry, Gareth,' she said. 'I don't imagine you think she was capable of it.'

He reached for his drink. 'On the contrary, my dear, I know damn well she was.'

*

Mission accomplished, Jason had time on his hands before his rendezvous with Carl. He drove back to the village. He'd spotted a couple of pubs on the way through and a pie and a pint would kill time nicely. As he sat at the bar, waiting for his food order, he noticed the table of three through an alcove, talking intently – a middle-aged slaphead, a young fellow with his back to the bar and, facing him, a girl. A pretty girl with one of those cropped hairdos that looked like someone had attacked it with garden shears. She had a pointed chin and wide-spaced eyes, and a gap between her front teeth.

It was her.

He'd never seen her in the flesh – it would have been daft to visit the yard if he'd met her before, say at Gallagher's office. He'd studied photos, however. The solicitor had given him a few and some of them had been pretty tasty – he could imagine what had been going on before they were taken. There were worse jobs than committing a face like Tara O'Brien's to memory.

Suddenly she looked up and caught him staring. He let his eyes slide away and then reached for his glass, as if he was just a lonely drinker, gawping the surroundings. But he'd been clumsy. He daren't look that way again.

'Number sixty-one,' called a voice and he turned to see the red-faced waitress emerging from the kitchen door.

He raised his hand and waited patiently as she laid the plate and cutlery on the bar before him.

'Steak and kidney,' she announced. 'You enjoy, my darling. Can I get you some mustard?'

By the time she'd finished fussing around him, the alcove was empty. He turned to squint through the window across the room and could just make out the three of them climbing into a battered saloon.

She'd gone but no matter. If Carl did his job right, they'd catch up with her soon enough.

There was little to do in the office to keep Tara's mind off the conversation with Rick and his father. Thinking of Kirsty's death was like picking at a scab that wouldn't heal and the picking made it less likely that it ever would. And Kirsty wasn't blameless. She'd had a talent for getting herself in the mire with men, though she always seemed to walk away smelling of roses.

The last time Tara had spoken to her was the night before she had left for Amana.

'I've got something to tell you.'

At the time Tara was halfway through a file on the mugging of an eighty-year-old grandmother. 'Can I call you back?' she'd said.

But she'd never made that call and she'd always regretted it. She wondered now whether Kirsty had been going to tell her she was pregnant.

She would never know.

There was a knock on the door and a lad she knew from the stud came in.

'Hi, Steve.'

'There was a bloke round here looking for you when you were at lunch.'

'For me?'

'Well, he wanted the girl who ran the office, said he had some equipment on offer. I told him Jean had left 'cos I didn't know you'd taken over. Sorry.'

'That's OK.'

Steve seemed reluctant to leave.

'He was a bit of a wide-boy salesman type. Sharp suit and flashy tie. Pretended to know Jean but he didn't. I reckon he was after you.'

255

'What do you mean?'

'He asked if she was blonde and a looker. Jean's OK, don't get me wrong, but no way is she a blonde.'

'What did you tell him?'

'Me? Nothing. But Lucy came back and said you were at lunch.'

Sharp suit and flashy tie. The man staring at her in the pub.

'Did she tell him my name?'

'Sure. I expect he'll be back because – if you don't mind me saying – you're the one who's a bit of a looker.'

Tara didn't mind – she'd stopped listening.

Chapter Thirteen

Danny got home from Hereford in a foul mood. There and back was around four and a half hours' driving and all for two poxy rides at a gaff track which, as he'd predicted to his mother, had both amounted to nothing. What's more, he'd picked up a suspension for over-zealous use of the whip.

'Would you like me to find someone else?' Christine had said in the face of his objections. 'I'm sure Rick would appreciate the rides.'

Of course he'd said no but now he rather wished he'd ducked the trip. Except it would have been a black mark against him, if not with Christine then with others at the yard. He didn't want it said that Mummy let him cherry-pick his rides.

The cottage was in darkness when he arrived and the door was double-locked. Tara must be out.

To his surprise, when he turned on the light he found her sitting in the front room.

'I tried to call you,' she said.

'Sorry, my phone's flat,' he said, noting with surprise that she held a carving knife in her hand. 'What's the matter?'

When she didn't reply he put his hands on her shoulders and looked into her eyes. 'What's going on, Tara?'

She appeared to come to a decision.

'Put out the light,' she said, 'and I'll tell you.'

*

Rick took the call from his father in his bedroom. He sounded tired, as if his exertions were catching up with him.

'Is it good to be home?' Rick asked.

'I can't deny it will be a relief to sleep in my own bed tonight.'

Rick could imagine. Mrs Turner's little bed in the attic was as hard as a wooden bench. But by his 'own bed', he knew his father did not mean the one he had shared for so many years with his mother. Their separate daily agendas extended to the nights as well.

'How's Mum?'

'She seems OK.'

In other words, there had been no great reconciliation on his father's return. Rick supposed that would be too much to ask. He'd bring forward his weekly call to his mother and ring her tomorrow.

'I tried calling Edwards,' his father continued. 'He's on leave this week.'

'What about the other one?'

'DS Harper? I haven't spoken to him in over a year. Anyway, they said he'd moved to a new division. I'd rather wait till Edwards returns.'

'Jesus, Dad, I don't know what I'm going to say next time I run into Patsy.'

'I'm sure you'll think of something. Just remember he's never told you he was stalking your sister at the time of her murder. I'd keep well clear of him.'

His father sounded unhappy. It seemed a long time since Rick had dropped him at the station in Swindon.

'OK, Dad. Listen, I think you've been incredible doing all this, travelling halfway round the world, living a nightmare over and over.'

'Are you trying to make me feel better?'

'You've done that for me often enough.'

'Well, thanks, son. I think I'll get an early night.'

Rick turned in early too. For all the good it did him.

Tara had often wondered how she'd tell Danny the truth about her flight from Manchester. In the event it was between quick gulps of panic as they sat together on the sofa in the dark with his arms tight around her. He listened with barely an interruption.

'You remember when I was working closely with Tom. I was in love, or thought I was, and it was all wrapped up in the work we were doing together. He was married with children and always went home at night and on the week-ends. I could never have him then but at work he was mine. And sometimes, often, work didn't end till very late. It doesn't upset you, me telling you this, does it?'

'It's OK. Carry on.'

'Well, I got to know a lot about Tom's cases and, of course, his clients. I mean, that was the point of me working with him, to learn the job. A lot of it was dire, grisly stuff, if you looked at it in human terms. But as a lawyer, that's not how you see things – it's part of the training, I guess. You put your personal opinion to one side and look at the situation through your client's eyes. It's adversarial and you're on his side. You look at the strengths and weaknesses of the case against him and, of course, you try to defeat it. And the more horrible the things your client is alleged to have done, the bigger the case and the better for you. People say, "How could you possibly defend Myra Hindley or Fred West or Harold Shipman?" but, as a solicitor in criminal practice, it's a no-brainer. You want the big ugly cases.

'That's one of the things Tom taught me, anyway. The biggest client he had wasn't in the weirdo killer league but he's the most frightening human being I've ever met. A drug baron called Benny Bridges. All smiles and charm on top but a block of ice underneath. He's a businessman and his business makes millions. He routinely has people tortured or killed as a management technique. When you get fired from Benny's firm you literally get the bullet.

'All the same, Benny was very important to Tom. He'd been working with him for years, from when Benny wasn't such a big fish. And as Benny became more successful at his business, so did Tom. Benny referred all sorts of other clients to the firm and Jack, Tom's partner, was delighted. He said the money that was coming in from the heavy-duty criminal cases enabled him to take care of the little guys. He was the firm's social conscience, taking on a lot of Legal Aid work. Jack's a good man but he's got a blind spot about Tom. He treats him like a son.'

'You've got a bit of a blind spot about Tom yourself, haven't you?'

His face was inches from hers in the dim light, pale and stern.

'I used to have,' she said. 'He had me on a string.'

'And it didn't bother you that he was older than you, married with children and all of that?'

'Of course it bothered me. But the fact he was so unsuitable made him more irresistible. Like a kid being told not to play with a box of matches – give him the opportunity and he'll burn the house down. Kids like me anyway. You think I'm cool and sensible – I wasn't with Tom Ferguson.'

'So why did you leave him?'

'Because I discovered he was corrupt. He was as much a part of Benny's criminal business as the dealers and enforcers he represented. He'd crossed the line and I realised that I'd be pulled over it too unless I did something.

'There was one morning we were in court. The judge was

taken ill and the proceedings were adjourned for the day. It was like being let off school. Instead of returning to the office we went straight to my flat. Anyhow, it was mid-morning and Tom's phone went off. I told him to leave it but when he saw it was Benny he went next door to take the call. I was furious so I listened in. It was obvious something serious had happened because Tom was telling him to keep calm and speak slower. Then he told him to go to a cafe round the corner from the office and to get there as quick as he could, he'd meet him there. He finished the call and dashed off, with me shouting at him. We were going to drive out of the city for a country lunch and I'd been really looking forward to it.

'That evening I heard on the news about the murder of a man walking a dog in Clementine's Park to the west of the city. The dogs had got into a fight and one of the owners had gone for the other with a knife. At least that's what the police assumed. There were witnesses but not close and the whole thing was over very quickly. The next day when I got to the office I found that Tom's diary for the day before had been altered. The scheduled day in court had been crossed through and marked 'cancelled due to judge's indisposition' and an eleven o'clock meeting with Benny had been inked in. Tom's secretary was ill that week and the office was in chaos. Nobody had any idea what Tom had been up to. But I did. I knew he was in my flat at the time. I also knew Benny Bridges owned a bull terrier he used to walk in Clementine's Park. The police knew it too because they hauled Benny in for an interview but he was able to prove he was miles away at the time – thanks to Tom.'

'What did you do?'

'Nothing. It took me a while to even think Tom could be capable of providing a murderer with an alibi. He was my employer. He was training me not just to qualify as a solicitor but to go places in the firm – that's what he'd said – and I was in love with him. It took me a few days to recalibrate my thinking. Then he made a big mistake. He turned up for work in a new car, a blue Ferrari, and insisted on taking me out in it, to make up for the week before, he said. He took me to a country hotel for lunch and he'd booked a room upstairs for the afternoon. When we were leaving, he opened the boot and showed me a sports bag. I thought it was the bag he took to the gym but when he opened it up I saw it was stuffed with banknotes. He held it open and told me to grab a handful.'

'Jesus.' Tara could tell Danny was hooked. 'What did you do?'

'I said I wasn't a whore and told him to drive me back to Manchester.'

'And that's when you broke it off?'

'That's when I realised I was fooling myself. I didn't know what to do. I agonised over how much I was compromised. And I started building a case against him. I took notes on calls and meetings, I went through any personal papers I could find and copied them. Tom used to bring his credit card and mobile phone bills to the office – so his wife couldn't go through them, I assume. I built up a little dossier and took it to a policeman I trusted.'

'That was brave.'

'I've never felt brave. I've been scared every moment since. Tom is due in court in June for conspiring to pervert the course of justice and I'm the chief prosecution witness. If he's convicted, the police have a direct line to Benny Bridges. I've just got to stay alive till June.'

'But surely the police can help you? Give you bodyguards or something?'

'It's called witness protection, Danny. But it's not foolproof. You're reliant on people you don't know.

Sometimes they're not as smart or careful as they should be. Or as honest. People die in witness protection.'

There was silence for a moment. Tara was conscious of Danny's strong arms round her.

She said, 'A man came to the yard today when I was at lunch. He said he was selling office equipment and looking for the yard secretary. He knew she was blonde. When I was in the pub I saw a guy in a suit staring at me. It could have been him. You've been brilliant, Danny, I probably owe you my life. If you give me a ride to the station I swear it's the last time I'll ask you for anything.'

The silence stretched on, then he said, 'You want to run away just because some salesman stared at you in a pub? No you don't, Tara. You're not going anywhere.' And his arms tightened round her in a reassuring circle.

When Gingerbread had the accident, the only consolation Rick could take was that he was riding. So he could blame no one else and, in all honesty, he couldn't really do that. It was one of those freak incidents that happen with horses and you just have to accept it. They weren't even schooling, just doing a routine canter up the grass gallop. Rick felt the horse's near fore give way about half a furlong from the finish and pulled him up immediately.

He dismounted, his heart in his mouth. He'd seen horses injure themselves on the gallops before and most of the time their hurts could be healed.

But not always.

Christine saw what happened. If she'd been a woman who cursed she would have sworn out loud. Instead she ran towards the stricken horse, scrabbling in her pocket for her phone.

She had Peter Fisher, her vet, on speed dial and told him to come straightaway as she knelt in the grass to examine the wounded leg that Gingerbread was now holding off the ground.

Rick clung on to the horse's head, fondling his ears and whispering to him. His face was pale beneath a coat of muddy drops.

'Oh Christ,' he said. 'Why did it have to be this one?'

Christine got to her feet. 'He's definitely broken it. I can feel the bone moving. Let's hope the vet gets here soon.'

Rick looked at her. 'What am I going to tell Hugh?'

Christine wasn't worried about Hugh. From what she'd seen of him he was man enough to take the ups and downs of racing in his stride. She was more concerned about Rick. Maybe Latchmere wasn't the place for him – it never seemed to bring him much luck.

The vet's estate car appeared on the gallop five minutes later – a long five minutes in which Christine had searched hard for some words of comfort.

'Sorry, folks,' said the vet. He only needed a cursory glance to confirm Christine's fears. 'It's a nasty fracture. There's no point trying to patch him up.'

Christine watched Rick bury his face briefly in the horse's neck. The animal stared at him stoically, though he was now shivering with pain and shock. The vet pulled his humane killer from his bag. Some vets preferred to use a lethal injection of Somulose but Peter preferred a gun.

'Are you sure there's no way of saving him?' she asked. 'It doesn't matter if he can't race.'

Peter shook his head.

'Only,' she continued, 'it's not just this horse. He's got a mate who's going to be lost without him.'

The vet considered for a moment, then said, 'I have to put him down straightaway. It's only fair. Can you get the other one up here? I won't have the body removed till his mate has had the chance to look at it and sniff it to see that he's dead.'

In all the time Christine had been training, this was something she'd never heard of but the vet recounted a story of a man who'd once had two Labradors from the same litter. When one had died, the vet had told him to do exactly what they were about to do with Gingerbread and it had stopped the surviving dog from pining.

She explained the matter to Rick and phoned the yard to get one of the girls to bring Treacle up from the yard.

Rick held on to Ginger while the vet did his sorry duty.

Given her panic, Tara was surprised she'd managed to sleep but she emerged from a dreamless slumber to the sound of Danny whistling in the bathroom.

'Tea?' he said as he popped his head round the door. 'See, we got through the night in one piece.'

She'd been aware, as she'd finished her tale the night before, that he had found her story hard to swallow. Now, she wasn't so certain of it herself. A salesman had turned up at the yard. A man had stared at her in the pub. It might not even have been the same fellow. And, though she wasn't a vain woman, she was well aware that many men found her attractive. She'd been ogled in pubs many times and survived the experience.

There was something else, too, that eased her mind as she sipped the tea and nibbled the toast that Danny had brought her. Steve, the lad who'd spoken to the visitor in the yard, had remembered one other detail. The man had said he'd come from London. Not Manchester. Maybe she'd got the wrong end of the stick. Certainly, in the light of day, she was glad she hadn't run away last night. Where on earth would she have gone?

She went down to the kitchen to find Danny reading the

paper. 'It's late for you, isn't it?' she said. He was usually off riding by now.

'I can't ride today, I'm suspended.'

Of course, he'd told her but she'd forgotten. He'd been fed up about the ban at the time but now he grinned at her. 'I thought I'd wait for you. We can walk up to the yard together.'

She smiled back, as much in relief as anything, and sat down next to him.

'Thanks for looking after me last night.'

'That's OK,' he said. 'What are friends for?'

She put her hand in his. 'You've been more than a friend to me, Danny. Much more.'

Danny hung around the yard, finding odd jobs to do but mostly keeping an eye on Tara. He was still taking in the extraordinary things she had told him.

His reaction, as he'd listened in the dark to her tale of persecution by gangsters who wanted to kill her, was that she was a fantasist. It had often occurred to him that sane people could harbour mad delusions which they nurtured in secret. How many racehorse owners had he met who seriously told him the horse he was about to ride would one day win the Grand National? He himself had harboured similar hopes. For weeks before his first Cheltenham Festival he'd tried to psych himself into a winning frame of mind by visualising a dynamic run up the hill to destroy the rest of the field in the Gold Cup. He'd thought of that sheepishly after his 250–1 outsider had dumped him on the turf on the first circuit. Thank God he'd not told anyone.

Of course, racing dreams were one thing and permissible for any rider with ambition. Tara's paranoid nightmare was of a different order. And yet, she had been working with violent and dangerous criminals, she knew what they were capable of. Maybe the nightmares went with the territory.

One thing that might explain the delusion was her affair with Tom. That had been real, all right. He'd seen the guy once, back when he and Tara had just been friends, out for a drink. She'd told him she was meeting her lover and he'd taken the hint, leaving the wine bar ten minutes before her rendezvous. On the way out he'd been passed by a tall man with dark floppy hair in a cashmere overcoat and he'd known at once just who it was. Out of curiosity, he'd hung back long enough to see the tall man approach Tara's table and greet her with a kiss – a more-than-just-friends kiss.

It was easy to understand Tom's attraction for a girl like Tara. You could tell he was a smooth operator at a glance: the commanding air, the effortless style and the light in his eye. Working side by side with him and learning your trade at his hands, a girl would be doomed to fall heavily if the chemistry was right. And, with Tara, the chemistry had obviously been spot on.

So, when the affair went pear-shaped, wouldn't it make sense for Tara to wrap it up in some fantasy about him being a crook? It was more likely, in Danny's opinion, that Tom fired Tara once she started becoming a nuisance. And she'd indulged herself in this make-believe about him alibi-ing a murderer and them coming to get her because, frankly, it was a whole lot more heroic than facing the truth. Which was that she'd screwed up her career by making a fool of herself over a married man.

After all, if she really was running for her life and due to star as a prosecution witness in Tom's trial, surely she would have gone to the police for protection? He didn't buy her excuses. He'd seen a TV programme about witness protection and it was heavy-duty stuff. And whatever its deficiencies, it offered a sight more security than hiding away at a racing yard. If this Benny and his heavy mob turned up at Latchmere, what did she think she was going to do? Fly for her life on Miller's Tale?

He'd thought all this through as he'd tended for Tara the night before. He'd made her eat an omelette and provided plenty of tea. She'd fallen asleep the moment he'd got her into bed, exhausted by the effort of unburdening herself, and he'd lain awake by her side, pondering her words.

She'd got herself into a state, that was plain enough, though whether she really wanted him to drop her off at the station to head off into the blue, he had no idea. In any case, it was out of the question at that time of night – where would she go?

He wouldn't have stood in her way this morning if she'd insisted on leaving, but he'd been relieved when she'd seemed happy to stay. For all her neuroses, he didn't want to be the one to give up on their puzzling relationship.

The accident to Gingerbread plunged the whole yard into a sombre mood. He'd never wish any harm to a horse, especially not as game an animal as Gingerbread. But if a fatal accident had to take place it could not have been better timed, distracting Tara from her imagined worries.

And, when the end of the day finally came round, there had been no sign of any grinning salesmen on the lookout for good-looking blondes.

How could you tell if a horse was grieving? Rick wondered as he contemplated Treacle Toffee in his box while the light faded over the yard. It was probably the same as any emotional trauma. They went off their food and lost interest in what was going on around them.

He'd been surprised by the vet's suggestion to take Treacle to look at Ginger's body. If he hadn't been in shock himself he might have objected. How do you know it might not make matters worse?

Would he have felt any better had he been magically transported to the Caribbean to look at the corpse of his dead sister?

He couldn't answer that. All he knew was that sending her off on holiday and never seeing her again left a hole inside him that could never be filled. A part of him forever expected Kirsty to walk through the door, suitcase in hand, saying, 'Did you miss me?'

Treacle had looked solemnly at the body of his stablemate then nuzzled the prone chestnut flanks. He'd licked Ginger's muzzle and circled his body, looking at him from every angle. Rick had given him all the time he needed, as Christine watched and the drizzle soaked into their clothes. Eventually Treacle had looked up and allowed himself to be led away.

Now, in his box for the night, he'd eaten his customary supper and seemed none the worse for the presence of the empty stall just next door. So maybe it was that simple – the mourning was over.

Rick knew that neither he nor his parents would ever come to terms with the death of Kirsty.

'So, Rick, how are you doing?'

The voice came from behind him, catching him by surprise. A familiar face, surrounded by thick dark curls, appeared at his side and an arm was hooked through his. Stephanie.

'Sorry about Ginger.'

They stood in silence for a moment, watching Treacle who came over to say hello to Stephanie and allowed her to scratch his nose.

'He seems fine,' she said.

'Yes. It's incredible how he screamed the place down when they were separated. But when Ginger dies he just gets on with life as if nothing had happened.'

Pity human beings couldn't act like that.

Stephanie gauged his mood. 'Come over to the office then and I'll make you some tea.'

That made sense.

Rick slumped in Tara's chair in the little room while Stephanie boiled the kettle. He'd not been able to talk to Tara since their lunch with his dad. He wondered what further conclusions she'd reached. He could see that Patsy's things were still in the carrier bag by the side of the filing cabinet.

'Steph, when you were in Amana, the time Kirsty died . . .'

She turned to face him, a mug in each hand. If she was surprised by the switch of subject, she didn't show it. They never talked of Kirsty's death.

'Was Patsy out there too?' he asked.

She placed one mug on the desk in front of him and sat down facing him, holding the other.

'No.'

'I thought not. It was just the family plus Kirsty, wasn't it?'

'Why are you asking?'

'I'm puzzled. What would you say if I told you Patsy was there at the same time?'

Her brow furrowed. 'I'd say you were wrong.'

'Suppose I could prove it?'

'I'd still say you were wrong.' She blew on her tea. 'What are you getting at, Rick?'

He got up and delved into Patsy's bag.

'Jean brought round some of the things Patsy had left at her place, which included his old passport.' He handed it to her, open to the page with the entry stamp.

'Should you be looking at that?' she said.

'It's an expired passport not some top-secret diary. Just tell me what you make of this.'

She took it from him and looked carefully at the page.

'September two thousand and six,' she said.

'Kirsty was killed on the fourteenth.'

'I know.' She stared at the page, her face a blank. 'I'm surprised,' she said finally.

'Just surprised? Don't you think it extraordinary that he should be there at the same time as you were?'

'Well, I didn't see him, if that's what you're asking. He was entitled to be in the Virgin Islands, I suppose. He came with us once before. Maybe he went on his own holiday and kept quiet about it.'

'That's crap.'

She laughed. 'You know my uncle. He's crazy Irish. I bet you he had some woman on Tortola he didn't want us to know about.'

Rick thought that was stupid but if Stephanie did not want to see the significance of this discovery he wasn't going to rub her nose in it. Of course, Stephanie did not know all that he did but he could tell she was not a receptive audience.

He downed his tea and got to his feet. 'I think I'd better be getting home.'

Gareth soaked his weary body in a hot bath. He was aching all over. It was his own damn fault. He'd spent the day in the garden clearing debris that had accumulated over the winter, forking the waterlogged patch of lawn at the bottom and digging the vegetable patch. The garden had been a source of enjoyment to him for many years, a hobby he'd poured his creative energy into even in the days when he was working flat out at school. It had been his contribution to the household, providing a leafy outdoor haven for himself and Margaret, not to mention a supply of home-grown fruit and vegetables for the table. But he'd scarcely set foot out there since Kirsty had died. He hadn't had the heart.

As he'd swept and dug, he'd turned the discoveries of recent days over in his head. And the question that kept ending up on top was, why would Patsy Walsh want to kill Kirsty?

Personally, Gareth didn't know all that much about Patsy, except that beneath his affable exterior he had the reputation of being a tough nut, that he was related to Christine's first husband, and he was Adrian Spring's right-hand man.

Adrian had to be the connection between Patsy and his daughter. Adrian, the soon-to-be father-in-law who enjoyed a 'special' relationship with Kirsty. Special enough, it transpired, to get her pregnant.

Oh Kirsty, couldn't you at least have avoided that?

This was difficult ground for him, as it would be for most fathers. He found it hard to think of his daughter as a sexual creature. The notion of his child bedding any man seemed a thought crime and would doubtless be branded as such by his wife if she ever found out about it.

Yet he was well aware of the boy-magnet Kirsty had become in her teens. And the kind of boyfriends who had squired her around Manchester were obviously not boys at all. Adrian was by no means the first man Kirsty had attracted who was considerably older than she was. It had been a relief to Gareth, and to Margaret, when she announced she was marrying Danny, a nice fellow of her own age.

But it turned out there had been an older man in the background – wealthy, powerful and manipulative. What Adrian had been thinking of in dallying with his stepson's fiancée, Gareth couldn't imagine. But the very rich lived by their own rules, didn't they? One reason being that they could afford men like Patsy to clean up their messes for them.

Gareth dragged himself from the cooling water and slowly towelled himself dry.

In the kitchen he found that Margaret had left him an enormous portion of shepherd's pie in the oven. Whatever their failures of communication these days, she evidently still regarded him as her responsibility. He padded into the front room to fix himself a whisky and water to go with it.

Margaret was watching the television. It looked like one of those property programmes.

'Thanks for supper,' he said. 'I won't manage all that, though.'

'I thought you'd be hungry after a day in the garden.'

So she'd noticed. It was a civilised exchange, at least.

To his surprise he did finish all his supper. By the time he'd cleared up, she'd gone out. He found his notes and reached for the phone. By his calculations it was afternoon in Chicago. Maureen Benson answered the phone. He apologised for the call and said he would understand if she did not want to speak to him.

'God forbid there's ever a day I won't be happy to speak to you, Mr Jordan,' she said.

All the same, it was an unhappy chore for her – it had to be. He promised to keep it short.

'If you could think back to that evening in the Cliff Tops bar, when you saw my daughter and thought she was pretty. Did you notice her companion?'

'Oh yes. A middle-aged man – attractive, though. That's Mr Spring, isn't it? Ron told me the other day he's buying into some racing concern in Kentucky.'

This was news to Gareth, though not surprising.

'Can you remember anything about how they behaved with one another? I mean, did you think they were together as a couple?'

'Like married, you mean? Sure. Or possibly older rich guy

273

with young girlfriend. It's the way of the world, isn't it? To be honest, it was Ron who was watching them more than me – I was facing the other way. All I remember him saying is something like, "You'd think a guy would be happy going out with a girl like that, but he looks as miserable as sin." Ron will tell you himself, if you want to call back later.'

'Thank you, Mrs Benson. I don't think there will be any need for that.'

Gareth sat by the phone and pondered everything he knew. Would Kirsty and her inconvenient pregnancy have so threatened Adrian Spring that he'd arranged to have her killed?

Maybe his own judgement was clouded by personal animosity, but he honestly didn't know.

Patsy groaned when he saw that Stephanie was on his doorstep. She wore one of her intense looks. There was plainly some bee in her bonnet she wanted to set free but, Jesus, couldn't she do that during working hours? Right now he wanted to grab a bite and get down to the pub. He opened the door all the same.

'I've brought some of your stuff,' she announced as she marched in, a carrier bag in her hand. 'Some things you left round at Jean's.'

'Oh really? I hope she's not been making a nuisance of herself with you.'

'I haven't seen her since you frightened her off.' Stephanie marched straight through into the kitchen as if she owned the place and dumped the bag on the table, next to his half-eaten plate of beans on toast. 'As a matter of fact, she left them in the yard office. Didn't she tell you?'

He shrugged. There'd been a couple of long, aggrieved messages from Jean on his answerphone and he'd erased them without listening closely to the details. Maybe there had been some reference to things he'd left behind and he'd missed it.

'I've been a bit busy, what with moving in here.'

The flat was a mess, full of unpacked suitcases and boxes. It was like that wherever he went these days. Since his marriage had gone south – and thank the Lord for that – he'd never stayed anywhere long enough to make himself properly at home.

He sat down at the table. There was no point in letting his food go cold. 'Do you want to make yourself a coffee or something?'

'No.' She stood by the table and began to unpack the bag, chucking a sweater and a couple of battered paperbacks on the table. Then she found what she was after.

'Rick knows you were on Amana,' she said, holding up a passport.

For a moment he was at a loss. He wasn't so disorganised he didn't know where his important documents were – he had his passport in his bedside drawer. Then he realised that this was his old one. It had been returned to him when he was shacking up with Jean and he must have left it behind. All the same . . .

'So what?' he said, chasing the last mouthful of beans around his plate with a wedge of toast.

'Look, you twit.' She opened the passport and pointed to a stamp on the page. The entry stamp to the British Virgin Islands in September 2006.

He got it now. It placed him in the BVI at the time Kirsty was killed.

'Rick's seen this?'

'Yes. Tara must have done too since she's running the place these days. I was in the office with him just now and he came right out and asked me about it. Did I know you were there at the time Kirsty died.'

'What did you say?'

'I waffled, to be honest. Said I knew nothing about it and maybe you had some secret girlfriend on Tortola – which wouldn't exactly be out of character, would it?'

Patsy didn't respond to that. He needed to think.

'How could you be so careless?' she went on. 'You know Rick's father's just come back from Amana, don't you? He probably went because Rick told him about this.'

'Will you give it a rest, Stephanie? I know what the implications are.'

'Do you really? Adrian won't be able to get you out of this, you know. If I were you, I'd think about packing my bags and getting out while I can.'

He didn't reply to that either. There wasn't anything to say.

Rick hid in his room. Downstairs he could hear shouts and laughter as Freddy and Tim resisted their mother's attempts to get them to bed. He'd not played with the boys tonight – he hadn't had the heart. He felt bad about that. They were just kids and shouldn't suffer because of his grumpy mood. It wasn't their fault Ginger had died – or Kirsty.

Their cries increased in intensity and now, in between the treble yells, he became aware of a lower, gruffer voice which certainly didn't belong to their mother, and their father was currently driving an HGV through France. The voice sounded again and this time Rick placed it. It belonged to the last person he wanted to see right now. Patsy.

A few minutes later, after a final explosion of jollity capped by a series of commands from Mrs Turner, the noise ceased. Children's bedtime had arrived. A moment later came a knock on Rick's door.

At least he'd had a chance to decide how to deal with

Patsy. He'd be friendly, keep their conversation on safe ground, aim to make it short.

And try to keep out of his mind the terrible possibility that he'd just discussed with his father. That Patsy had murdered Kirsty on the orders of Adrian Spring.

'Rick, how are you doing?' Patsy filled the doorway of the room. 'That's a poor business about your horse Ginger.'

'Yes.' There wasn't anything else to say on that subject.

'I thought you might like a shoulder to cry on down at the pub.'

'If it's all the same to you, Patsy, I'll pass on that. It's been a long day.'

It sounded lame and, as was apparent as Patsy produced a brown bottle from inside the bulging folds of his coat, it was also a miscalculation. Patsy was not to be denied an interview.

The Irishman shut the door behind him and magicked two glasses from another pocket. 'I thought you might not fancy going out so I came prepared. You shouldn't let a good horse go without saying a proper goodbye.'

Rick went along with it – what choice did he have? He watched as Patsy poured an inch of Jameson's into both glasses and handed one over.

A crazy thought burst into Rick's head. *The drink is poisoned – he's come here to kill me.*

'God rest the poor feller's soul,' said the Irishman solemnly and drained his glass.

Rick shook the thought from his head. He was becoming paranoid. All the same, he sipped cautiously.

Was Patsy's sentimental act genuine?

They sat down on either side of the fireplace. Patsy suddenly seemed less sure of himself. As if, now his planned theatrics were over, he was at a loss for words. Rick was not inclined to help him out.

Patsy finally spoke. 'So you saw my old passport.' It was not a question.

Rick was taken by surprise. How did he know that?

Stephanie, obviously. It had been a risk to mention it to her – she must have run straight to Patsy.

'Yes,' Rick said. 'I also saw the entry stamp to the Virgin Islands when Kirsty was killed.' There was no point in playing dumb.

'I know what you're thinking,' the Irishman said, 'so I've come to set the record straight before the police come for me. I don't deny I was out on the island when your sister died, but I want you to know I didn't kill her. In fact,' he poured himself some more whiskey, 'you must believe me when I tell you that she was the last person in the world I would have wished to come to any harm.'

'Really?' Rick could feel the anger starting to churn in his guts. Did this sanctimonious thug think he could get him on his side with his teary-eyed toasts and hypocritical expressions of affection? 'As I remember it, you didn't think much of Kirsty. You didn't even deny it the other night.'

Patsy shook his head. 'That's what we wanted you to think.'

'Why bother? Who cared what you thought of each other?'

'A few people, as it happens. As I explained to you, it wasn't a smart move to get involved with the girl who was going to marry the boss's son.'

'Come off it, you weren't involved. You told me so yourself.' Maybe the whiskey had loosened his tongue but Rick couldn't see the point in hanging back any longer. 'Listen to me, Patsy, there's no need for you to carry on protecting Adrian. I know what happened. He was having an affair with Kirsty and when he got her pregnant he decided to get rid of her. And that's where you came in – to do Adrian's dirty work like you always do. You can deny it to me, Patsy, but you'll have trouble explaining yourself to the police.'

Patsy appeared unmoved. 'So you know about the baby.'

'My father read the post-mortem report. He's only just told me.'

'Why do you think it was Adrian's?'

'Because I know it wasn't Danny's. Who else could it be?'

Patsy drained his glass with a sigh.

'Me,' he said. 'The baby was mine.'

Patsy put his glass down on the table. He mustn't drink any more. He had to keep a clear head to dispel the disbelief and suspicion that he read in Rick's face. There was anger there too. At times the lad looked uncannily like his sister.

'Is that a joke?' Rick said.

Patsy shook his head. 'I fell in love with your sister the moment I set eyes on her. She was sharp and funny and completely fearless – she didn't care whose toes she trod on sometimes. But you'd know that better than me.'

Rick nodded. 'Yes.'

'That's why she got on so well with Adrian. She'd make fun of him, tell him the truth to his face and laugh at him.'

'What truth?'

'That he was a dirty old man having the hots for his son's girlfriend – but she didn't care. That, if he liked, she'd text him the colour of her underwear every day. That, if he bought a thirty-inch plasma screen for the cottage, she'd model her new bikini for him. That kind of thing.'

Rick's face flushed pink. 'That's disgusting.'

Patsy chuckled. 'They both got a kick out of it.'

'You're saying Kirsty was just a little tart.'

'Indeed, that's pretty much what I told her. We had a big row about a horse, Diamond Jackie, one of the young stallions over at the stud. He'd been complete murder one afternoon. Kicked one of the girls so bad she was off for a week. I had to give the little bastard a fair bashing to get him back in his stall and Kirsty came in at the end of it. She called me a whole string of names – a bog-stupid, bouffant-haired, bullying dickhead who ought to be prosecuted for animal cruelty. Or something like that. I told her to sod off back to her lamp post in Manchester or wherever she peddled her fat fanny before she picked on our yard. Then she smacked me in the face – a fair wallop it was too, I had the bruise for ten days after. I'd have thumped her back but Stephanie had heard the shouting and came running. So it got about that we hated each other's guts, which turned out to be handy. Sort of.'

'You're going to tell me how?'

'Sure. I got a text from her that night, saying let's make peace. I bought her a drink to make up for calling her fanny fat and she said sorry for jumping to the wrong conclusions about the stallion – she'd heard about the girl who'd got kicked. She never apologised for socking me one, though.'

'And you're saying you had an affair?'

'We tried not to, if that makes any sense. I was still married then but the marriage was on its last legs, for which I hold up my hand. And, of course, Kirsty was engaged to Danny, not to mention keeping Adrian on a string. But she was just my kind of girl and the other two didn't seem to give her everything she wanted. Danny was far too safe and Adrian was a daddy figure. I guess I turned out to be her bit of rough.'

'How do you know the baby was yours?'

'I knew it had to be. She said she'd never slept with Adrian and I believed her. She teased him outrageously but she swore a tease was all it was. And, well, from what you say I assume you know about Danny's accident.'

'I just found out.'

'Kirsty told me about the pregnancy just before they were all due to fly off to the Caribbean on their holiday. She said, congratulate me, Patsy, I'm going to be a respectable housewife with kids and then she told me she was having a baby. I said, it could be mine, couldn't it? And she said that as far as she was concerned it was Danny's.'

'She didn't know about his accident?'

Patsy shook his head.

'And you didn't tell her?'

'No.' Patsy paused. It was difficult to know how to explain, especially to Kirsty's brother. She'd told him the day before she'd left for the West Indies. He'd been at the stud that afternoon and she'd found him in an empty stall. She'd hurled herself into his arms. 'Quick,' she'd hissed urgently, placing his hand on her breast. It was obvious what she wanted and there was no time to debate. 'One last time,' she'd whispered and he'd not refused her. He was glad he hadn't. Ever since, he'd clung to the memory, trying to recreate in his mind the feel of her skin, the smell of her scent, the breathy murmurs of her excitement. It was getting harder to keep those moments alive.

After, they'd barely had time to get their clothes in place before a couple of lads came back from their break.

'You know that expression, "There's no such thing as a free lunch"?' she'd said as she got into her car. 'Well, I'm your free lunch.'

If only.

That evening, she'd rung him and told him she was pregnant. And she'd rung off before he'd had a chance to explain about Danny.

'So you're saying Kirsty went off on holiday thinking the baby was Danny's?' Rick wasn't enjoying this conversation but he was determined to see it through.

'That's right. I went along with it at the time. Then I started thinking. If Kirsty had just been drawing a line under our bit of fun I could have stood that. But the idea that she was going off to marry another man carrying my baby brought all my feelings to a head. It came to me that this was my one chance to persuade her to leave Danny. Your sister was made for a man like me, not a nice lad like Danny who she'd twist round her finger and end up making miserable. He'd be shocked when he found out he was going to be a father after all but I had no doubt she'd get round him somehow and they'd be bringing up my child together. And if I wanted to carry on here at Latchmere, I'd just have to keep my mouth shut and watch them do it. I wasn't sure I could handle that.'

'So you went after her?'

'Yes. I got a room along the coast from where they were staying. I didn't want any of the others to know I was going, I just wanted one more chance to make a pitch for her. Explain the child had to be mine. I'd promise to leave my wife – well, she knew that was over anyway – and offer to marry her and bring our baby up together. I'd have blown my chances at Latchmere but I'd do that for her and our child. We could go anywhere in the world she wanted. This was the most love-crazy thing I'd ever done and probably the most foolish. But I knew I'd never forgive myself if I didn't try to persuade her.

'So, the day after I arrived, I followed her, looking for an opportunity to get her on her own. It was hard just hanging around, trying to avoid getting spotted. And she never went anywhere without one of the others. Finally, in the evening, she went to the bar above the beach with Adrian. I followed and waited on the path where I knew she'd have to come back. Frankly I thought I'd blown it because she'd be returning with Adrian but I couldn't bring myself to give up and start all over the next day.'

'But she did come back on her own,' Rick said. Kirsty had left Adrian taking a phone call in the bar and headed back to change for dinner – that's what his father had told him.

'Yes.'

'So what happened?'

Patsy lifted his head and stared into Rick's face. 'The only thing I'm going to tell you is that I didn't kill her.'

Rick looked at him in disbelief. 'But you saw what happened?'

'Yes. And I tried to save her, believe me. But it was over in a flash. I've often thought I should have done better but I couldn't. She was dead when I got to her.'

'So who killed her?'

'I can't tell you that.'

'Jesus, Patsy. I don't believe a word of this. You got her on your own and tried to persuade her to leave Danny, like you said. And when she turned you down you bashed her brains out. That's the only explanation that makes sense.'

Patsy got to his feet. He shook his head. 'I understand how you feel. But that's not how it was. I just wanted to tell you face to face that I loved your sister and I did not kill her.' He had his hand on the door.

'The police will want to talk to you. You'll be arrested. You'll have to tell them.'

Patsy shook his head. 'I'll tell them the same as I've told you. Because it's the truth.'

And then he was gone.

Chapter Fourteen

'Where's Tom?' Jack Gallagher rampaged through the office, up and down the stairs, ignoring his pounding heart and shortness of breath. 'Where's Mr Ferguson? Has anybody seen him this morning?'

But nobody had and maybe, given Jack's condition, it was a good thing he could not be found. Or else Jack's system might have combusted in an apoplectic seizure and he'd not have survived the day.

'For God's sake, Jack, calm down.' Eileen insisted he take a seat in her office and fetched him a cup of water. 'It's bad for business for the senior partner to have a heart attack in reception.'

'I'm in no mood for jokes,' Jack grumbled. He sipped his water and willed his pulse to slow. He'd had a shock, maybe the biggest of his life. That snake Tom Ferguson had betrayed him in the foulest, most craven sense. Tom, his protégé and professional partner, the lad he'd invited into his firm and trusted to take it on to prosperity. He'd just discovered that Tom was – and he could barely think the word – corrupt. The sense of betrayal was worse than if he'd discovered his late wife in an infidelity. And he, the cuckolded partner, had refused for months to read the evidence there in front of him. He felt a damn fool.

It had only taken one phone call, out of the blue that

morning from Northern Ireland, to pull the rug from his partner's deceit.

He'd not expected Kelvin Connelly to come on the line. It had been some weeks since he'd rung round his old pals on the off chance that Tara might have pitched up in their orbit in Belfast. Kelvin had been away at the time and had, so he said apologetically, only just got round to calling back. He had no news of Tara, which was not surprising as Jack now knew she'd never left the country.

They'd chewed the cud, as you did. Jack had made reference to the terrible sectarian murder of Tara's uncle, Des Monaghan. Kelvin had agreed that it had been an ugly business but not, he said, sectarian in origin.

'I know some of the detectives who've been working on it,' he said. 'They've been leaning on their paramilitary snitches and they're sure the assault was ordered from the mainland. There was an Englishman in the baker's that afternoon hassling Des, some big bruiser with a northern accent. They're not sure what it was all about but they're fairly certain it wasn't sectarian.'

But Jack reckoned he did know. He'd pieced together the sequence of conversations he'd had with Tom. How he himself had brought up Tara's uncle's name. And how Tom had behaved when he showed him the newspaper with an account of the murder just a few days later. Tom's surprise had convinced him at the time – but not now.

One phone call from Tom to his client Benny Bridges could have despatched a killer to Belfast.

It made Jack look at things in a new light – lots of things, starting with the police charges against his partner and against which he had defended Tom stoutly. It all came down to who you believed and, suddenly, he didn't believe Tom any longer.

Jack dragged himself to his feet with a thank you to

Elaine. She watched him with concern. He brushed aside her suggestion that he go home and rest and plodded slowly up the stairs. It might not be a bad idea to take the rest of the day off. But first he had a call to make.

He found the card in his desk drawer and the number he needed written in last year's desk diary. To his relief, he was put through at once.

'Hammond,' said the Scots voice as he answered.

Jack introduced himself – unnecessarily, it turned out, for the detective knew his name.

'It's about Tara O'Brien,' he began. 'May I ask if she is under your protection?'

'Why do you want to know, Mr Gallagher?'

'Because I believe she is in terrible danger. And I can tell you where she is.'

And then he gave DS Hammond all the information written on Adrian Spring's business card.

'I don't see why I have to be involved in this.'

Tom directed the words at the man driving the car, the individual he least wanted as a companion for the afternoon, with the possible exception of Benny Bridges. Of course, spending time with Jason was the same as spending it with Benny since the slimy sod operated entirely as his master's voice.

'You've got to come and make the ID,' Jason replied.

'But I was told you'd already identified her.'

'I saw a girl in a pub who looked like the photo of your bit of fluff. Very likely it's her but you're coming to make it a hundred per cent certain.'

'But what if she sees me?'

'What if she does? You're going to be about the last bloke she does see.'

Tom let the implications of that remark sink in. He was

part of an assassination squad. It was unreal – and terrifying.

Jason seemed to read his mind. 'Bloody well open your eyes. You soft buggers sit around in offices and stuff your faces at fancy eateries, you never go down in the sewers. There's always some lowlife underling to wade through the shit and piss for you. Welcome to the sticky end, mate. You might not enjoy it but I'm going to get a kick out of seeing you mess your pants.'

God, was he in trouble.

Danny spent another morning nurse-maiding Tara though, if he were honest, he was beginning to feel a bit foolish. A day and a half had gone by since she'd spotted a so-called hitman sent by Tom Ferguson and life was going on just as usual – except that he was hanging around being her guard dog. Lap dog, more like, shadowing her every move, waiting for the occasional stroke.

It was obvious that her worries were just the product of her imagination – she'd been watching too many reruns of *The Sopranos*. The more he thought about it, the more he concluded he was simply pandering to her neuroses. Was their future together going to continue like this? Did they have a future together? So far in their quick-fire romance he'd resisted thinking about the long-term. Perhaps now was the time. He wasn't sure he wanted to be shackled to a hysteric, no matter how lovely she was.

There was another thing that ate away at him, however hard he might try to overlook it. He could tell Tara wasn't as passionate for him as he was for her. She wasn't as exuberantly loving as Kirsty, of course, but he didn't expect that. Every woman was different in revealing their emotions. Maybe being shy and elusive was part of her nature.

But she'd been passionate enough about Tom Ferguson.

The story about him taking a phone call at her flat had the ring of truth. He'd bet they were naked in bed when that call came. Making love without inhibition.

Screwing like rabbits.

He tried to erase the image from his mind. Why be jealous of a boyfriend she now loathed?

But he was jealous of a capacity to love that she had never revealed to him. Jealous, though he hated to admit it, of the possibility she might even here, supposedly in fear of her life, be on the lookout for a man who would suit her better than himself.

She'd ridden out with Rick, slipped away for quiet lunches with him and kept quiet about it. Perhaps it was time to face up to his fear that he might lose her. Time for a serious talk. He'd do it this afternoon when they were back in the cottage.

Jason parked up by the crossroads without explanation. If the poncey bugger by his side wanted to know why, he could ask and Jason would consider whether or not to provide an explanation. He didn't like Tom Ferguson and he didn't see that there was any need to hide it. Especially in these circumstances. Benny had given him his orders and Jason thoroughly approved. Whatever the success or failure of their mission to find this Tara woman, Tom would not be returning to Manchester.

The rear door of the saloon opened and Carl chucked a holdall on to the back seat and climbed in.

'All right?' Jason said.

'A damn sight better now I'm out of that dump. Another night in that bed and I'd be walking with a limp.'

But Jason had not been referring to the B&B where Carl had been staying.

'I meant the girl,' he said.

'She's there, don't worry. She's in the little house. I saw her and the boyfriend go back there about half an hour ago.'

'How long will she stay there?'

'I can't say for sure, can I? I don't have a flaming crystal ball. But she only goes two places as far as I can tell – up to the stables and then back to the house. The stables is busy from first thing and it packs up in the afternoon. So, with luck, she'll be in the house for the rest of the day.' Carl sniggered. 'Probably bunking up with chummy right now. I hear she's a bit partial to that kind of thing.'

Jason glanced at Tom and was rewarded with the sight of the lawyer's snooty face lit by fury. He kept his temper bottled up, however. Only a fool would mix it with a meathead like Carl.

'Let's hope you're right,' Jason said. 'If she's got her mind on chummy's dick then she won't be expecting visitors.'

It occurred to him that if Tara really was in the sack with the boyfriend it might make a neat solution to the Tom situation. Jealous ex-boyfriend bursts in on girl with new lover. He puts a bullet in both of them then blows his own brains out. Good story.

He turned to Tom. 'All set for your big moment?'

Tom glared at him. 'Let's get on with it,' he muttered.

'I'll take that as a yes,' said Jason and started the car.

His cocky lawyer friend didn't have a clue how big his moment was going to be.

Danny was determined to have his make-or-break conversation with Tara but was still looking for the right opening.

As Tara laid out lunch on the kitchen table she laughed about a misunderstanding she'd had on the phone in the office that morning. It was rare to see her in such a good mood and, for a moment, he indulged the thought that maybe things could continue like this.

'Are you all right, Danny?' Tara asked as she cut the bread. This was his cue and he was framing his words when the doorbell rang. Jesus.

'Don't worry, I'll get it,' he said, barely able to hide his exasperation.

He strode to the front door and flung it open.

Rick stood there. 'Is Tara in?' he said.

'Yes. We're about to have lunch.'

'Do you mind if I have a word with her?'

'Go ahead,' Danny said, taking his jacket from the hook in the hall. 'She's all yours.'

Tara was surprised to find Rick standing on his own in the hall.

'Danny let me in,' he said. 'Then he rushed off. Is everything OK?'

'He'll be back soon enough, I expect,' she said, wondering where he'd gone. 'I see he's left his things.' Danny's phone and house keys sat next to each other on the hall table. She hoped he wouldn't be long. She wanted to go back to the office later and he wouldn't be able to get in.

'I'm sorry for barging in,' Rick said, 'but I've got to talk to you.'

Danny stormed out of the house and up the path. What a fool he'd been, allowing Tara to walk into his life so completely. Just because Kirsty had brought them together, there was no sane reason to think Tara could take her place.

Obviously they weren't suited. Or maybe he wasn't suited to her. Plainly there were other men she preferred. It wasn't Rick's fault he was one of them. All the same, he wasn't going to hang around the pair of them and watch which way the wind blew.

Perhaps Rick would like to take her over full-time. The silences, the weird neuroses, the fantasies. He'd be better off without her.

He was striding out blindly, unaware of the direction he was taking, just keen to put some distance between himself and the cottage. He followed the drive as it curved away from the yard and wound in a long loop around the paddocks up to the main road. Danny was about to turn right at the gate when a car slowed to turn in.

He recognised the man in the passenger seat as he passed just a few feet away. It took a few moments, however, for him to place the firm jaw and dark hair. Tom Ferguson. Tara's former lover from Manchester. And in the car two other men, a bony-faced driver and, in the back, a shaven-headed hulk.

He watched the car as it receded from his sight down the driveway.

In an instant he realised that Tara's fears might after all be real. Tom Ferguson from Manchester and two menacing companions were coming to visit.

Suddenly, the contempt with which he had treated Tara's story of persecution seemed misplaced. Maybe he had got it wrong. She had not been deluding herself. Ferguson and two thugs had come to find her, just as she had feared.

And he, whom she had trusted to keep her safe, had deserted his post.

Christine's hand shook as she put down the phone. It had been a short conversation and almost entirely one-sided. Her caller had done the talking.

Though not a conventionally religious person, she had prayed that this day would never come. And, just recently, she had allowed herself to think it never would.

So, fate being what it was, what should she do now?

She had several courses of action open to her but the most important was undoubtedly to talk to her son.

There was no time to get back to the cottage, Danny was too far away. Help lay, if it lay anywhere, in the opposite direction.

He ignored his bruised thigh, now screaming in protest, and ran as fast as he could, trying to keep a rein on his panic.

He was running for his life. Or rather, Tara's.

Tara led Rick into the front room and he sat on the sofa along the back wall, refusing her offer of tea. She took the easy chair opposite.

'Patsy came to see me last night,' he began. 'He knows we've found his passport.'

Tara felt a surge of guilt. She'd been so wrapped up in her own drama she'd scarcely given a thought to her dead friend and the discussion she'd had with Rick and Gareth in the pub.

'He admits he was there?'

'Oh yes. He says he was in love with Kirsty. He said the baby was his and he'd flown out secretly to persuade her to come away with him.'

'What!'

'And he says he knows who killed her.'

A ring at the door interrupted them.

'Who was it?' she said.

'He wouldn't tell me.'

She was speechless.

The doorbell rang again.

'That'll be Danny,' she said.

Rick got to his feet. 'We can't tell him any of this. Dad is getting on to the police – let them handle it.'

He went to answer the door.

Two men stood in the porch, both wore suits. The nearest, a short fellow with a lurid yellow tie, held a card in his left hand. It was too far away to be legible.

'Excuse me, sir, but I'm looking for Miss Tara O'Brien. We had an appointment up at the yard. Is she available?'

'Tara,' Rick called over his shoulder.

'Thanks, chum,' said the small man and barged past him into the hall.

'Hey.' Rick put his hand on the man's shoulder, intending to haul him back but he was held by an irresistible force. A third man, a giant who must have been standing outside the porch, had him in his grip.

Tom watched as if in a dream. He couldn't believe he was part of this barbarism. What would his children think if they could see him?

But what would they think if he was sent to prison? And that's what would happen if he didn't go along with these two gangsters. It was his only chance to avoid ruin.

He stepped into the hall of the cottage.

In a corner of the living room to the left of the passage, Carl held the man who'd opened the door. Carl's weight pressed the lad to the wall by the side of the window, his arms wrenched upwards, his face squashed against the wallpaper.

Tara was standing by the fireplace. Tom had not seen her with her hair cropped and it made her features bigger. She was skinnier than he remembered, a stick thing with a white face and enormous eyes which drilled into him as he stepped into the doorway.

'Tom,' she screamed. 'Tell them to stop.'

'I take it we have a positive ID?' said Jason by his side. He was looking at Tom but the gun in his left hand was pointed at Tara.

'Yes,' Tom said. 'That's her.'

'Don't kill me, please.'

Tom had heard people plead for their freedom before but never for their life.

'I'm not going to, sweetheart,' said Jason. 'He is.'

And Tom saw there was another gun, in Jason's right hand, which he was holding out, the hilt nuzzling into Tom's side.

'Take it,' he said.

Tom obeyed, suddenly alert to a new horror.

'You know what to do, don't you?' said Jason.

The thing was small but heavy. He took it and fitted it to his hand, like a child clutching a toy. He'd never fired a real weapon or killed a living thing but he raised it now and took aim.

She stared at him defiantly, the woman he'd once thought he loved, daring him to shoot.

'Hurry up, you wanker,' said Jason, 'or I'll do her myself.'

Christine saw the other car at the top of the lane. Had the police arrived already?

She speeded up, in time to see a tall man in a suit disappear into the house.

No, it couldn't be allowed, she had to get to Danny first. She ran down the path and looked into the house through the open door.

The man was standing there, looking into the living room. He had a gun in his hand. She knew at once he was no policeman.

As Jason had suspected, it looked as if Tom was too shit soft to do it.

Go on, smart arse, pull the sodding trigger. Or else I'll kill her and you'll be next.

*

Christine picked up the little stone hedgehog from the porch and ghosted down the hall.

The man didn't see her. His hand was shaking.

Christine brought the stone down on the back of his head, cracking open his skull.

It was easy to do.

After all, she'd done it before.

Jason's first thought, as Tom toppled forward, the gun spilling from his grip, was that the idiot had fainted. Then he saw the blood on the back of his head.

A woman was standing where Tom had been, something in her hand.

She shouldn't have been there and she was holding a weapon.

He shot her.

She crumpled to her knees.

'Jason!' Carl screamed. The guy in his grip was twisting and struggling. 'Watch the girl!'

Tara was on her knees, scrabbling for the gun on the floor.

As her fingers closed on it, Jason stepped on her hand. He put his weapon to her head. Like he should have done in the first place.

Rick fought with all the energy he could muster against the man squeezing the breath out of him. It was like trying to uproot a tree with bare hands. Pointless.

He saw clearly what was going to happen and there was nothing he could do to prevent it.

There was a noise from outside the house. A loud sharp crack.

Jason's head jerked backwards. Blood flowered over his yellow tie.

The noise came again and he fell backwards.

For a moment there was silence.

Then, suddenly, the weight crushing Rick against the wall was gone. He was free. He lurched towards Tara and wrapped her in his arms.

Danny had no idea what he would find as he ran into the cottage.

'Wait! Be careful!' Patsy called from behind him but he took no notice.

Two of the men he'd seen in the car were lying motionless on the floor. One of them was the man Patsy had shot with his rifle. The other was Tom Ferguson. He didn't know whether they were dead or alive but he didn't care.

Rick and Tara were kneeling by the side of his mother. She was propped up against the wall.

The surprise was almost as great as the terror he felt at the sight of her. She was clutching her stomach, blood bubbling through her fingers, matting the grey wool of her sweater.

He dropped to his knees. 'Mum, what's happened?' In the background he could hear Rick's voice demanding an ambulance *now*.

'She saved my life,' Tara said. 'Tom was going to kill me and she saved me. They shot her.'

From outside, up on the lane, came the sound of an engine starting. That would be the third man getting away. He didn't care.

Christine was looking at him intently, her face chalk white. 'Danny,' she murmured.

He held her gently by the arms, frightened of hurting her. 'Don't talk, Mum. We're going to get you to hospital. You'll be fine.'

She shook her head.

Tara was there with towels, pressing them round the stomach wound, trying to stem the flow.

Christine gripped his hand. 'Listen to me. I'm sorry about Kirsty.'

Kirsty? What did she have to do with this? His mother was rambling.

'Patsy knows,' she said. Her voice was faint. 'He'll tell you. Just say you forgive me.'

'Of course I forgive you, Mum. But there's nothing to forgive, is there?'

Danny left Adrian with his mother's body and went downstairs to a private room the hospital had made available. Outside, a man who identified himself as a policeman, DS Hammond, offered his condolences before allowing Danny to go in.

Tara, Rick, Stephanie and Patsy were sitting round a table. His arrival appeared to have interrupted a silence. They had been waiting for him to arrive.

Patsy gave them all a tight grin. He was the man with the explanations.

He looked at Danny and began to tell him a tale that seemed not only irrelevant but tasteless. Of how he had had an affair with Kirsty beneath everyone's noses while she flirted outrageously with Adrian and scandalised the whole yard.

'Do we have to talk about this?' Danny said.

'Yes,' said Stephanie. 'You never told Kirsty about your accident, did you? And that you couldn't have children.'

'Jesus, Steph,' he exclaimed, looking around with embarrassment.

'But you told me, didn't you?' said Tara.

There was no avoiding the subject. 'When I proposed to Kirsty, the first thing she said was that she never wanted to have kids, so it didn't matter. I knew you felt differently.'

Tara gripped his hand. 'I wish I'd been as honest with you.'

But when she had told him the truth he did not believe her, so maybe they were even.

Stephanie said, 'Kirsty was pregnant when she died.'

Danny wasn't shocked. He was beyond that by now. 'She never told me.'

'She was working out the best way to break the news. She said you had an agreement not to have children but, in the circumstances, she'd changed her mind. I knew it couldn't be yours. I didn't know what to do so I told Mum. Big mistake. I'm sorry.'

'I don't follow.' And he didn't. This whole conversation seemed irrelevant to the situation they found themselves in.

'Mum assumed, like me, that the baby was Adrian's. We'd all been unhappy about the way Adrian went around after Kirsty with his tongue hanging out. Mum didn't say anything but she was burning up inside and Kirsty didn't care. I'm sorry, Rick, but your sister sometimes behaved like she was the only person in the world who counted.'

Rick said nothing. Danny thought listening to this must be tough for him too.

'So what happened?'

'The day Kirsty was killed, Mum and I had been to Tortola. On the boat back I told her about Kirsty being pregnant and she said, "It must be Adrian's." After that, she shut down, hardly said a thing. When we got back to the chalets and found Adrian had taken Kirsty off to the bar, she said, "I'm going to sort this out now," and went after them. I honestly don't think it was in her mind to kill Kirsty.'

So this was what the conversation was leading up to.

Patsy said, 'I was waiting for Kirsty on the path, sitting on the other side of the wall, out of sight. I didn't expect she'd come but suddenly there she was. I was just about to show myself when Christine came up the other way. I thought she might carry on to the bar and I'd still have a chance to talk to Kirsty on her own. But the two of them stopped. I didn't hear what was said. Christine said to me later that she'd told Kirsty to take her claws out of the family, to pack her bags and never come back. Apparently Kirsty laughed at her, called her a dried-up old witch and said she wasn't going anywhere. Then she turned her back on Christine. Christine picked up a stone and hit her on the back of the head. It was over in an instant. I rushed up the path but there wasn't anything I could do.'

Danny wanted to shout out, 'No!' It was ridiculous. His mother couldn't kill anybody.

Except she'd killed Tom Ferguson that afternoon. Smashed his head in, just the way Kirsty had died.

Stephanie laid a hand on his arm. 'When Mum came back to the chalet she told me she'd hit Kirsty and that Patsy had seen her. We couldn't think why Patsy would be there. Then Kirsty's body was found and I said Mum was with me all the afternoon. We kept waiting for Patsy to come forward and say what had happened but he never did.'

Patsy spoke up. 'I just got on the next plane home. When I realised Kirsty was dead I simply walked away. But I knew I'd been seen. Even if I'd wanted to, I reckon if I'd spoken up I'd have been held responsible. And in a way I was. If I hadn't got her pregnant it would never have happened. Later, when we were all back in England, the three of us agreed to keep it quiet. After all, we couldn't bring Kirsty back. We never talked about it again. At least, not till I called Christine today and told her that Rick knew I'd been on Amana and his father would be telling the police. I guess that's why she went to the cottage. She wanted to tell you herself, Danny.'

Danny sat stunned. His mother's life and death seemed to take on a new meaning.

'What happens now?' he said. 'Is all this going to come out about Mum and Kirsty?'

'I think,' said Patsy, 'that's up to Rick. And his father.'

Epilogue

Standing in the shadow of Patsy Walsh, as ever Tara felt safe, though today his presence was more of a talisman. Since her miraculous escape she had come to believe she was living a charmed life. And today, surrounded by the throng of race-goers who had made the pilgrimage to the Cheltenham Festival, she felt happily insignificant.

'The bookies don't fancy Treacle much,' said Patsy, 'though I can't say I blame them. You'd be mad to put your mortgage on a horse that's run once over hurdles and performed like he did at Haydock.'

'You're not going to put your mortgage on him, are you?' she asked.

'Don't have a mortgage, my darling. But I've lumped on him all the same.'

'So you really think he's got a chance?'

The big Irishman grinned at her. 'As it happens, I do. He's a different animal to when he came. Ever since his mate died, he's been busting a gut. And now we've got Rick back – well, it's fate, isn't it?'

Tara would settle for that.

Before the start, Rick took Treacle up to the first hurdle for a sighter, as was traditional. He was trying hard to focus on the race ahead. The Triumph Hurdle for four-year-olds at the Cheltenham Festival was, by some measure, the best race he had ever ridden in yet it was hard to keep his mind on the job.

He'd sworn, after the shootings in the cottage and the discovery that Christine had killed Kirsty, that he would walk away from Latchmere and its people for ever. But in the end the ties that had taken him back there at the beginning of the year continued to bind.

He'd returned to Shrewsbury and the sanctuary of his childhood home. It seemed to him that his parents instinctively made an effort to behave as they'd always done, as a married couple united by trouble. He'd not brought it up directly with his father but he'd detected that the distance between them was closing.

His father had decided not to take his new knowledge of Kirsty's murder to the police. They'd talked it over long and hard.

'If I thought it would provide justice for Kirsty I would,' Gareth said. 'But Christine is dead and I don't see that punishing Patsy and Stephanie would serve any purpose. They have to live with what they've done. Besides, there's other considerations.'

Rick had known what he meant by that. In the aftermath of the deaths at the cottage the newspapers were in a frenzy of speculation, centred on the heroic actions of the celebrated trainer Christine Clark. Her cool self-sacrifice had elevated her to near sainthood, which Gareth pondered with black amusement.

'It's funny,' he said. 'I read a newspaper every day of my life, yet whenever the papers report on a matter of which I have personal knowledge, they always get the facts wrong.'

Many theories had been floated to account for the murders. The most popular posited a plot to kidnap Adrian Spring's stepson and his girlfriend and hold them to ransom. The dead Manchester solicitor, a man known to be linked to the criminal fraternity, was suspected to be the brains behind the scheme.

In the circumstances, it made sense not to spoil the entertainment. Rick and Gareth were well aware of the field day the media would have with the real story – Christine guilty of murder, the promiscuous behaviour of her son's previous fiancée and sexual high jinks at Latchmere Stud. The story would run for ever. And the damage it would do would be irreparable.

'I don't think your mother would be able to cope,' Gareth had said to Rick. 'And I feel for your friend Danny, too. None of this is his fault.'

So they'd kept quiet and Rick had no doubt that had been the right thing to do.

And, as an indication that that was the case, his mother and father were in the stand together about to watch him ride. He hoped he wasn't about to make a fool of himself but, frankly, that really didn't matter a jot.

Danny found a television screen. It would give him a much better view of proceedings than trying to watch the race out on the course itself. And these days scrutinising every detail was important. Since the death of his mother, the success or failure of the yard was down to him.

In the numbed shock that had gripped them all after the shootings, Adrian had said, 'I'll get someone to take over the yard.' But Stephanie had objected. 'That's not what Mum would have wanted. Danny should run it.' And Adrian had agreed that was the right thing to do.

Having a big responsibility thrust on him had helped Danny. Frankly, it was the only way he could cope. Horses didn't know or care about human tribulations and running a racing yard required urgent attention every minute of every day. Living in the now – that's how Danny was coping with the loss of his mother. And everything else.

The four of them – Adrian, Stephanie, Patsy and Danny – had sat down after Christine's funeral and put everything on the table, about Kirsty and Christine and what had happened on Amana. A part of him was still in shock and he didn't want to think about murder and betrayal and the aching void that was the loss of his mother.

He could have turned bitter. Hated all of them – certainly Patsy and Adrian – but he was determined not to go down that path. The funny thing was that he now felt closer to his stepfather than he'd ever done before. The man was in pieces inside, just like him. He felt responsible for so much and so he should.

Adrian no longer treated Danny like an employee. He sought out his opinion. He was asking Danny's permission to launch a charity in Christine's name. Danny was in favour, though he hadn't yet said yes. He was still talking it over with Jean, who'd come back to the office at his request. He trusted her judgement. The police had taken up a lot of Danny's time. There had been the suggestion that he might be prosecuted alongside Patsy for the murder of one Jason Price, the gangster Patsy had shot. But he'd been told the CPS had shelved the file, probably on the grounds that they'd look like idiots if they went ahead. Press and public sentiment was squarely on the side of the cavalry who had arrived in the nick of time.

The runners were off. Danny scanned the screen anxiously, looking for Rick's white cap amongst the mêlée of horses. At first he couldn't see it and a sudden moment of panic was only quelled when he saw that Treacle Toffee was leading the pack over the first. What was he doing there? That wasn't in the script.

It had taken some persuasion to get Rick to accept the

ride. He'd not shown his face at Latchmere in the weeks after the deaths and Danny had barely managed a few words on the phone to him. He'd left it to Stephanie to keep the lines of communication open.

Then Hugh, Treacle's owner, had suggested that Danny rode the horse in the Triumph. Though Danny had stopped riding to take on the training duties – frankly, he was better at it – the notion of a swansong at Cheltenham was tempting.

All the same he'd said no. 'Rick's got to do it. I'll fix it.'

First, Danny had got approval from Gareth and after that it was easy.

'Ride for Latchmere one last time,' he'd said to Rick. 'Think of Hugh and Gingerbread. Do it for them.'

Rick had sighed. 'Actually, mate, I'll do it for you.'

But when Danny had legged him up in the parade ring and wished him luck, making all the running had not been in his mind.

Tara was puzzled. 'Is Treacle meant to be in the lead at this stage, Patsy?'

'I wouldn't have thought so. Maybe your Rick's got some cunning plan for him.'

Tara thought about what he'd said – mostly the 'your Rick' part.

When Duncan Hammond had finally got his hands on her, he'd insisted she go into the witness protection programme. 'Like I told you to do in the first place,' he'd said.

She wondered whether her refusal to cooperate had led to the deaths of three people. But who was to say Benny's men wouldn't have found her in police protection? And maybe she would have been one of the corpses.

Then things changed. Hammond told her gleefully that a

certain Carl Harris had been arrested on the afternoon of the murders while doing 110 mph on the M42. She picked him out of an identity parade as the large man who had held Rick while Tom and the other man threatened her. Duncan said he matched the description of the Englishman who visited her Uncle Des's tea shop in Belfast and, a few days later, he confirmed that Harris's blood had been found in Des's kitchen.

Carl Harris had turned out to be a cooperative interviewee and, shortly afterwards, Benny Bridges himself had been arrested and charged with murder, conspiracy to murder, drug trafficking and a variety of other serious offences.

'If you're lucky,' Duncan told her, 'you might only have to testify against Harris.'

So Tara had extricated herself from the soulless hotel where the police were keeping her a virtual prisoner 'for her own safety' and headed to the only place she felt certain of receiving sanctuary – Latchmere. To her surprise, the family had welcomed her without hesitation. She would have understood if they'd rejected her – 'Got any more hitmen on your trail?' Stephanie had remarked. Adrian had privately apologised to her for checking up on her with Tom Ferguson; his suspicions had caused fatal consequences. And all of them had insisted that she stay.

She'd been allotted a room in the farmhouse where, on her first night, she'd woken in the grip of a familiar panic. Returning had been a terrible mistake. Benny would know where she was and word would go out from his prison cell. More Carls and Jasons would be arming themselves to have another shot at her, and this time they wouldn't miss.

She'd considered going down the hall to where Danny was sleeping. They'd made their peace and she'd apologised over and over about not telling him the truth in the first place. She wished now that she had. He would have taken her in willingly out of friendship, she realised that now.

But she couldn't dump on Danny again. So she'd called the number in Shrewsbury that she had for Rick. They'd talked for most of the night and the next day he'd come to take her away.

'Uh-oh, I think he's had it now.'

Patsy's words focused Tara's attention back on the race. Rick's horse was no longer in the lead.

'That's the favourite that's gone past him,' said Patsy. 'Oh well, I've had a fair run for my money.'

'Mug punter,' she said.

'So what makes you an expert?' He was laughing.

'I'm the jockey's girlfriend, that's what.' She was laughing too. But she wasn't joking.

When The Prophet overtook him on the inside, Rick saw the irony. That was Sean Boyle on board, the champion jockey who'd made such a fuss when he himself had done the same to him at Wincanton.

Rick had not intended to lead the field round almost two miles of the Triumph Hurdle course. But Treacle had felt so comfortable beneath him, easy and powerful and working within himself, that he was content to let him go.

This was the first time he'd sat on Treacle since the day of Gingerbread's accident. He'd been told he was a changed horse, more serious, less skittish, eager to work. And riding him today he could understand what they had meant.

But now they were at the business end of the contest and he feared the show was over. The ground was soft and sticky, draining the life out of tired legs. One had gone past him already and he had little doubt the rest of the field would follow. The hill ahead, the killing slope that sorted the

309

champions from the also-rans at Cheltenham, would be the real test of the new Treacle.

But, to Rick's surprise, his horse buckled down to his task. Rick shot a glance over his shoulder. A line of horses was there all right, the nearest three lengths behind, but none of them looked like they were about to burst past.

Maybe Treacle could hang on to second. That would keep the smile on Hugh's face for the rest of the week.

They had one more hurdle to jump now. The Prophet, a couple of lengths ahead, seemed to hesitate and made a meal of scrambling over the obstacle. Treacle skipped over it, just as he had every other hurdle in the race. But jumping had always been his strong suit. Ploughing on through heavy ground, gutsing it out to the finish like Ginger, had been the test he'd always failed. Until now.

To Rick's astonishment, Treacle put his head down and, inch by inch, hauled himself back into the lead. He beat The Prophet by a short head.

Hugh would be smiling for the rest of the year.

Sean Boyle was the first to reach him. He held out his hand in grudging congratulation. 'Well done, mate,' he said. 'I heard you'd given up again.'

Rick grinned back. 'There's no chance of that.'